monsoonbooks

ROGUE RAIDER

Nigel Barley was born south of London in 1947. He originally trained as an anthropologist and worked in West Africa, spending time with the Dowayo people of North Cameroon. He survived to move to the Ethnography Department of the British Musem and it was in this connection that he first travelled to Southeast Asia. After forrays into Thailand, Malaysia, Singapore, Japan and Burma, Barley settled on Indonesia as his principal research interest and has worked on both the history and contemporary culture of that area.

After escaping from the museum, he is now a writer and broadcaster and divides his time between London and Indonesia.

ALSO BY NIGEL BARLEY

The Innocent Anthropologist
A Plague of Caterpillars
Not a Hazardous Sport
Foreheads of the Dead
The Coast
In the Footsteps of Stamford Raffles
Smashing Pots
Dancing on the Grave
The Golden Sword
White Rajah

ROGUE RAIDER

THE TALE OF CAPTAIN LAUTERBACH
AND THE SINGAPORE MUTINY

NIGEL BARLEY

monsoon

monsoonbooks

Published in 2006
by Monsoon Books Pte Ltd
106 Jalan Hang Jebat #02–14
Singapore 139527
www.monsoonbooks.com.sg

ISBN-10: 981-05-5949-6
ISBN-13: 978-981-05-5949-6

Printed in Singapore

10 09 08 07 06   1 2 3 4 5 6 7 8 9

To the eccentric Mr Hedden

INTRODUCTION

The life of Captain Julius Lauterbach was so extraordinary that no one would dare to invent it. Juli-bumm, as he was known to his friends, was very much a real person although he lives on chiefly as the myth he was transformed into. The *Emden* was a real ship. The events described here – for the most part – really happened, though they were later hushed up, especially by the British authorities.

The First World War left Germany feeling a little short of classic heroes. The circumstances of the land campaign were not conducive to gentlemanly conduct and it was only in the air and at sea that a space was left for the conventional hero the public still demanded in an age of callous *Realpolitik*. Hence the continuing importance of SMS *Emden*, a light cruiser of the Far East squadron, commanded by Lieutenant-Commander Karl von Mueller, whose story has often been told and is something of a cult in Germany, neatly offsetting that of the negative 'Rape of Belgium,' just as frequently repeated in the rest of Europe. Von Mueller was of military family and noble blood, cold, distant, ruthlessly correct and punctilious in the interpretation of the articles of war. In 1914, the *Emden* was sent as a raider into the Indian Ocean to prey on Britain's merchant fleet. It was not expected she would return. In the course of three months, however, she sank sixteen merchant ships and two warships and carried out daring raids on the harbours of Penang and Madras, making a mockery of British naval supremacy, paralysing trade and making the Allies fear for their crucial troop convoys from Australasia. In the course of this, barely a life was lost. Von Mueller devoted himself to looking after the welfare of enemy crews and liberated them in safety and good health whenever circumstances permitted. Often, they cheered him as the *Emden* sailed off. His reputation and popularity throughout the Empire became a personal embarrassment for the First Sea Lord, Winston Churchill, who had seventy-eight vessels of British and allied navies searching the world for the enemy ship. In Germany, the legend of the *Emden* remained alive long after the war and spawned a whole series of vessels of similar name, becoming the official, acceptable face of the German navy.

But there is another side to the ship of legend – Captain Julius Lauterbach of the naval Reserve. His memoirs were written up as war propaganda and he too was portrayed as fearless, fanatically nationalistic and inevitably devoid of individual, intelligent thought. Yet, if we strip him of such conventional pieties and try to transform him back into a realistic human being, it seems likely that, for every austere virtue of von Mueller, Lauterbach possessed the corresponding vice. He was gross, beer-guzzling, cigar-smoking and uxorious, a seasoned filcher, braggart and – above all – a survivor. Lauterbach was made prize officer of the *Emden* in charge of loot. Rarely do navies match a man so ideally to his job. Lauterbach stuffed the warship with luxuries and one may suspect that, like others in his position in other navies, he had an eye to his own comfort and profit at the same time. When the *Emden* was finally shot to pieces Lauterbach was snugly installed in a prize ship a safe distance away.

Captured by the Allies, he was imprisoned in Singapore. In 1915, making opportunistic use of a mutiny amongst his Indian guards, Lauterbach made good his escape. His account of his involvement in that mutiny is inconsistent and shifty and has invited speculation. He now embarked on a protracted series of adventures as he tried to head back to Germany with a price of £1,000 (later inflated in his memoirs to £10,000) on his head and sought by all the British and Japanese agents in the East. He had contacts all over China and the Pacific from his sailing days as well as on German vessels interned in all the neutral harbours. He spoke Malay, pidgin Chinese, Dutch, Swedish and English as well as German. Beneath the flag of patriotism, Lauterbach performed several feats of great physical endurance and bravery, mixed with low cunning and self-interest. He was not a modest man. Often, when he had fooled or tricked anyone, he sent them a gloating postcard. After many adventures, he managed to return to Germany from the other side of the world and resumed an active role in the navy, though again one resting as much on deceit and cunning as military bravery.

Oddly, Captain von Mueller refused to write his own story, feeling it would be a base profiteering that would dishonour so many dead comrades. Lauterbach's tale has been told several times. It appeared twice in German, with a deadly patriotic twist for wartime propaganda purposes, first under his own name as *1000Pf Sterling Kopfpreis – tot oder lebendig* in 1917 and again as *Als Fluechtling um den halben Erdball* by Reinhard Roehle n.d. Then, in 1930 Lowell Thomas, an American journalist, took up the story and reworked it for the German-American market as *Lauterbach of the China*

Sea which went back into German as *Mein Freund Julibumm* by Graf Luckner. It is with the luxury of hindsight that we can now see him as a far more interesting character than the nationalistic obsessions and hatreds of the time allowed him ever to appear. Thomas calls him 'Falstaffian' but we should perhaps nowadays see him as more 'Flashmanesque'. Any truth about Julius Lauterbach goes far beyond the extant straightjacketed patriotic renditions. The version given here is no more than a possible version but to offer it is in no way to denigrate Julius Lauterbach. If anything, it seeks to humanise an exceptional man who has been caricatured as a fanatical martinet and return to him his deserved human condition. He is a man for whom I have a particular fondness. I hope readers will feel the same way.

Nigel Barley

BOOK ONE

THE SWAN
OF THE EAST

CHAPTER ONE

The hard heat beat down upon Tsingtao. No one could remember a hot season like it. For week after week, the black-white-red of Germany hung limp in the air till the meteorological station's equipment, fresh from Berlin, gave one final, desperate click and locked solid. With a thousand brass hammers the sun cracked the red rooftiles of the Chinese shophouses and bleached out the features of the Kaiser's portraits, nailed patriotically above all cash registers. It mined and split the concrete of the new German harbour and sucked the very life from the roses planted by homesick Europeans in the gardens of their villas. On the roof-terrace of the *Dachsaal* beergarden, the troops bleared wistfully at the cool but distant Laoshan mountains, grew tearful and confused at the unwonted tropical vigour of the imported German pinetrees there, drank another beer, sang another "Muss i Denn" and fumbled absently at the breastless Chinese serving wenches whose *Dirndl* bodices flapped limp with unfulfilled expectation. Colonial life was a thin membrane of glory stretched over a yawning pit of boredom.

"Bloody mockery," snivelled Captain Schulz, gulping fizzy beer and belching. Another month and he was due for the more solid forms of German home leave. He would be there now if it hadn't been for the last-minute malaria. Instead he was on his jack, on this roof, in this mockery of a town, that yodelled with dumpy south German towers and all the gingerbread cosiness of Bavaria. A lissom Chinese waiter in *Lederhosen* minced past on hairless legs and Schulz shook his head in pain.

At the neighbouring table sprawled a bunch of young naval officers, empty steins discarded around them in puddles of beer, sporting a muddled variety of uniforms, military and merchant, that meant nothing to Schulz. The whole of this Kiaochow Chinese protectorate was treated like some bloody great ship of the Reich, Admiral Tirpitz in charge, another popinjay captain as governor. Even the soldiers were called 'marines' and only he and a few other officers were real army men, stuck like bored housewives in the stinking barracks at Fort Bismarck while the navy went off to play their silly games at sea.

"Bloody mockery," he snarled again.

Tsingtao, the capital, was a model city, the teeming humanity of mainland China tamed and dammed by German colonial efficiency and the pouring in of millions of marks – water, roads, street-lighting, hospitals, schools, a railway, a floating drydock, and everywhere great naval guns poking at sky and sea. Undersea cables linked them to the wider world of Shanghai and the Pacific colony of Yap. The other side of the bay, disappearing in blue haze, was German too but under Chinese administration, a convenient muddle that gave excuses for military intervention whenever Germany needed them. The wind shifted and blew a sweet miasma of excrement, *Chinese* excrement over the town. Costive European dung was disdained as poisonous and fed into the maws of proud modern sewers to be belched out beyond the lighthouse but Chinese was traditionally composted for manure on one of the harbour islands and shovelled lavishly over their food. One way or another the Chinese made them all eat their shit. Schulz belched again. The wind shifted anew and now it was loud, beery conversation that blew over from the next table.

"There is absolutely no doubt about it. A missionary assured me ... with his own eyes ..."

"Ah, Juli-bumm, missionaries ..."

Missionaries had a certain mythic power in Tsingtao. The protectorate had been seized following the murder of a couple back in 1897. German righteous outrage had led to an armed landing, a fine exacted in silver coin, raising of the German flag and the establishment of a profitable trading colony – all in search, not of gain, but allegedly to teach the Chinese a well-deserved moral lesson.

"No, no, a reliable man of experience – with a long white beard – I have known for many years, a Dutchman, a bishop even ..." The speaker was huge, a great bear of a man, well over six feet, 18 stone of bullish flesh, bone and luxuriant fat, barrel-chested, vast Bismarckian head topped by a crewcut, full moustache and beard and little piggy eyes that gleamed like the colonial dollars the sailors were paid in. In his late thirties, he was far older than the clean-cut and pared young men at his table, a sea-dog amongst sea-puppies. He sighed and wiped his sweaty face with a pink, hairy hand, gestured for another round and poured it down as if dousing a fire in a waste-basket.

"I picked the Dutchman up in Talien, the end of the Trans-Siberian railroad." With a finger, he drew elegant cartography, as in a primary school, in the slops on the table.

"He'd come through from the West and everywhere, he said, Russian troops were moving back the other way. Germany, Austria. Great trains full of them – pale Ukrainians and Siberians – stuffed with rifles. Thousands more shunted into sidings. I tell you there's a war coming."

Howls of derision. "Juli-bumm, rubbish. Who are the Russians going to fight?" The Japanese had given them a bloody nose just the other year and sunk their navy. There would be no war. The boys had just come from the beach. The sun was shining. Their skin was taut and tanned. Hair bleached and sleek. Just last week that British navy had dropped by for football, horseracing, horseplay. The admirals had gone snipe shooting together and chortled in their clubs. The ratings got drunk and danced fraternally entwined. There would be no war. The big man sighed and wiped the ruined railway away, flicked the drops from his palm onto the floor.

"It's this way." He leaned forward, his voice growling and booming over their boyish piping "You know I have my two months' reserve duty to do, same as every year?"

Yes, yes, they nodded. "And if a war starts, they can assign me anywhere?" Yes, yes. "But if I'm already serving on a ship they automatically make me part of that crew? Well, if it comes to a war, I can't think of a better berth than the *Emden*, or better, braver mates to serve with ..."

"Oh Juli-bumm ..." Comradely tears started to their eyes for no heart is more sentimental than the caloused heart of a sailor, riven by a hundred reluctant farewells and with no second home to suborn its affections and Lauterbach knew that the constant presence of a disdainful sea and sky made men on ships huddle together against the cosmic chill.

... Softly ... "So I wonder if maybe we can fix it that I

start my reserve with you boys right here and now ...? What do you think?"

"Oh Juli-bumm. Don't worry. We can fix it." Hugs, manly choking. Their smooth, young faces lit up with pure joy. "Franz Josef can fix it. You know, the Kaiser's nephew. On the *Emden*, a technician looking after the torpedoes. A word with the admiral and he can fix *anything*. But there will be no war." Still – a war – their eyes shone with bright excitement as they rolled the word round in their mouths. It would mean medals, bugles, cowboys and Indians, promotions ... They pouted, "But we're all headed for Mexico on a dull official cruise, haven't you heard?" There could, after all, be no war. Other arrangements had already been made. "Have another little beer."

It was pointless to argue. The young knew themselves to be confidently immortal while the fat man had attained a terrible awareness of the fragility of human flesh. A fat man has limited options in this world, reduced to the choice between embodying the virtue of joviality or the vice of greed. But Lauterbach, while he might slip in and out of either of these roles, could not make them permanently his own. In truth, he was horribly sensitive and as the years rolled by, he needed ever more flesh, piled up as a barrier against the world, just as he needed money and possessions to protect him from its bruising reality. Among the wildly gesturing boys, he sat back provisionally satisfied, like a man who had spent all day working his way against the wind and finally made it to a safe port. On the *Emden* he would be safe. Over the swimming table, Schulz caught his eye and a strange knowledge flowed between them. The big man stroked his moustache and smirked boldly into Schulz's crazed grey eyes.

"Of course," he said, staring, half-challenging, half-sharing cynical insight, "I suppose joining the *Emden* would mean a quiet war. After all, they won't risk the Kaiser's nephew's life on anything too exciting. But one thing I've found from all my years in the Eastern seas." He laid a hand melodramatically on his heart and used the sort of flattery he normally used on women. "It's comrades that count more than excitement. Just great comrades like you fine boys."

"Oh Juli-bumm." They simpered, bathed in rugged mutual respect. Another little beer. Another little beer. A toast to Julius Lauterbach, the best mate a bloke ever had.

Schulz coughed and tittered. Lauterbach. There was a cheap little song that had gone round the world by squeeze-box. In English it ran "Oh where oh where has my little dog gone ..." In German it was "In Lauterbach I lost my sock. / I won't be going back there. / But if I went to Lauterbach, / I'd once more have a pair there."

Schulz guffawed and lah-lahed secretly under his breath. "Socks," he sniggered to no one in particular and stared gleefully down at his boots. Lauterbach raised his glass and smiled peacefully. He had heard it all before. It had no power to upset him. Safe. On the *Emden*, he was safe.

"One for our friend over there," he smirked with fat generosity, pointing with fingers like pork sausages. "The navy must not totally forget the army." It was young von Guerard's round anyway. In such circumstances, generosity cost nothing.

The wind shifted again and the sweet stink of the new brewery doused them in its catholic blessing. It did not smell that different from the dungheap really.

Julius Lauterbach was thirty-seven years old and life –

thus far – had been good to him. He would have been the first to admit it. He was a Baltic German, born within sight of Mecklenburg Bay – the same name as that fancy sanatorium up in the Laoshan hills. Bloody mock ... No, wait, that was someone else.

A Baltic twang still salted his speech. Six years of military school at Lichterfelde had demonstrated beyond all doubt, to himself and the world, his unsuitability for the intended career in the army or the law. He could still feel the knuckles of his Latin master as they pummeled his shaved, schoolboy skull. "Examinations, Lauterbach, Are-Not-For-You. I fear that when the time comes you will have to resit your post-mortem."

The death of his father, which had seemed at first to cast something of a shadow over the preparations for his eighteenth birthday, had been the making of him. He was free. Not the army then, not the law, not even the navy, but the merchant marine! In those days, it was still all sail. Sixteen months back and forth around the Horn at two dollars a month had hardened his hands and coarsened his speech. He had a pet monkey and a parrot. To be the complete sailor, all he needed was a wooden leg. His bourgeois family had withdrawn into shocked silence. Over the years, he had swopped ships and women, soft berths and hard, got a mate's ticket, switched astutely to the new thing of steam, gone three times round the world and settled in as quartermaster on the China run of the big smug steamers of the Hamburg–America line. In the East, everything was big but the people and Lauterbach had begun to absorb that bigness into his own unshakeable flesh as quiet peculation lined his pockets from the company's coffers. There were hurricanes and mountains, elephants and snakes. Once, six of them had wrestled a huge python back into its cage in a darkened cargo hold in a force nine gale, having stupefied it first with goat. At twenty-nine, finally, he was master of his own ship, the *Gouverneur Jaeschke*, a trim vessel with a gaping Chinese crew that he ruled with a rod of iron as he worked it round every port and up and down every river in the Orient. Shanghai, Tsingtao, Manila, Vladivostok and Hongkong were his regular fare.

He liked the Chinese and learned the simplicities of survival from them, that to die was always bad, to live much better and to live with money best of all. He quietly turned a blind eye to their little scams that hurt only the customs service or the money-changers, deliberately did not notice the odd, too-intelligent, new face among the crew when the nationalist forces were on the move. But he was prepared to pay them out a good thrashing too, with his own hands, often the best-appreciated currency on the coast. He prided himself that a German thrashing was worth three times a Britisher's. While they feared him, they knew that if the worst came to the worst he would never simply tip their bodies over the side, like so many European captains, for burial at sea, so that they would end up as hungry ghosts. He could be relied upon to take them to a port where they could be properly buried and decently furnished with burned paper copies of the goods they would need on the other side. So he toiled with them, called them dogs and whores' sons in fluent pidgin, fought them with his fists and gambled with them, drank them under the table in a hundred, filthy dockside bars and nursed them when they were sick. If they did not exactly love him, they at least respected him as a man to be reckoned with and wreathed him round with silken myth. He was the product of a drunken union between a mad sailor and a witch who had assumed the form of a fox. If roused to wrath he could turn into a bear. He had been seen to eat iron rivets, chomping them down with his great teeth. There was even a Chinese version of the Lauterbach song whose darker linguistic points he did not seek to elucidate. In those years he had crushed life's grape against his palate and happily spat out the pips. He was young and glad to be free and touched the earth very lightly for such a heavy man.

In the East any white man became upper class, regardless of his origins. He had stayed at the best hotels, dined at the best restaurants and drunk the most subtle vintages. In Shanghai, Lauterbach had sipped pink gins with Kitchener in the International Club and wore a gold ring on his finger given by the Emperor of China, or sometimes it was the other way around. There had been girls – bony Chinese with bodies like bicycle frames, voluptuous, hairy-backed Russians down on their luck. Once, in a casino in Shanghai, he had won a pair of blonde Swedish twins with huge pink breasts like blancmanges and extraordinarily complex underwear you needed a chart to fathom. They had drunk and sung and danced and made love and finally he had recited to them Swedish poetry, remembered from Baltic childhood, and made them cry. To the crash of waves and the throb of mighty engines, Lauterbach had obliged many a lady passenger on the slow Pacific swell, always a generous and unfussy lover, fervent but discreet, so that they usually came back for more of his tasty beef on the bone. As a sailor, he had always prided himself on his bedside manner and his couplings were as efficient and dispassionate as a naval docking procedure. A fat moustache and a touch of gold braid proved an irresistible aphrodisiac to colonial wives who appreciated his discretion which, in fact, rested on his inability to remember any of their names or faces so that he was frequently astonished to wake and see that of a complete stranger on the pillow beside him. But he always retained an encyclopedic memory of the feel of their thighs as they gripped his comforting bulk and scrambled giggling to his summit. The top drawer of his dresser contained a pile of the conventional gold watches, most of them too tight for him to wear, given by unimaginative but grateful women. He made them the small change of friendship to departing Chinese crew, inscrutable but litigious. Sometimes, he knew, these ran a sweepstake on his exploits, especially on the dull Shanghai stretch. Long faces or grins at breakfast showed who had hit the Lauterbach jackpot on the last night. And towards the end of a run, Ah Ping, the steward, had a way of damping down his boilers or opening his throttle wide to guide his efforts towards the desired total. "You take this boi' egg. You need keep up your strength. I think you get old." Or. "You only get porridge today. No boi' egg. Need rest yourself. You do too much." Sometimes the Lauterbach torpedo was so unpredictably trigger-haired, he thought they must be slipping him other stuff, more than boy eggs or even girl eggs, in the food.

But now war was coming and it was time to batten down the hatches and get under cover. Regulations obliged Lauterbach to serve two months a year in the naval reserve and normally it was a welcome break from the routine of restless motion. They gave him a new uniform, lots of fancy saluting, there was riding, hiking, swimming and banging about with guns. Usually it was here in Tsingtao where the cold inshore winds spared you the humid horror of a summer in Shanghai. You could afford to rent a room, lay in some wine, fix up a comfortable mistress at long-term rates. The onboard food was awful but often you could eat at the Cafe Floessel, run by a fat Duesseldorf lady with a roving eye, and the only really bad part was being under someone else's orders again, corseted by childish discipline and the starched collar of regulations. It was as good as a holiday. Now Russia would put an end to all that.

Not just Russia, naturally – who would probably just support the Serbs against the Austrians as always. The real enemy in Europe would be the French if the lazy British could be kept out. But the most immediate danger out here in the East was the bustling Japanese. Maybe they would fight the Russians again. Last time, half the Russian fleet had run away to hide from them in Tsingtao. No fools, when they had looked to the West for models, the Japanese had based their army on that of the Germans and their fleet on the British Navy. But their spanking new warships were already arrogantly jostling those of the Western powers in the harbour of Shanghai and the real goal for Japan would be the precious city of Tsingtao itself. Tsingtao and all the German colonies of the Pacific – that was what they would want to join the grown-up nations of the world and there was precious little to stop them. A cruise to Mexico? He thought not. The whole world and all the certainties of this new twentieth century were about to blow up in their faces. Not just a war, a world war. Time to get under cover.

Lauterbach's rickshaw rattled over the railway tracks set into the cobbles and wheeled to a halt in a great arc. It was a comfortingly nautical way to stop. The sweat-soaked rickshaw man slumped on the shafts in a theatrical demonstration of exhaustion and despair as Lauterbach heaved himself creaking down and looked up at his new ship, the harbour water sucking and slapping at her sides while she gently peed bilge from a rust-rounded hole. Sailors were rubbing down and repainting her sunburned nose. All about were stalls selling food, cheap souvenirs, and great heaped crates snarling with German military and technical reference numbers. Around them, hundreds quacked and shrieked in dialects of Chinese, carried things up, carried things away – maybe the same things – scraped pans, smashed bottles, performed unspeakable acts of mutilation on screaming pigs. A woman was throwing greasy water over a wailing child that danced with rage. China had always been a bad place to have a headache and there was no shortage of headaches this morning. Debauched and stubbly sailors, newly mobilised with kit bags on their shoulders, took queasy leave of their local amours in tones of tragedy or relief to the chink of Mexican dollars. Lauterbach's civilian uniform, provoking neither respect nor salutes, bestowed blessed invisibility. Having newly sacrificed beard and moustache to naval discipline, he seemed, even to himself, like an impostor.

They called His Imperial Majesty's ship *Emden* "the swan of the East." Lauterbach shouted and gesticulated to a stall for hot dumplings and looked her over. He danced the hot food on his tongue, swallowed and grunted, unimpressed. He had visited too many "Pearls of the Orient" and "Venices of the East", that lay choking in their own garbage, and paid court to too many "oriental beauties", who turned out to have pyrrhoea and scabies, to pay heed to any of that. Swans, anyway, he had always found to be unpleasant and pointless creatures – like aristocrats. He had looked her up in the naval records, rattled the skeletons in her closet, seen her with no clothes on. She was nothing to write home about.

He knew that, technically at least, the *Emden* was less a swan than a white elephant. Her keel had been laid a good eight years back in 1906 in Danzig as part of the Kaiser's first petulant arms race against his British cousins. A policy had sought to cultivate local enthusiasm by naming each vessel after a particular German city. That of Emden was informed, in suitably inflated language, that it had now a ship of its very own and had tried to rise to the occasion with a rash of civic receptions and declarations of patriotism that fatigued both givers and receivers but allegedly pleased the Kaiser. In those days of peace and posturing, the navy's main duty was to please the Kaiser and numbers were everything as nations fought with reviews of the fleet like little boys showing off their collections of marbles.

She was obsolete when built. The old stove-pipe funnels had a quaint air of tipped top-hats and her torpedoes were of outmoded design and sorely limited range. The prognathous bow echoed a time when ramming was a standard naval manoeuvre while the old piston-driven engines were cumbersome and unresponsive. Ships were split into categories – battleship, destroyer and so on – so that they could be matched between the various nations but then a sort of cheating blurred the distinctions so that a cruiser could be heavy, light or medium. The *Emden* was a decidedly 'light'cruiser. Those of foreign navies already had smooth-running turbines and were faster, better armoured and more heavily gunned than this white-painted swan. They had more watertight compartments and were less easy to sink. Never mind. She had one great charm for Lauterbach. She was not intended to stand and fight other armed vessels but prey on helpless merchantmen. She was designed to be the school bully that kicked little kids and took their sweets off them. If anyone her own size or a teacher turned up, she was to run away.

"You givee one piece dollar I takee travel box inside ship-ship." The rickshawman was there, interrupting his thoughts, grinning through broken teeth and holding out his hand confidently. Lauterbach paused and sighed. Those young puppies had spoiled the market. He roused himself, deliberately stood against the sun so the great shadow of his bulk fell in the driver's eyes and pointed to the stack of old, well-used luggage, generously embossed with supplementary straps and reinforcements, raised his fist and gobbed a stream of pidjin in the expectant face.

"I reckon you one piece fella him savvy box velly bloke. Chop-chop you takee bloody travel box. You no takee I givee bloody bamboo chow-chow, damn right."

The scrawny driver quailed, seized a suitcase, clapped it on his head and jogged off up the gangplank at the exaggerated pace they called "the imperial trot."

Lauterbach watched him with a satisfied smirk and moved gently up the plank himself, clamping the rail with huge, serial, slow hands. Gangplanks could be slippery and dangerous. This one bent under his weight but that was just a comforting proof of his own solidity. Later, he resolved – point made – the Chinese should have his tip. He was, after all, far from being a harsh man. He just liked things to be clear.

His cabin was tailored for one of those slim boys, a thing

of louvred lockers and stick furniture, a doll's house. Back on the *Kraetke*, his own command, he had a double bed screwed to the floor and chairs of leather and brass. Here, there was a slim monastic bench of leatherette that, he could foresee, would be too short, too narrow and preclude all hospitality. He sat down on it with a groan – that it returned – lit up a cigarette and stared at the pile of luggage, like a new schoolboy waiting for his feeling of blank emptiness to turn into the inevitable homesickness. Only now he was not moving forward to some new stage in his life, with new experiences and privileges but backwards towards adolescence and loss of power. Already the leatherette was sticking wetly to his buttocks. There was a smart tap at the door and young von Guerard was there, grinning through flawless teeth, beckoning in another rickshaw driver with more luggage.

Lauterbach sat his ground, puffed smoke aggressively. "I think you must have made a mistake, Lieutenant von Guerard. They told me this was my cabin."

Von Guerard laughed with confident charm – threw a fencing foil twirling into the corner, seized and piled boxes and tennis raquets, gave too large a tip. He sprawled back, legs apart, on his boxes and grinned up at Lauterbach. He had been perfectly and expensively finished in all the best schools of the Reich and acquired gentlemanly accomplishments. Great wealth brought with ir great irresponsibility. He had the ability to drink a bottle of champagne standing on his head whereas Lauterbach, more pedestrian, merely prided himself on drinking one while still standing on his feet.

"Surely you don't think you're having this huge cabin and all this space to yourself, Juli-bumm. We're lucky there are just the two of us. Will you take the bench or the hammock?"

"The hammock." He could get one of the men to stitch two of them together lengthwise. The mere thought of trying to sleep through rough weather, swinging there like a bat sent a stab of dyspepsia through his stomach and stuffed suffocation up his nostrils.

"This is going to be such fun." The boy quivered with excitement. "We'll give the Brits a pasting."

"Yes. Such fun."

Wherever he went, von Guerard expected to be loved and to feel himself immediately and effortlessly at home. He was like some big-footed puppy that had been petted and cosseted all its life. Lauterbach lacked such certainty. He had never found it easy to simply belong or even be accepted. Feeling old and depressed, he rose on shaky feet to stagger to the heads across the way and slam the clanging door shut and sat, fat, mottled knees crammed up hard against the warm metal and held his head. There were the usual pathetic pencilings, "Long live the Kaiser" and "Up the Boys in Blue." Along the top was a line from a von Eichendorf poem, "Whom God truly favours he sends out into the wide world." They did you a good class of poems in the navy. Down in one corner, was a further text in a small crabbed hand. He bent to decipher it as von Guerard's clear happy laughter rang out again in the cabin across the corridor, accompanied by the sound of tennis balls thudding against the bulkhead. It was the optimism and cheerfulness of the young that made them insufferable. "Turpitz fucks pigs," it read. In support, was offered a sketch of the admiral, hat rakishly askew, engaged in one of the less common forms of congress. It was clear that the artist had studied at no formal school of anatomical drawing and impressed by verve rather than draughtsmanship. Lauterbach sat back and breathed with relief. He was not totally alone in a conformist world, then. To settle and reassure himself further, he reached into the special, waterproof pocket a cunning tailor had sewn into his waistband and pulled out a fat wad of currency and started counting his money out onto his knees. "Ten, twenty, thirty ..." There were slick dollars and curlicued marks and arrogant pounds but somehow most reassuring were the fat Chinese notes – soft, thick and friendly as bedsheets. "Forty, fifty, sixty." A comfort blanket against the world. As he counted, his breathing steadied and his heart slowed back to its accustomed pace. He would survive.

"The situation is as follows ..." Von Muecke, the First Officer, was enjoying the chance to perform in public. He raised his pointer with trim authority and rapped firmly on the map pinned to the wall. Early thirties, focussed, a mind devoid of doubt and humour, he reeked of hard beds and cold showers. In his presence, Lauterbach was oddly aware of the dandruff on his own collar. Dandruff was a sort of unpardonable inefficiency. There was no need, he thought with irritation, for von Muecke to rap. Did everything have to be a military parody? At the messroom table, he had noticed him attacking the dumplings in their serving dishes with the sequenced motions of a bayonet charge. He shifted fat buttocks uncomfortably on the hard wooden chair. Von Muecke had made them heroically fling all cushions overboard as part of the change from peace to war footing. The curtains over the portholes had gone too and they had been blacked out with paint . A good nautical fug of armpits, fags and fish supper was building behind them. When on war watch, men slung their hammocks by their stations, slept in their clothes for days and had no time to wash. The stink of a warship was like that of a prison – all balls and boredom. Lauterbach hated it.

"The war is nearly won. Berlin reports that our forces have already scored significant victories in France and Belgium ..." Von Muecke's pointer coolly moved whole divisions effortlessly across borders through barbed wire and machine guns. War was then not a thing of rotting green corpses and foul decay but of crisp lines etched on a map. "It was feared that the British, unable to confront Germany as an equal, would take the coward's route yet again and fight its battles through others. Luckily that has not occurred and Britain has let slip the mask and we see, at last, the naked face of our enemy's jealous hatred. English greed for wealth and power has deceived and humbled France and Russia, now also enemies, and reveals the sole purpose of that perfidious nation to be nothing less than the total annihilation of peaceful Germany." His beaky little nose pecked the air with satisfaction. Its silhouette fell across the map of Europe seizing Paris in an ambitious pincer movement between nostrils and upper lip. The eyes gleamed fervently. "Our glorious victory is certain. The land war will be over in a matter of months. Our mighty fleet has gained the open sea. Tsingtao is an impregnable citadel, a secure part of the fatherland, that will vigorously defend the honour of German arms. If we are to deck our beloved vessel with a champion's laurels we must all lend ourselves swiftly to that great purpose, before our foes bend on trembling knee to sign their unconditional surrender" The pointer became a sword for the flourishing. "Three cheers for the Kaiser!"

The ratings leapt to their feet, crying out lustily, fisting the air, cheers ricocheting around the steel walls like shrapnel. Lauterbach flourished his pipe silently in token participation, mimed cheers slack-mouthed, being irrelevantly distracted by the irritating image of foes trying to sign while on bended knee. He had no hatred for the British. He had met lots of decent British seamen and the world for him was divided along a simpler line – that between sailors and landlubbers. The sea belonged to no state, neither did sailors so that a seaman's vocation was its own nationality and brotherhood. One of the turning points in his early life had come with the realisation that his father's mind was irrevocably decayed when he developed a sudden rabid interest in national politics.

"Three cheers for Admiral Graf Spee!"

The situation was bad then, much worse than he had thought. The rest of the Pacific squadron had got out of port fast and sailed for German Samoa to avoid being bottled up by the British. Tsingtao was undefended and would fall if the Japanese came in on the other side. In a few short months Germany would have no coaling stations left in the East and the entire fleet would be immobilised for lack of fuel, whereas the whole British empire could be reduced in naval terms to a series of heaps of Cardiff coal, dumped arrogantly all over the face of the planet. Earlier that day they had passed through the lingering wakes of a big flotilla of ships and there was noisy wireless in code. It could only be the British foolishly chattering and giving their position away. Germany had eight cruisers, Britain alone had thirty-four, not counting their French, Russian and Japanese allies. A less skilled card-player than Lauterbach could see that those were not great odds. But he would not mention Japan. These happy boys would not want to hear it and would hold it against him as a mark of his negative thought and lack of team spirit.

"What about Japan?" he asked. The words fell into a deep, deep silence, like a depth charge tumbling in still blue water after the initial splash. Von Muecke wheeled round, sneered briefly and opened his mouth to speak. Before he could do so he was flung to one side and his pointer sent clattering as the *Emden* veered hard over to starboard. Lauterbach hardly had time to feel the pleasure of Number One's discomfort before the rising revolutions and an abrupt thrumming through the steel deck gave sign that the ship was running at full speed. "Action stations" rang out and the audience disappeared in a thunder of feet that reminded him of boys stampeding at the sound of the bell that marked the end of the school day. Lauterbach – Lieutenant Lauterbach – rose to follow at a more measured pace. This was the navy so there were rules of course. Everyone's precise status was defined by the rings on his sleeve and precedence and rights of way up and down ladders and corridors were clearly marked in the handbook. Lauterbach's bulk made such rules redundant for he filled every stairway and gangway and moved like a whale through the ocean, leaving smaller fish to avoid him as best they could. Younger men hitched their elbows into the rails and coolly slid down ladders, leaning back and without touching the treads with their feet. Lauterbach plodded down step by step. Ladders were dangerous. You could hurt yourself. He had seen it happen loads of times.

As acting navigation officer his place was on the bridge and he moved solidly along the passageways and upwards to glowworm illumination. The nighttime waves were rough and heavy and the decks were awash. Rain squalls lashed his eyes, reducing vision still further. An eerie phosphorescence glowed from the sea and the prow was rhythmically dipped in running gold sending long dark shadows ghosting through the water. The men would be up, panicking, spotting non-existent submarines all night. As he struggled along the open deck and up the ladder, the wind plucked nastily at his tunic so that he gathered it around him. Important not to catch a chill. He knew they were in the Straits of Tsushima, between Korea and Japan. Japanese ships they could not yet touch. Russian they could and would seize. He passed through the door and saluted.

"Lieutenant Lauterbach on the bridge, sir." Von Muecke was there before him, saying, "I think it's a Russian, sir, the *Askold*." The *Askold* would outgun them, blow them to pieces. Bloody hell. Pangs stabbed through his stomach. The captain turned slightly and smiled a superior smile. It was not the *Askold* then.

"Mr Lauterbach, yes. Take a look, please. The Russian heavy cruiser *Askold*?" The voice was hushed, little more than a paper-thin whisper. Von Mueller was the most ethereal captain he had ever met. "*Mr*" Lauterbach? They had been at naval college together but, even then, von Mueller exuded aristocratic Prussian austerity, played no team games, rode alone or performed cool gymnastic exercises in unsweating geometric isolation. His tall gaunt form was shrouded in a long, shapeless overcoat, so that his feet were invisible and he seemed to float. His face was that of an honest preacher. The granitic features emerged pale and haggard and his fingers, as he passed the binoculars, were cold and unfleshed. Lauterbach shivered.to their touch.

He peered through the rain-blurred glass and at first

could see only sea and sky, then between gusts of rain caught a sudden glimpse of something else. There was colour out there. Straining his eyes, he could just make out an all-black steamer with twin yellow funnels running fast without lights. Thank God, a civilian.

"Russian Volunteer Fleet, the *Rjaesen*, built in Schichau, a fast new mailship." He knew her well. He knew just about every ship on the coast. He had drunk in most of them and blotted his copybook in a few. "Captain Ausen, a fine seaman." The man was a prat but kept good scotch. Last time he had been on board there was some sort of a disagreement at cards – the reasons were hazy, it had been a long night with drink taken – and Lauterbach had been violently ejected. He had ended up full length in the mud, his hat tossed after him by laughing tars. At least they had thrown him off the landward side and it had taken three Russian sailors to do it. That signified a little respect.

"Confirm Mr Lauterbach that we are in international waters."

It was touch and go. Sod Ausen. "Confirmed, captain. Well inside."

"Number one, make a signal. 'Stop at once – do not wireless.'" Von Muecke barked orders, stood to attention. Soon he would be rapping on something.

"Sparks reports she is sending wireless, requesting help, sir. She's running for Japanese waters."

"Jam signals. A blank shot across her bows, Number One."

The Russian response was to put on more speed, belching black smoke that obscured their view and aim. A shot thudded dangerously close to her bows. Any more of that and they would sink the stupid cow by mistake. Lauterbach settled back in fat contentment bracing himself against the wheel housing.

"Another round, Number One." Lauterbach had a brief bewildering vision of them back in the Dachsaal in Tsingtao bibulously ordering more beer. He was recalled to reality by a third sharp crump, an exasperated puff of smoke and the clang of a shellcase on the metal deck. Because of the smoke, that shot too had gone closer than politeness allowed. Von Muecke was panting and dancing on the spot with excitement like a dog watching a squirrel up a tree. Lauterbach's eyes never left the captain, fascinated by his detachment. The thin lips parted then closed and he had a mouth as tight and snug as a cat's bum.

"Live rounds, commence fire."

Only on the tenth, after another near miss, did the Russian slow. On the twelfth she stopped entirely. The cold blue eyes swivelled round as in a gun turret.

"Mr Lauterbach, arm yourself. Take the cutter and a boarding party of twenty men. Examine the documents. If all is in accordance with the conventions of war, declare her a prize of the Reich. You are her new master. Pray apologise to the captain for the closeness of our shooting. I will have a word with the gunner. Assure him that I take full responsibility for it. We shall escort her back to Tsingtao for immediate conversion to an armed auxiliary. If we sight enemy warships you will scuttle her immediately and without compunction."

Lauterbach paused. It would be good to see Ausen's ugly face as he lost his ship. Maybe he would resist a little and he could have him pitched over the rail by three rough sailors and here there was no landward side. Less cheering was the idea of himself labouring up the slippery steel hull of that great ship, in this filthy weather, swinging like a fat clapper in a bell, and then going down with the vessel. As for apologising to that Russian bastard – forget it.

"Sir. As you know I care nothing for my own discomfort and safety but perhaps the honour of the Imperial Navy requires that the senior officer have the opportunity of performing this historic task. It is, after all, our first prize."

Von Muecke's whole face collapsed into surprised sentimentality. "Oh I say. Damn decent of you Lauterbach. May I please sir? Please?"

Von Mueller traced a thin smile. "Sorry, Number One. Your place is on board. Next time perhaps. Mr Lauterbach, if you please. Do not forget to take our flag."

He looked at that wet steel cliff, heaving in the darkness and fearful sweat gushed copiously from crotch and armpit. For Julius Lauterbach the war had just begun.

CHAPTER TWO

Pagan and the other islands of the Northern Marianas had been bought from Spain in 1899 as a particularly extravagant act of impulse shopping. The natives, of course, had not been consulted in the matter and found the overnight change from Spanish to German disconcerting. Language was like a sink plug that suddenly did not fit any more. Magellan, on his voyage around the world, had given them the irksome name of the Island of Thieves but their principal importance lay now in being the Island of Coal. The entire coal-hungry German Pacific Squadron had gathered to feed in the sheltered bay beneath the volcano that, secure in its own fuel, smoked above them in peaceful parody. Admiral Graf von Spee had surrounded himself with the star vessels *Sharnhorst*, *Gneisenau* and *Nuernburg* with a complete supporting cast of attendant colliers and auxiliaries. In the admiral's presence, von Mueller had become still more ethereal, disdaining normal meals, spending long hours alone in his cabin doing one knew not what. Sometimes his ghostly voice would whisper through the speaking-tubes calling for a map or a book or soup and rolls. In Pagan he finally became fully invisible. It was rumoured he had been whisked away in the early pre-dawn for endless strategic conferences aboard the flagship. Fearful of British naval dominance in the Indian

Ocean and the China Sea, Graf Spee had determined to take his fleet on the long voyage to the West coast of the Americas. All were coaling in preparation.

Von Muecke had always had an odd obsession with making the men swim to improve fitness. In the filth of the port it had been compulsory. He could be seen and heard shouting instructions through a megaphone as they wallowed and gulped in bilge and sewage. With the logic that dogs all navies, bathing was now forbidden in these smooth and limpid waters. The previous night Berlin had radioed through the promotion of the officers' class of 1911, which had led to a major bout of sewing and some minor celebration of the new badges of rank. Many men were the worse for wear, red-eyed and green-skinned but the sea was allowed to bring no relief. The ratings stared glumly down into the flawless blue depths and sweated as they waited their turn to coal. "Sir, sir. Just a quick dip sir?"

Lauterbach had no intention of involvement in either coaling or swimming. He already swam well enough and anyway, he had an old salt's conviction that to swim *too* well was to invite shipwreck. Moreover, he had other fish to fry.

The assigned colliers that moved slowly out to sandwich the *Emden* were the commandeered *Staatsekretaer Kraetke*, his own ship, and the *Governeur Jaeschke*, his previous command. Coaling was the most hated occupation in the entire navy. In harbour, it was only ever done by coolies and only a dire emergency would force European sailors to do it for themselves. It involved hours of backbreaking manual labour in the hot sun, choking on dust, digging and hauling sack after sack of the hated stuff with slashed knuckles and bruised shoulders from one ship to another.

Serious accidents were frequent for each bag contained about a hundred pounds. Heatstroke posed a permanent threat. At the end of it, the entire ship was full of grime and had to be scrubbed clean. At the beginning, men did the job in their oldest clothes. As heat and wear and tear took their toll, modesty gave way to exhausted practicality. The bolder natives who paddled out to view this strange spectacle were shocked to see white men transformed into blackface demons, shovelling, spitting and swearing in a state of total nudity. In terror, they swiftly dumped the coconuts they had come out to sell, not even waiting for payment, and fled. Outside, a rhythm established itself – the accelerating pace of feet on a descending gangplank – thud, thud, thud – followed by the rush of falling coal, followed by a groan. Only the nature of the groan was subject to variation.

"Oh, Juli-bumm, your face." His former officers on the *Kraetke* stared at him as at one desecrated. "Your beard. Your moustache."

"It's the war. They chopped down all those expensive pine trees in Tsingtao for the war. My beard's the same thing. They're turning it into socks for the infantry."

Lauterbach sat in the saloon sipping iced beer and jawing comfortably with his former officers as dust rattled like hail against the sealed portholes. It was good to be with grown-ups again. Von Guerard was nice enough but it was hard to share a cabin with someone who regarded every day as an opportunity for achievement and growth rather than something to be simply got through intact. Losing a glorious beard was one thing, yet he was appalled to see his ostentatiously immaculate craft reduced to the fate of a common collier. It broke his heart to see the mahogany stairrails scored and pitted with grime like a miner's face, the paintwork copiously chipped and gouged and everything defiled and cheapened. It was a world from which elegance and style had been brusquely put to flight as battleship grey had been sloshed over the whole of social life. It sent a little frisson of regret up his spine that they still called him 'captain' here, not 'lieutenant.'

And the chatter too was all of war, war, war. At least, in the cabin, von Guerard sometimes talked about sport and horses even if shy of talking of women. They were entranced by the westward thrust of the Reich's army but worried by what the Russian peasant troops and their bayonets might be doing to their relatives in East Prussia. What else, he asked, was happening in dear old Tsingtao? The coolies were leaving, streaming out in thousands on foot, by sea, by rail. Like rats. German soldiers were driving them back at bayonet point. Bayonets again. The Austrians had scuttled their old cruiser, the *Kaiserin Elisabeth*, outside the harbour. There had been a run on the bank. Lauterbach was pleased to have prudently arranged the transfer of his own funds to sit snug in a dollar account in Shanghai. But the sinking of the *Emden*, he now learned, had already been confidently announced by Reuters. Another rumour had it that the Russian heavy cruiser, *Askold*, was sunk by them. Then again, they had been clearly identified fearfully fleeing from Tsingtao, flying the British flag, in the face of a lurking Japanese force blockading the harbour. In the eyes of most of the world the *Emden* was already a ghost-ship.

Lauterbach cared little for such wounds on the face of truth. Wars were fought from the backside up. His crackling leather armchair was a rare treat to the rump after the Mueckeimposed austerities of the *Emden*. During the journey from Tsingtao, with iconoclastic zeal, the sea-puppies had ripped out the ship's wood panelling, as a fire-risk, fed it to the boilers in proof and painted the walls a bilious green that troubled his equanimity. The measure of his stoked-up discomfort, it seemed, was to be the measure of their patriotism. Since all volatile chemicals had been diverted for military use, the paint would not dry. It dribbled and ran icontinently and formed a crusty patina of grime and human hair. Everyone had it on their hands and shoulders. Enough. He drew a mental line under this war and promptly made arrangements for the surreptitious transshipment of his wine-cellar, his library with its gentlemanly works of sepia pornography and a set of comfortable deckchairs to the *Emden*. Henceforth, he would make it a matter of self-respect that he should always be more at ease than his superiors.

When he returned to the *Emden*, several hours later, Lauterbach was calmed and refreshed – indeed he was refreshed to the point of befuddlement. As he made his way carefully down the difficult and boisterous gangway from the collier, he saw young Fleischer, a subaltern expert in dumb insolence, sweat streaking his black body like huge tears, hunched brokenly over the rail and looking wistfully into the cool water as von Muecke shouted on about duty to the fatherland and the inexpressible glory of one shovelling team beating the other shovelling team that was shovelling from the other vessel. With a stumble, Lauterbach sent their coal-sacks, stacked on the rail, flying into the water where the ebb tide began to carry them circling away towards the open sea.

"Don't just stand there, you clumsy swine!" he screamed,

winking – von Muecke on his blind side. "You men, jump in and fetch them back. That's navy property, that is. Any lost sack gets docked from your pay. Jump to it, lads!"

With a cheer they dropped shovels and leaped into the sea, knees tucked under their chins, plunging deep. Von Muecke looked on suspiciously. It would take a good fifteen minutes of swimming and diving and laughingly throwing sacks from man to man to get them all back. He was, he felt, very far from being a harsh man.

In the waist of the ship were the three Chinese washermen, known simply as Boy One, Two and Three, sitting on knotted bundles of laundry and waiting with oriental patience. Lauterbach, it seemed, was the only white devil with whom they would speak.

"We go Tsingtao, chop-chop. Boom-boom no good. We no die-die dead. Too long no getee dollar." Their faces were set and blank. Of course, they were wearing their best shirts and trousers and new wooden clogs and clutching straw hats, dressed to leave. Those bundles there were not just washing, then, they were these men's few treasures. They were talking of life and death but pidjin English turned everything into one of those stupid comic operas the British loved to perform in all their outstations of empire. But this, he knew, could not be rushed, would require long, slow excavation with buttressing at every point like an archaeological dig. He leaned on the rail and settled gently into the discussion.

"Where Joseph?" Joseph was the fixer, the middleman, the *compradore*. The only one you could argue with.

"Joseph in Tsingtao. No givee dollar."

"How? When?" Lauterbach had negotiated with Joseph for the washermen at the same time as they had dispensed with the coolie stokers. It had been understood that dapper, sharp-faced Joseph was first amongst them, that he was entitled to levy a tithe on their pay and that his personal duties were not to exceed a little light starching.

"He go pilotman ship, hidee in laundry."

"I see." So he had not been on board at all for days. He had taken the advance pay and run. A very smart Chinese, young Joseph, mission-educated of course.

"How much you wantee?" He said it to each of them in turn, hoping to divide them, one against another. Obligingly, they immediately began to quarrel. He let the babble run its course for a minute or two, then returned to the one who had spoken first. Small, thin, strong muscles on light bones, a sharp, intelligent face.

"One, how much Joseph say he givee you?" Sloe eyes appraised him cautiously.

"I no One. I Two."

"Alright Number Two. How much Joseph he payee you?"

"Five dollar." He told off the sum on fingers red and sore from constant immersion in hot water. He was lying of course. Lauterbach inhaled sharply and shook his head.

"Okay. Four dollar. Number Three getee three dollar. Four getee two dollar."

Four? Who the hell was Four? They pointed to the little fat one with the currant-bun face who squirmed and blushed coyly at such unaccustomed prominence. If he was Four, then who the hell was One?

Two looked at him evenly. "Mr von Muecke, he Number One. Captain call him Number One alltime."

"That," insisted Lauterbach calmly, "is different and you

know it. Which one you Number One Washboy?"

They looked at each other and suddenly erupted in giggles, struck out at each other's shoulders, collapsed in a general hug and fell among the washing, kicking and screaming with their feet in the air.

"Is no One. No one Number One. One no live. Joseph he just takee dollar for Number One." They screamed in hilarity.

Lauterbach looked on them with love. He liked Chinese. He sat down on the laundry or rather their luggage. Something cracked sharply inside beneath his weight but he ignored it. It was the moment to let them actually see money to focus their minds. He dug in his pocket and extracted a pile of Mexican silver dollars, lined them up on his fat knee, counted them out. They immediately fell silent and looked grave, eyes fixed on the silver, the way chickens are said to stare at a chalk line drawn on the ground.

"Okay. Maskee. I fixee. Likee this way. Number Two getee six dollar, Three getee four, Four getee three dollar. I givee dollar chop-chop" They put heads together, brooded darkly under bobbing pigtails. NumberTwo turned back, clasped his hands together primly.

"How bout One?" he asked. Lauterbach grinned.

"Number One still workee for us. One getee six dollar. Me takee half. You takee half." They relaxed. This was a world they recognised. If he had killed off non-existant Number One Washboy they would have lost all respect for the white man. They nodded, content. Four whispered an overlooked objection. There was another outburst of quarrelling static.

"One thing-lah." Two looked worried. "Six dollar only not enough. You payee me six dollar. So you payee Number

One eight dollar. He number One Boy – cannot getee same as me, cannot losee face." Lauterbach held his gaze, stared into the unblinking black pupils. There was no quiver of irony there. He *really* liked Chinese.

Von Mueller returned silently from the *Scharnhorst* and slipped, without particular gratitude, into a cool, freshly laundered and ironed tropical tunic. That night, the entire squadron raised anchor and set sail. The bustling lagoon was suddenly empty, haunted by a ghost of black smoke that was the end of German imperial possession, for another message from Tsingtao announced that Japan had declared war on Germany and that its vastly superior fleet was on its way south towards them with a force of occupation. The natives did not yet know that they would now have to throw away their relatively new German grammar books and learn to speak Japanese.

"*Emden* detached. Good luck."

Lauterbach read the signal flags on the *Scharnhorst* and watched carefully as a further signal detailed the collier *Markomannia* to attend them.

He was reclining in his new cane-backed planter's chair with its adjustable headrest, extendable footrest and armrest pierced to receive a reviving glass. It had been specially strengthened to bear his weight. Prudence had required that he send an only slightly less desirable example to the captain with his compliments. Von Mueller had taken to it at once, installed it on the bridge, lived in it, slept in it. God knows, with over four hundred men aboard, there were takers enough for a spare cabin. On the captain's chair, the drink receptacle held ruthlessly sharpened pencils, not gin.

Both ships wheeled south south-west in a smear of foam, as the rest of the squadron steamed off to their rendezvous with destiny. In November they would annihilate the British naval squadron in Chile. In December the same would happen to them. Thousands would go down in a neat balance of slaughter that would be a matter of simple pride to both navies.

Lauterbach knew at once what it all meant. They had all argued their options in the vomit-green wardroom. The *Emden* was to become a lone raider, preying on enemy merchant shipping in the great British lake that was the Indian Ocean, living on its wits, knocking on doors and running away, a constant irritant. Since the intended enemy would be unarmed all would be well until they met their inevitable nemesis in an encounter with some bigger vessel of the Royal Navy. Everything depended on what would happen then. Von Mueller was an old-fashioned man and a fine old naval tradition existed of a discreet gentlemanly comparing of the size of one's ordinance followed by just heaving to and quietly accepting a defeat that seemed inevitable. After all, in naval encounters, the outcome was almost always predictable in advance, barrel inches being everything. Yet there was also a nasty, modern idea that honour required a fight to the death with as many as possible going down with their ship and Lauterbach could all too easily picture the captain's insubstantial form being sucked down with no more complaint than a great air-bubble. If he were incapacitated, von Muecke would assume command and he was even worse. He would have them doing bayonet charges on the poop and singing "Die Wacht am Rhein" as the sea washed over them. Lauterbach ran his hand over the comforting materiality of his own thigh and stomach and saw big trouble coming. At least the other ships had not given them three cheers, the usual public acknowledgement of a suicide mission.

This would mean setting a new course. He sighed. Before the summons came, he hauled himself to his feet and headed for the bridge. Inside, it was crowded. There was chaos and confusion on all sides. The rest of the squadron was observing radio silence. The German island of Yap could not be raised. The message of a Japanese declaration of war was – it now seemed – garbled and unsure. They travelled cocooned in perilous ignorance. Von Muecke devised an elaborate set of training exercises that kept the men's hands out of their trouser pockets around the clock. Junior officers were set to erecting anti-shrapnel screens around the guns. Made of woven hemp, they would later prove splendidly incendiary. Gnarled engineers dismantled the boilers, one by one, and replaced their fouled tubes. Prince Franz Josef tinkered whistling with the torpedoes and reset their warheads. And everywhere was coal. Not only the bunkers were full, but it had been piled everywhere on the decks in great tottering stacks, so that the men squelched through it in trenches like on the Western Front, their feet dragging through filthy coal slurry. The ladders and companionways were gritty with it. Soon it was trekked all over the ship. It was under their nails and behind their ears and when they blew their noses, there it was again embedded wetly in their snot.

"A course for the Palau Islands, if you please Mr Lauterbach, port of Angaur." Von Mueller, endeckchaired, serenely above it all, a board set across his knees with a homely clutter of charts and papers, watching as men poked rifles up the big gun barrels to check their aim without wasting shells.

Von Muecke had thought of that. The captain was swaddled up against the weather, like some millionaire invalid on the Atlantic run, though it was warm enough in these latitudes. "And keep us well to the east of Yap. They may well have been taken by the enemy." Bloody right. He took them a good seventy miles out.

With 6,000 tons of coal aboard, the *Markomannia* wallowed heavily in their wake, painted in the colours of a British Blue Funnel liner, irritated to be constantly used as their practice target. At the economical steaming speed of twelve knots, it would take them six days. The sea was horribly vast, the ship suffocatingly tight. On the heaving bridge, Lauterbach felt the chords of feat twang through his guts. The whiff of death was borne incontinently on the wind like the smell of excrement in old Tsingtao. He would soon have to go and count his money again to be soothed.

In Angaur, the *Princess Alice* was an old friend from Tsingtao. She had come from Yap and brought the news that the British had given three hours' warning there before shelling the radio tower from the sea, blasting it to pieces. Having nosed into the harbour at Angaur, she could not anchor, being a 10,000 tonner, because of the great depth of draft and held her position, screws wastefully turning against the current. Civilians from the local phosphate company came out to beg supplies but the *Emden* had none to spare. Prince Franz Josef was doing his own more practised aristocratic begging aboard the *Alice*, pocketing up drink and cigars without formality or embarrassing signs of gratitude. The American newspapers she had brought reported that a great naval battle had occurred in the North Sea with no less than 28 German and

16 British warships sunk, including Jellicoe's flagship. It was all rubbish of course, an ill-judged attempt to manipulate the stock market. Lauterbach scanned the prices anxiously. He was heavily into American stock and doing nicely.

The *Alice* was to be commandeered and become an auxiliary but Captain Bortfeld was far from pleased, insisting on a meticulous documenting of every militarily appropriated match and safety pin. Meanwhile the *Emden* coaled again. And when they set sail, the *Alice* was mysteriously missing. She had no coal. It had evaporated. Her boilers were suddenly fouled and inoperative. She became accidentally lost. It was regretfully impossible to rejoin the flotilla. The 'vons' and other swans on the bridge raged and cursed such low bourgeois concern for property and self-preservation that went against the demands of patriotism. Lauterbach thought of his own besmirched command and understood only too well.

"A course for Portuguese Timor, if you please, Mr Lauterbach."

They crossed the steamy equator somewhere near New Guinea but no time now for japes and duckings, no courtly panoply of King Neptune and hairy-legged mermaids with rolled socks for breasts. Supplies were running low. For days, the cooks had rung every possible change on corned beef and rice. They had fried it, boiled it, roasted it and made it into pies but it was still rice and bully with a lingering aftertaste of flat metal and everyone was sick of it. To add insult to injury, as they headed down for the East Indies, they came upon a fat

Japanese passenger ship, stuffed with supplies. They paused, considered each other, neither entirely certain if they were actually at war, and passed with mutual curtsies expressed in the language of punctiliously dipped flags.

Off Timor they stopped to coal again. A supply ship should have been waiting but wireless rendezvous never quite worked. The sailors were becoming petulant. They had been promised excitement, the fun of rough boyish games and glory to follow. All they had got was the grime and boredom of coaling, foul food and an empty sea. In a magnificent gesture, Prince Franz Josef stripped off his imperial tunic and joined in the coaling. Lauterbach, more cautious, offered a bottle of champagne to the first man to spot a prize ship. If it were von Guerard, he could drink it standing on his head. Too late, they finally heard the Japanese declaration of war reported on wireless from Siam.

There are over thirteen thousand islands in the East Indies, from huge masses such as Java and Sumatra to tiny uninhabited outcrops of coral and sand, a perfect maze to hide in. Another rendezvous off Tanahjumpea. The *Emden* and the near-empty *Markomannia* glided into the paradisal anchorage, and prepared to drop anchor

Suddenly heavy radio traffic bleeped from the bridge and everyone's hair stood on end. Action stations rang out. There was no way of working out the Morse code's point of origin but operators could tell by the signal's strength whether it was near or far. This was very close and the chances were it was a British warship. A smudge of smoke and suddenly, in the thickening late-afternoon sun, there was a pocket battleship coming at them from a range of 3,000 yards, guns trained and thrust towards them.

Lauterbach scrambled for the armoured bridge. At all costs the open decks must be avoided in a battle. Anyone out there would be shredded in seconds. The men rushed to their posts as the two ships, like knights at a jousting, charged either side of a low-lying spit of land, furiously scanning each other with glasses. Battleflags were hoisted. Full speed ahead was rung up. As the men stood in their asbestos gloves, waiting for the order to open fire, the flags were recognised. It was the *Tromp*, a warship of neutral Holland. Speed clanged to dead slow, the flags were hauled down, the guns were pointed straight over the bows and the stiff minuet of internaval courtesies began again. Lauterbach sweated and trembled with relief. Von Muecke cursed. "Infernal bad luck. Thought we had a scrap on at last."

As master of the smaller ship, etiquette decreed that von Mueller had to pay a call on the Dutchman. Boys Two, Three and Four hastily preened and pressed dress uniforms for the captain and the crew of the steam launch while the men scrubbed down the grimy ship's boat out of sight.

Salutes, piping aboard, a glass of beer in the wardroom. Mynheer must know he was in Dutch waters. It was not permitted for belligerents to be in Dutch waters for more than twenty-four hours every three months for purposes of coaling and repairs. A German supply ship had been detected lurking here in Dutch waters for an excessively long period and been ordered to leave. Mynheer must know that a longer period risked compromising Dutch neutrality and involved the sanction of internment. Von Mueller politely withdrew and the *Tromp* escorted them to the three-mile limit. More extravagant salutes, courtly farewells. And don't come back. Von Muecke raged against Hollander pusillanimity, rooted no doubt in English perfidy. Lauterbach saw things more simply.

"The Dutch have no choice but to be neutral, Number One. Theirs is a country where, if you dig a trench, it fills with water and becomes another damned canal."

That night in the listless heat of the wardroom, as they forked greasy corned beef fritters and grey rice around their plates, von Muecke seemed preoccupied. They still dined, with cruel mockery, off rather fine monogrammed china, linen cloth, with a silver cruet set in the middle of the table. Lauterbach had a little something tucked away in his cabin he could eat later but he had his eye on that slice of beef untouched on von Guerard's plate. Von Mueller would be in his deckchair, above them, sipping soup. Finally, von Muecke made a face and pushed the food away with decision.

"Did you know, Lauterbach, that I am musical?" What was this? Was he going to do the "Lauterbach" song? Were they to clear the table so that he could leap upon it and hammer out a hornpipe? It might be a trap. Lauterbach looked into the ice-blue eyes and hedged.

"No, Number One, I did not. And what form does this musicality take?"

"Oh," he smirked self-deprecatingly and flutterd thin, blue-veined hands. "Piano, flute, a little bit on the trumpet." The trumpet? Von Muecke? Surely not. A piccolo man if ever there was one, just as he himself was destined, in any band, to parp and wheeze on the tuba.

"In my student days, I was most attracted by the romance of the theatre." Lauterbach was appalled. Von Muecke a starstruck thespian? Young von Guerard winked wickedly, his generous smile plucking any sting from his words.

"We should have a concert party. Number One, you can play the organ and you, Juli-bumm, can put on a bear suit and dance." Cheers, laughter. Incongruously, in the midst of this tropical sea, miles from land, the sound of sheep bleating blew in the porthole. What enchantment was this? Of course. It was the *Markomannia*, following their stern light too close. Aboard, she still had two pigs, six cattle and a few well-travelled sheep. Converted into roast joints and sausage, they had begun to play a role in the men's dreams. Dr Schwabe there, a follower of the latest psychological fashions, was becoming interested in the subject. Professor Freud was, after all, an Austrian, therefore a sort of ally.

"My principal concern, naturally, was less with acting than with directing others." Yes, thought Lauterbach, he could see that. Von Mueke with his pointer and wall charts ... "and an important part of this was to agree the scenery with the painters, some of them quite talented men but in need of guidance, an overall vision, you understand. They were to produce the large painted backcloths – what we in the theatre," he blushed, a real insider now, "would call 'the flats.'" He cleared his throat. Except for long political tirades against the British, this was the longest speech Lauterbach had ever heard him make. "Now, von Guerard. You remarked this evening that you had picked up a Dutch wireless message that mentioned a four-funnelled British destroyer in the Sunda Strait." Von Guerard nodded, intrigued. "Our principle defining feature, when seen in silhouette," he turned sideways on, "is our possession of three funnels – not two or four like the British and French – but three. So why do we not rig a fake fourth funnel of canvas – a flat – to confuse the enemy?" Cries of "Brilliant," "Well done Number One."

The blue eyes turned to stare at Lauterbach who was pursing his lips. "You do not," he challenged icily, "like the idea?"

"Oh it's not that, Number One. It's an excellent suggestion." God knows, he would vote for anything that would avoid their being blown out of the water a little bit longer. "God knows, the British papers always claim we hide behind a fake British flag anyway. But what about the old man – I mean the captain? He can be – well – a bit of a stickler in matters of honour. We'd be mutton dressed up as lamb. He wouldn't like that at all."

Von Muecke considered. "But the *Markomannia* sails under false colours."

"She is not – strictly speaking – a vessel of war. Anyway, she was already that way when assigned to us."

"True." He got to his feet, put on his cap. It had a smear of the still undried green paint on it. "I will just go and ask him, then." They were speechless. It was like suggesting one should just nip up and ask God for a clarification after an argument over the mystery of the Trinity. Lauterbach noted with distaste von Muecke's athletic, feline step towards the door, the mark of a man with an excess of energy.

When he was gone, they had another round of beers drunk in shocked silence – small, parsimonial bottles, not the elaborate, foaming steins of shoreleave.

"He won't go for it," opined Franz Josef breaking the silence and pushing a pile of ten silver dollars across the table. There was an explosion of bets and counterbets. "You hold the pot Juli-bumm."

"It is not seemly to gamble on the ethics of war," he grinned piously. Howls of derision, lip-farts. He gathered the money in his hat and stowed it, out of sight, on his fat knees under the tablecloth then reached across and forked von Muecke's left-overs into his mouth.

Von Muecke returned, frowned, sat down. Frustrated thespian that he was, he knew how to work an audience. Silence tautened. Finally someone spoke.

"Well ...?"

He broke out in a broad grin and threw himself back in his chair. "He said it was a great idea. The treacherous British always talk about their great sense of humour. It would be," he explained earnestly, "a sort of English joke."

What sounded like a squeal of laughter floated in across the waves, one of the pigs aboard the *Markomannia*. "Must have flown into something," thought Lauterbach, astonished and belched. That last slice of bully beef had been very nasty.

They sailed through the narrow straits between Bali and Lombok, in four-funnel disguise, heading south of Java and Sumatra with the *Markomannia* a safe distance behind. The churning, crowded water and its many prying eyes were the greatest danger they would face in this part of the world. The endless, undisciplined chatter of the British over the radio gave away another of their warships following a similar course at similar speed that they might otherwise have fallen foul of. They coaled once more in Dutch waters and again were caught and ordered to leave. The Dutch official, observing strict neutrality, neither declared their own identity over the radio nor revealed that they had passed within 30 miles of HMS *Hampshire* and certain annihilation. And there were final additions to the crew. The ship's cat gave birth to five kittens.

They had been at war for some two months already and achieved virtually nothing. But now the whole of the Indian Ocean and its rich sea lanes suddenly lay open to them. No one even suspected they were there.

CHAPTER THREE

There is nothing so romantic as the stern light of a ship on a moonless night, bobbing on an ink-black sea. Even better when the whole side of a ship is carelessly lit up like a Christmas tree, with copious coils of smoke belching back from a single funnel. But romance was not on their minds. They were sharks. This was prey. The *Emden* leapt forward, slicing through the water. Real action stations at last. Lauterbach sighed in the tiny cabin and pulled on his boots, tottered as she cut speed again and crept close to fire off two blanks. "Stop engines. Don't use wireless." The other ship, shocked, stopped dead in the water. Lauterbach was already on the ladder over the side, ready to board, a torch gripped, for want of a cutlass, between his teeth.

Proximity banished romance still further. She was a small vessel, low in the water, her own good thick ladder on the side, thank God. He examined her papers, ignoring the phlegmatic captain who smelled of garlic and chewed melon seeds, spitting out the shells onto the filthy deck and shouting occasionally to no one in particular, "Greek. Neutral. *Pontoporos*. Greek." Wait, what was this? Yes, she was Greek but had been chartered by the British Government to carry 6,000 tons of Bengal coal. That coal was fair game, could be called contraband, and badly needed for the boilers. But if the ship itself were sunk, the German government would receive a hefty bill for it and von Mueller would be furious. A dilemma. Never mind. Lauterbach he fixee.

"Captain," he said, slipping an arm matily around the chubby, doubtless hairy, shoulders. "I think, as men of the world, as fellow members of the merchant marine, we should have a little talk in your cabin. Do you, by any chance, have any of that very fine brandy for which Greece is justly famous?"

"Eh?"

Twenty minutes later, the brandy was finished and the charter of the *Pontoporos* had been switched, with a stroke of the pen, to the German government. It was an intelligent compromise. A wad of US dollars crackled comfortingly in Lauterbach's hidden pocket. He was the only member of the crew developing a paunch on slim rations. The ship would not be sunk. Instead, the coal would be paid for in full by the Kaiser. The news was flashed in Morse back to the *Emden* and the dumpy vessel, with a galling top speed of a mere 9 knots, fell in behind her new mother ship. They were elated to have coal, not yet knowing – as Lauterbach knew – that Indian coal was of terrible quality, soft, fouling the boiler tubes and producing huge amounts of treacherous smoke that betrayed their position twenty miles away. In the cabin he had found another treasure, an Indian newspaper with an obliging list of local shipping movements. Von Mueller would love that. Now they could pick and choose and stop sodding about all over the place.

The first victim was the *Indus*. With her aerials and odd white structures on deck, they thought at first she was a warship but when she cheerfully raised her flag to greet what she assumed was a fellow British vessel, it was a blue ensign not the white of an auxiliary. Her captain cursed as the *Emden* ran up her own German battleflag and fired the usual warning shot. She turned out to be a troopship and the odd structures were stalls for horses. Soon her crew were being ferried across to the *Markomannia*, the 'junkman,' whose job was to house prisoners and unwanted cargo that could not be sunk. The *Indus* was crammed with supplies but, as yet, no troops and the inexperienced prize-crew wandered through her like bumpkins at a fair, seizing all and sundry with their hands. When von Mueller saw bright silk kimonos, cushions, knitting wool and bundles of stationery tied up with pink ribbons being brought aboard his ship, he knew it was time to send over Lauterbach to supervise the looting and so save the men from mindless haberdashery.

His eye was discriminating. He knew what was militarily useful and what would appeal below decks. Soon there was fresh food, and fine conserves, drink and tobacco and a wealth of fancy equipment – including a whole radio station. The deckhands were soon kitted out in slick oilskins and binoculars. Instead of coal, the decks were now heaped with the untold wealth and benevolence that flowed from Lauterbach's cornucopia. A Father Christmas in mufti, he dispensed sausages and sweet bon-bons filled with brandy, rained jam and pilchards down on the men. Hams were strung across the ship in a cheery bobbing display and a saucy tar had seized a supply of female undergarments to be converted into more gay bunting. Twists of tobacco reared up in benodorous mounds and the British now supplied them with fresh bread and live hens. Ironic toasts were drunk to good King George in brandy, as supplied by royal appointment, and then to Lauterbach as his prophet on earth. They sang the Lauterbach song. They were happy. *He* was happy.

Most sought after of all was soap. The *Emden* had run so short that the precious suds of the men were collected for the use of the laundrymen, and those of the laundrymen used to scrub the sleazy decks. A few days before had been Prince Franz Josef's birthday. The band had oompahed patriotically, in his early morning honour, outside his cabin, but best of all was the present of a complete bar of soap mysteriously preserved by Lauterbach. Now the *Indus* was awash with soap, whole cartons of it. Two, Three and Four fell on it and squirrelled it away with little cries of joy. Cigarettes were so plentiful that von Muecke was found staring at his fake funnel. "How would it be," he mused, "if the off-duty stokers were to light up in there and get a bit of smoke going?" It was almost a joke. As the day wore on, a glutted torpor fell over the whole ship. The air thickened. Eyes unfocussed. Reflexes slackened and sagged.

Von Mueller watched from the bridge, sipping milkless lapsang soochong from a paper-thin cup and matching saucer. The men had been good and loyal, had borne danger and deprivation with courage. They must receive their due in the only language they understood, the things of the senses, and must have their fill of laughter, cognac and greasy sausage. He regretted only that he had no women to issue them and that bitter masturbation and those informal practices to which the navy turned a blind eye must for the moment suffice. Dr Schwabe was down there pursuing one of the ratings who had slipped on a bright female kimono, trying desperately to get down an account of his childhood as he waltzed around the deck to screams and catcalls. Von Mueller smiled wanly upon him as upon them all. But every minute spent here was dangerous. A British dreadnought could come over the horizon at any second and catch them napping. There must now be an emotional purgation. He called action stations.

To deliberately sink a ship is a terrible thing. They had been trained to think of themselves as fearless stalkers and hunters of wild beasts but to destroy a captured ship was more like beating a placid cow on the head with an iron bar until it died. The seacocks on the *Indus* were brutally smashed so that water shot into engine room and bunkers in great grey geysers. As soon as the scuttling crew had themselves scuttled clear, the forward gunners coldly pumped six shells into the vessel. A terrible hush fell over the spectators lining the rails of the little fleet, suddenly horribly sober. The *Indus* shivered as though with a spasm of sudden internal agony, steadied and settled a little lower in the water. Then, as the crew watched in suspense, she seemed to fight for life, showing a terrible will to survive her implacable fate. As the minutes ticked by, little by little, she started slipping down, accelerating as she went, gulping down great final draughts through hatchways and stairs and coughing them back out through open portholes. With a groan she twisted on her side and blew huge gouts of filthy oil through the ventilation shafts like a dying whale and the funnels screamed as they were torn apart and rushed to the bottom in a terrible whirlpool. When it seemed that nothing was left but a monstrous vat of boiling water, mighty beams, ripped loose in the depths, shot up in the air and crashed back into the sea and a terrible funereal belch.roared up from the abyss to envelope them in a rank stench of gross decay. Lastly, the lifeboats surfaced, righted themselves correctly according to design, and bobbed cheerfully in the sun. They would give away the fate of the vessel so the *Emden* tried to run them down like puppies in the road. They swept playfully out of the way, twinkled their sterns and floated happily off towards India. Never mind. They would not be found for several days. The *Emden*, *Pontoporos* and *Markomannia* turned and sailed on towards Calcutta. The captain of the *Indus* stood on the deck and wept openly and without shame. It sent a shiver up every seaman's spine.

The next day they sank the *Lovat*, another troop transport. The crew were courteously allowed time to gather their personal effects before being installed on the junkman. Just off Calcutta, perilously close to the harbour entrance, they took the *Kabinga*, carrying British goods to North America. In fact, they were so close to land that they mistook a temple stupa in Puri for a ship and steamed towards it. Lauterbach had never been one of the world's great navigators and now he was the butt of shipboard humour with lookouts spotting the Brandenburg gate and the Eiffel tower in mid ocean. The *Kabinga*'s goods were deemed neutral so that the ship could not be sunk. Lauterbach rebuked his own crass sentimentality – the master had his wife and child on board – for settling for only a very small sweetener to explain to von Mueller the need to spare the vessel.

Then they took the *Killin*. More foul Indian coal, unwanted, so she would be sent straight to the bottom. The morning was ended with a pleasant lunch, the officers playing bridge or sitting in Lauterbach's easy chairs thumbing Lauterbach's books – young von Guerard, – himself the ship's pet – tousled, unshaven, giggling in delicious agony at the kittens boiling in his lap and poking their tiny claws through the thin stuff of his uniform and into his thighs. Their fur had already added itself as the latest crust on the sticky green paint.

"We have given them names Juli-bumm. Ah! Eee! They are Pontoporos, Indus, and so on – one for each of the ships we have sunk. What do you think?"

"Find more cats," growled Lauterbach.

Then the brand-new *Diplomat*, smelling of paint and full of costly imperial tea, the apoplectic British captain outraged that they would not porter across his golf clubs, sporting trophies and Indian curios. Lauterbach disliked his braying, patrician tone of voice, that transported him back to the childhood days of tight-arsed respectable relatives. They would all go to the bottom and the captain with them if he had his way. Yet part of him was endlessly intrigued by the bizarre objects by which people defined their own identities, the things they prized and wanted to save. Portraits of wives and children, of course, but there had been a man aboard the *Indus* who brought only a pair of knitted mittens and several gnarled old tars came aboard tenderly clutching debauched teddy bears. He would mention it to Schwabe.

Then a neutral Italian ship that was allowed on its way but hastened to improperly denounce the *Emden*'s position to the British authorities. Why? Lauterbach had always liked Italians. He had never done them any harm. Shipping in the area was promptly suspended and five British and Japanese cruisers were called out in emergency to search for them. The Italian captain, they heard later, was given a gold watch and chain by the grateful British.

They headed east, culling the *Trabboch* on the way, and finally released the *Kabinga*, now crowded with prisoners, to return to India. As they were freed, the captive crews crowded the rails and stared at them.

"What are they doing?" asked von Muecke, nervously. "Are they going to try to board us? This is madness. Shoot anyone who attempts to approach the side." Then …

"Hip, hip hooray!" Caps were tossed in the air, smiles waves. They were giving their astonished German captors three hearty cheers. In captured newspapers, the crew would now begin to see a legend take form that would cast the *Emden*, and more particularly von Mueller, as exponents of a gentlemanly and courteous kind of warfare that marked a return to the rules of knightly chivalry and was totally at odds with the emerging horrors of the Flanders trenches. The squalour and despair of the land war had led to a contempt for life that often included one's own, so that only in the air and at sea did conditions allow men to retain that sense of self-worth that bred humane behaviour and honour-governed, gladiatorial combat. It was, naturally, von Mueller's high aristocratic principles that received all the credit for this. The Germans, it seemed, were fighting to preserve British values.

Lauterbach smiled to himself, the latest newspaper from a victim vessel across his knee. It was full of the doings of the *Emden* and threw around words like "sportsman" and "fair play," "gallantry" and "gentleman of war" as if war were a genteel match of golf but, as a man of the material world, Lauterbach knew such abstract virtue rested squarely on the abundant supplies delivered by his own astute looting. It was his low purpose rather than their high principle that kept this ship afloat. He folded the paper and bent to enjoy a plate of puffed-up, high-principled Apfelstrudel, conjured up specially for him by the cook to whom he had given looted British flour and base grease.

"Mmm. Just the way I like it." He tongued through the outer carapace. "... dry and rough to on the outside and smooth, moist and sticky within."

He opened his eyes to see Schwabe looking at him excitedly, notebook irritatingly poised, pencil ready-licked for the taking of notes. Lauterbach glimpsed odd little sketches in the margins and thought of that of Turpitz in the heads. Surely he could not be the artist? It was an intriguing thought. Her would return to it in moments of contemplation in the latrines. Before Schwabe could say anything, Lauterbach struck first.

"Tell me Schwabe. What does your Dr Freud say on the subject of people who lick the tips of their pencils?"

"Er. Well ..." He stowed it rapidly away, blushing.

"Have you read this?" Lauterbach chuckled, swallowing dabbed-up crumbs, ostentatiously finger-licking and flourishing the paper in a great paw. "'There is no doubt that the German cruiser *Emden* had knowledge that the *Indus* was carrying 150 cases of North-West Soap Company's celebrated ELYSIUM Soap, and hence the pursuit. The men on the *Emden* and their clothes are now clean and sweet, thanks to ELYSIUM Soap. Try it!' They are using us to sell soap to Indians."

But an attentive eye would have seen that Lauterbach's tunic, taut now over his swelling paunch, unlike those of his slim fellow-officers, was not just clean and sweet. It was discreetly starched at cuffs and collar and the buttons were hand-burnished. Before delivery, the top pocket had received a final dressing of four chinking silver dollars, half the pay of non-existant Number One Washboy. Lauterbach felt he was finally beginning to get the measure of His Imperial Majesty's navy.

He felt breath on his neck and turned to see von Muecke reading, incredulous, over his shoulder. "We are the most popular ship in the Indian Ocean even though we are their enemies. The English are truly mad." Von Muecke, headshaking. "They speak of our campaign as if we were shoppers."

"Ah, yes, Number One, but not just ordinary shoppers. We are at least carriage-trade."

But the water in these latitudes was getting too hot for comfort and they would head south for a coaling in the remote Andamans, peopled by neutrally hostile aborigines who fired their arrows at all visitors with an easy indifference to nationality. On the way they picked up the *Clan Matheson*, more by habit than design. She made the mistake of running before them and they chased her as unreflectingly as a dog does a fleeing cat.

"Are you English?" they called across.

"Scottish, damn and blast ye."

Von Mueller was crisply punitive. "For failure to comply at once with my orders, the vessel shall be sunk immediately."

The cathedral-like holds were an echoing treasurehouse of rich and useless manufactures, luxury cars, typewriters, locomotives that gleamed silently in the dark. Lauterbach stroked the sleek Rolls Royces in quiet reproach, then kicked their tyres in a mixture of respect and vandalism. He was a sword of austerity from the desert, a punisher of the sin of pride and all this vanity was born but to die. But wait, what was this? In a well-strawed stall two nervous and immaculate racehorses thudded their hooves on the planking. Lauterbach considered them in horror and confusion. Never had he seen creatures of such impractical beauty, pared and delicate, uncompromisingly aristocratic. Compared to their sinuous lines and rippling flanks, the boxy Rolls Royces were merely cheap tin toys. He looked into those great liquid eyes and could not bear to think of their terror at an invading wall of cold, hard water surging towards them. If they had been women he would have mounted them, ridden them hard, forced and whipped them over the fences of his pleasure and they would have loved him for it.

"Lieutenant Schall, shoot the horses."

He went about his business on the upper decks, evacuating the crew, checking the contents of the captain's safe, pocketing up any useful dollars, trying to block out from his thoughts the inevitable shots that his ears were straining for and it was not until they were embarking in the boats, the explosive charges already set to blow the ship apart, that he asked again whether it had been done.

"Sorry, Juli-bumm. I just couldn't."

He climbed back aboard, padded quietly to their stall and shot them down with a single bullet each to the brain, as he kissed their hot foreheads with pure, sad love. They shuddered and died at his fatal lips. It was the first shot he had fired in the war – they the first casualties of the campaign. Barely had their boat cleared the ship, when the charges went off and blew a huge steel plate clanging over their heads. By the time they made it back to the *Emden*, the *Clan Matheson* was already taking its proud cargo swirling to the bottom.

Von Muecke showed an unexpected gift for stand-up comedy.

A ship at sea is a closed, incestuous community, a sweating mobile factory of love, hate and rumour. Newspapers from captive vessels were sent straight to the bridge as a useful resource. But there was a fear also that access to the propaganda put about by the enemy, for the consumption of their Indian subjects, might unsettle the men. Von Muecke knew that the wildest tales were circulating. It was time to sink them with a few well-placed charges.

He adopted the tactic of reading to the men totally contradictory accounts of the same events from different papers and the more deadly serious he was, the funnier it became. He read out descriptions of their own sinking and imaginary exploits that placed them firmly anywhere from Rangoon to Australia. He reduced them to tears of laughter with stories of simultaneous naval battles with the rest of their squadron in parts of the world they had never even visited. He totted up the casualty figures on the European front and proved that twice the population of Germany had allegedly perished there already. Best of all was a composite picture of British plans for the Reich after their victory. It was a vision of home with the Reich collapsed, penitent generals shooting themselves by battalions and the complete colonial dismemberment of Germany with Bavaria independent and only Thuringia being left intact. The Thuringian stokers rose spontaneously and stalked and pranced up and down arrogantly, as the only true Germans, before these contemptible new foreigners.

They steamed across the Madras-Rangoon and Singapore-Calcutta shipping lanes, horribly aware of the lingering smoke they were making from the foul Indian fuel. The crew were in fine form. Lauterbach had saved them most of the horrors of a recent coaling by secretly hiring the Indian crew of their latest prize to do it for them. Ships of all nations were run on imperial lines, white officers at the top, Chinese stewards between and, in the engine-room below, toiling brown helots. The money had come from a magical inventory of the safes of prize vessels that converted gain into loss and loss into gain by an act of twinkling numerical prestidigitation learnt from doing company accounts. He called it "tickling the kitty."

"Rather noble of those Lascars to volunteer for such a job," commented von Muecke. "Just shows what could be done to the British Empire with a few home truths. After just a few days with us they already love Germany. After the war, we shall take charge of India and rule it with a firmness they will appreciate."

The slow *Pontoporos* was sent off to a distant rendezvous, like an irritating granny with a gammy leg. A passing Norwegian disembarrassed them of prisoners – again three cheers – and obligingly gave details of the movements of enemy warships about the island of Penang. Von Mueller carefully stored that information away. Anyway, sloppy British security and uncoded radio traffic allowed them to keep easy track of their pursuers and so avoid them. Von Mueller took clean, hard coal aboard from the *Markomannia* and sent her too off to a rendezvous. For the moment the captain exulted in his restored freedom of motion for he had another bold scheme he was itching to realise.

The *Emden* started in from the east, sailing into darkness, straining to her full speed of 24 knots with her fake fourth funnel in place. The sea was like a mirror. It parted in glossy marcelled waves on either side of the bow while the men's heartbeats accelerated to match the pitch of her thrusting screws, so that all the world was one great visceral maelstrom moving to the same rhythm. The lifeboats had been filled with water. Everyone had been ordered to take a freshwater shower and change into clean underwear. To sailors that meant they were going into a battle where wounds were expected. Numbers Two, Three and Four disappeared under an avalanche of washing.

The lights of Madras blazed immoderately, not from bravado but sheer stupidity. The harbour was strung with bulbs and illuminated beacons guided the raider conveniently into the main channel where the waterfront welcomed them with fat open arms. Lauterbach alone was worried about the sudden crackling sheet lightning that lit them from behind but all these excited boys had their eyes fixed firmly in front. They would make a good target as they sailed away – *if* they sailed away. This was, after all, a defended harbour.

"The guns will be big but old, nothing but museum specimens that fire a shell the size of a dustbin," so von Muecke at the briefing, thinking he was being encouraging. Lauterbach found he had a particular dislike of being hit by a flying dustbin full of explosive. At 3,000 yards they stopped dead, a big easy target, and switched on their huge searchlights, probing the hillside for their goal, the great oil tanks of the Burmah Oil Company, painted an obliging shade of white. Von Mueller had done careful homework with his charts and maps. It seemed like an age before they began to move again. If he lined up his vessel with the six bulging tanks and the flashing navigation lights, he would have the biggest possible target with the smallest risk to local civilians. They brought all the starboard guns to bear and fired off twenty-five crisp salvoes. The noise was like thunder. A tank was hit.

Blazing kerosene exploded and gushed as from a volcano, starting other fires, while rockets of burning carburant shot into the sky and flame and thick black smoke danced over the hillside. Lauterbach raised his fine new British binoculars and stared at the city in disbelief. This was a new wonder. Instead of fleeing, excited sightseers – Indian and British – were hurrying down to the harbour to watch openmouthed, clogging the roads with cars, bicycles and rickshaws, blocking the fire-engines and the troops running around like headless chickens. The whole event had become a carnival. After ten minutes, the *Emden* coolly ceased fire and steamed off to the north east.

"In sea engagements," von Muecke had pointed out when putting his men through their paces at swimming, "nine tenths of the casualties are from the sea, not the guns. No one would get killed, if sea battles were fought in the harbour or on dry land."

"For that to happen we would have to have Lauterbach navigating, Number One."

Well, they were still in harbour and death was still on offer. The defences were finally brought to bear. Nine shots were returned. Lauterbach counted them all. None of the British shells hit anything. There were no casualties. In a later paper they would discover that most of the guns were unmanned as the British were at a special dinner celebrating yesterday's hot news – the sinking of that German cruiser, *Emden*, confidently announced on the wireless. The attack on Madras had been intended to demoralise the Indian population. Instead they laughed. They laughed at the British. Insurance rates on the London Market went through the roof.

They rendezvoused with the *Markomannia* and headed

south towards Ceylon over smooth seas. For most of the day, the pall of smoke on the horizon was visible as the oil of Madras continued to burn. The whole ship was still crackling with excitement and exultation. The crew spoke in grins. When you brushed against them, they tingled with electricity and when von Mueller appeared, unsmiling, from the bridge they cheered like British prisoners. Tars liked, Lauterbach realised, to be sent to their pointless deaths by a proper gentleman. But he knew this exploit meant not glory but trouble. They had singed the British lion's beard, shown it to be toothless and stupid, roused native contempt against it. Now it would stop at nothing to get them with its great grasping claws.

They gathered in a few more ships, gleaned just off Ceylon. Most were in ballast or uninteresting. With so much documentation imperfect or destroyed, it was often difficult for a prize officer to reach a rapid decision about the neutrality or contraband status of a vessel and its contents. Lauterbach always hoped for some moment of wordless understanding with fellow seamen but mostly the captains could not, or would not, understand that their vessels might just be favourably viewed by a well-disposed and adequately lubricated assessor. He lived a metaphorical being in a painfully literalist world where everything had to made laboriously explicit. One waxed insulting, shouting of dishonesty and peculation and Lauterbach had him arrested for fomenting military indiscipline, slapped in chains and his vessel sent to the bottom without compunction. This might have made him more cautious but did not. Peculation was his art. It possessed him and he could no more forsake it than any other artist could his particular muse.

Their supply of coal was running low. If a British warship happened across them, they would not even be able to lift their skirts and run. And then they took the *Buresk* with 7,000 tons – a whole month's supply – of hard Cardiff coal aboard her, the best in the world. An hour or so's wheedling and headshaking and a little well-placed money produced an excellent result. The British captain, officers and steward would stay aboard, with a crew hired from amongst the Arab prisoners of the junkman, and follow German orders. The remaining crews of the latest six victims were shipped off to freedom – or at least India. Von Muecke would insist on making the distinction. There was a final coaling from the *Markomannia* in the Maldives and she too was sent off to rendezvous with the *Pontoporos*. The men were finally permitted to send mail to their loved ones at home, that would be posted by her in the East Indies. By the time it arrived, many of them would be dead.

Von Mueller knew that troopships were being sent from Australia and New Zealand via Aden, hauling more fodder for the insatiable land war to chomp on. On the outward voyage they would have a heavy escort but on the way back, as empty vessels, would more than likely be unaccompanied. By sinking them, he could break the circle and cause widespread havoc like a man who refuses to send back his empty beer bottles. What he needed first was a quiet place for rest and repairs for, from radio traffic in code and in clear, it seemed that no less than sixteen enemy vessels were now scouring the seas for the *Emden*. Von Mueller scanned the charts. And his eyes lit up. Diego Garcia, that little dot of coral and sand in the most remote part of the Pacific, would do nicely.

The expat population of Diego Garcia was not large. In fact its total was two, an Englishman and a resolutely francophone Malagasy. Twice a year a small sailing schooner put in and brought supplies of tobacco, bully beef and strong drink and bore off the copra – delivered by the pretty and philoprogenitive inhabitants – that justified the imperial presence. It was not an eventful life. They ate fish, drank coconut milk and coconut sap and their many derivatives, alcoholic and not, and read and re-read the same few books beneath a benevolently distant British rule.

The *Emden* hauled itself on four clogged boilers into the coral bay and dropped its greased and fouled anchor into the limpid water as the sailors looked around at the waving palms and the gently pulsing waves and sighed. The *Buresk* slipped in and anchored coyly alongside the *Emden*, tucked behind its apron. Peace. Calm.

Then action stations rang out. A Union Jack rose suddenly above the trees at the edge of the shore. They all scrambled for their posts again. Glasses scanned the shadows for the feared battleship about to emerge from around the curve. A splash, another flash of British colours ... and a small rowing boat slid into view near the shore, pulled rapidly across the smooth water by two bare-chested natives. In the prow sat two obviously benign human beings, one waving a holed straw hat above his head like a halo, the other brandishing a large bunch of bananas Even to von Muecke, it did not look like hostile military action.

"Ahoy there ..."

"Bonjour messieurs ..."

"... Hallo chaps. Get out of my way you damn Froggie fool."

"... Do not push. Always you push."

Rose and Privett, respectively over- and under- manager of the copra plantation, clambered aboard with rheumatoid difficulty and comic synchrony, the *entente cordiale* become Feydeau farce. Rose was rubicund and very British, Privett an old Malagasy Creole, grown wizened and wattled under tropical sun. They dressed alike, much like the popular vision of an artist in the south of France, white flannels, cotton shirts, straw hats, espadrilles. One spoke only English, the other only French and being much rubbed together, they had been reduced to a bitter parody of an old married couple, each finishing the other's sentences and speaking of the other in the tones of withering contempt usually reserved by a wife for talking publicly of her husband.

Lauterbach took his hand off his pistol butt to aid them aboard and switched awkwardly back and forth from French to English as appropriate. They grinned, they beamed, they chuckled aloud at the sheer pleasure of seeing the enemies of their nation. The native rowers, too, waved and smiled up at Lauterbach with those incredible white teeth you can only have if you have a mahogany face to set them in. Lauterbach realised at once that in the Arcadia of Diego Garcia nobody even knew there was a war that was larger than their own domestic feuds. Ergo there was no war. Innocence was its own reward. In this palm-fringed paradise they were finally, totally, safe.

"I bring eggs," explained the Creole expansively in highly accented English, "Fruit, fish, turnips ..." Turnips?

"He calls them turnips – excuse his stupidity – he means yams." They were handed aloft from the bottom of the boat There had been no schooner for many months, they explained.

They knew nothing of world events, had no radio. Pray give us some news. We are thirsty for it. Lauterbach whispered orders. Newspapers were to be hidden, the captain to be informed of the situation. Men from the *Buresk*, including its British officers, to be confined to the vessel, their hopes of female diversion dashed.

"A drink," Lauterbach invited, stony-faced as a butler. "Have the gentleness to please come into the wardroom for a drink. Whisky and soda? And now – *ice*?" They slavered at that "ice".

Being His Britannic Majesty's consular representative, Rose had put on a tie and claimed the right to go first. As they moved into the wardroom, he froze, sniffed the air like an old dog.

"Hang on," he said, adjusting wire-rimmed glasses and staring at the framed portrait of the Kaiser. "That's not King George. You're not Brits. You're Germans."

It had never occurred to Lauterbach that anyone could mistake them up close for a British vessel. Perhaps von Muecke's false funnel was an unnecessary ingenuity. Now they sat, side by side, in creaking Lauterbach chairs, tinkled cubes of unaccustomed ice, rapturously, in pale Scotch – supplied by German appointment – sipped, gulped, drained. Another?

"Well, monsieur is too kind."

"Jolly good don't mind if I do but don't give *him* too much."

Privett scuffled awkwardly under his buttocks, with one hand, like a man having trouble with his underwear, wrestled out a crushed and forgotten newspaper and spread it out. Alas he knew not to read the English but perhaps he might pass it to his colleague over there whose tongue it was. Now that word there 'Crisis' what was that all about then?

Lauterbach completed servings of scotch with his own hasty hands, clumsily shovelled ice into the runners like a stoker Cardiff coal, whisked the paper away. "Excuses. Fouled by cats. Steward, please destroy at once this shockingly besmirched newspaper. The Pope," he said. "His Holiness Pius X has – alas – died. It is said he choked on a wafer biscuit."

"Good God!" cried Privett, toasting then crossing himself. "The Pope? What else?"

"There was a great fire in Madras, started by a hail of flaming meteors that ignited a chapati factory and the oil depot."

"Madras? Chapatis? Merciful heavens," cried Rose. "What else?"

"Great sadness. A British ship was lost not far from here. Apparently the crew tell a tale of being beguiled by German-speaking mermaids."

Privett gaped. "Mermaids is it? And in German? Such a thing has never made itself heard of. Drink had a hand in it I declare."

"Terrible drinkers the people round here," confirmed Rose, glaring at Privett. "Might I have a little more of that there …? Not so much for my under-manager. So many disasters. But is there no good news?"

Lauterbach furrowed his brow in concentration. "Oh indeed. The Queen of England, by the grace of God, has been delivered of a multiple birth – quintuplets I believe."

"But that is extraordinary," cried Rose. They both gulped, as in shock, and held out the glass for more, a patriotic toast.

"Is she not a lady advanced in years?" asked Privett, amazed.

"That is the wonder of it," affirmed benign Lauterbach. "The children have been christened Pontoporos, Indus ..."

Lauterbach suddenly felt an icy presence tickle the back of his neck, as of a ghostly manifestation and the eyes of his visitors grew wide, looking over his shoulder. Turning swiftly to see what this materialisation might be he found von Mueller, floating in one of his long coats.

"Enough news, I think, Mr Lauterbach, for our guests," he whispered huskily. "But I see they are thirsty. Please see to their wants."

It is often only when receiving guests that one becomes truly aware of the failings of one's own home. The *Emden* was no longer the trim, white-scrubbed craft that had left Tsingtao just a few months earlier. She was streaked with corrosion, coal-grime and oil. The rails were bent and broken from the impact of coal sacks and old automobile tyres hung down her sides to shield her from collision with colliers. In more immaculate days, von Muecke had wanted the men to paint them white but such affectation was now a thing of the past. Weekly inspections had been reduced to a visit to the heads to declare them either 'sweet' or not. The scored deck gleamed with treacherous bare metal. Electrical wires were draped dangerously over handrails and now fishing-lines trailed through every porthole. As they sat in the bilious green wardroom, a chicken wandered in and looked at them, scratched at a hole in the lino and wandered out. A sailor walked past, whistling, with a duck tucked casually under his arm.

Von Mueller offered yet more scotch, thirstily accepted, while he gripped his own, as yet untouched and embarked on an epic tale of their part in friendly joint world manoeuvres by the navies of Britain, Germany and France. The appearance of the vessel must be forgiven. They had put down an armed uprising in German East Africa, been ordered without warning on a trip to the other side of the world, been damaged by a freak wave in a huge storm and come here for emergency repairs. They were suffering too from an accumulation of barnacles that had affected their speed and manoeuvrability. At the very least here, they hoped to flood underwater compartments of the vessel and so cant it to allow them to have their bottom scraped.

"Yes, yes," cried Privett, misunderstanding, gesturing with ice-tinkling glass. "The ladies here are most obliging. They will do that for you for a few shillings."

"Shut up fool."

It was with deep regret that they arrived with no prior notice but the British vessels with which they co-operated had spoken so highly of the hospitality of the residents that they hoped they would be welcome.

"Ah yes. Co-operation." Rose slurped whisky, sluicing it back and forth through huge yellow teeth like mouthwash. "Delighted to receive you I'm sure, but do you by any chance have a chap on board who knows about motorboats? Mine's a sound enough old thing but the native mechanics have no sympathy for its little ways. You know what they say, 'Give us the job and we'll finish the tools'" He paused expectantly, awaiting laughter but von Mueller stared blankly. "Well, anyway, co-operation and all that ..."

Von Mueller smiled with a shark's smile that involved

only his mouth. "Of course. As His Majesty's representative, Mr Rose, it is hardly seemly that you conduct business from a rowing boat. Our machinist, Kluge, will attend you forthwith. Pray let me have you conducted back to your home in our own launch. Mr Lauterbach will attend to facilitate conversation." He flashed a significant look. Lauterbach understood at once that his job was to frustrate all communication.

"Oh I say, most frightfully grateful." Rose leapt to his feet, whisky slopping on crotch, teetered, overbalanced, put his hand to his head. Privett leapt up, canoned into him, spilt more on his lapel, was slapped angrily away.

"Damn and blast you."

"Pushing. Always the pushing." They swayed like two stage drunks.

"It is the canting of the vessel," von Mueller smiled calmly. "Already they are tilting her over. This, I think, is what is troubling you. It is a matter of a few days only. A little more scotch will steady you. And then, Mr Lauterbach … if you please."

Lauterbach swayed comfortably in his hammock, shaded by rustling palms, only one bare leg extending into sunlight, the better to appreciate the cool darkness of the rest. A cognac bottle nestled comfortably in the crook of his paunch, half full and providently corked. He had feasted on fresh fish, beach-baked in glossy banana leaf, and yam and cloudy palm toddy that tasted faintly of sheepdog. He had swallowed hot lobster and sea urchin and fruits that had no name in any European language. A cool wind, salted by a thousand miles of ocean, ruffled his hair and he thought fondly of the good, earthy sex he had also enjoyed the night before, betokened by the slight satisfied bruising of groin and thigh. Sex with a new race was always the most satisfactory. It was not the thrill of forbidden fruit, more the fact that – despite his cultivatedly bad memory for partners – he found that, with increasing age, the world was gradually filling up with faces that reminded him of other faces, faces that were quite inappropriate to sexual excitements. A girl in a Shanghai bar had recalled inopportunely and disastrously his grinning Foochow steward, Ah Ping. Whilst engaged in recent play with a Russian countess and studying the back of her neck, he had remembered absently the coiled hair of his great aunt as she sat before him in church, when he was a child. Hopeless. Even one of the more approachable ladies here had suddenly seemed to have von Mueller's purposeful nose and mouth. Unthinkable.

Over the other side of the paradisal lagoon, the men, sexually unshriven, were earning their bread in the sweat of their brows, in the hot sun, heads under knotted handkerchiefs, scraping, scrubbing and repainting such parts of their capsized mistress, the *Emden*, as were made available to their attentions. With the exhaustion of regulation navy off-white, a range of different shades had been produced by mixing together all remaining paint dregs on the vessel, so that the former swan now looked like a thing of patchwork. Lauterbach lay back and smiled and yawned. Newly emptied and filled, he loved to watch others work. It relaxed him.

He had gone over the top, he now saw, with his invention of news to satisfy Rose and Privett. The diminutive Japanese cricket eleven, none over four foot six, currently touring Great Britain and defeating all comers including the MCC, had been a step too far. Rose had bristled with disbelief. Similarly, the

French Academy's decree announcing the complete abolition of adjective endings in the French tongue throughout the empire in the interests of wartime economy had been ill-judged and rankled with Privett. Never mind. These had been smoothed over with the gift of a case of scotch and the repair of the motor launch, an antique thing of polished wood and brass more suited to Thamesside regattas than the Pacific Ocean. Rose and Privett had chugged off on a long overdue visit to the other side of the island, visibly still drunk, voices bickering above the soft putter of the recalibrated engine. "Do not push. Always you push." They remained ignorant of the outbreak of hostilities and this fact had somehow irked von Muecke who felt dishonoured by it and took it out on the men. But then von Muecke believed that wars happened for a reason. Lauterbach, on the other hand, knew they just happened, with all the lack of purpose and indifferent inevitability of earthquakes. The thing to do was keep your head down and wait for them to blow over.

There was an itch around his little toe, that one out there in the sun. Probably a mosquito bite. There was always a serpent in paradise. Perhaps he would scratch it later but it was, for the moment, simply too far. He yawned again, smiled and dropped into a contented doze.

Chapter Four

Lauterbach was by now used to three cheers from departing crews, as they headed back to freedom, with all their personal effects intact, and a tale of adventure to tell. But it was something of a surprise to be cheered while boarding a British vessel for the first time. The *Ponrabbel* was a dredger, small, ugly, a real pig of a ship, shoving its snout into the high waves and wallowing in the deep troughs with a nasty sideways shaking of the tail. The crew were there, grinning, lined up on deck with their bags ready packed and the captain stepping forward with a blushing handshake.

"Come right aboard you is it?"

She was built for harbour work in sheltered water and they were bound from Cardiff for Tasmania at a top speed of four knots. Every one of them had been seasick most of the time and they expected her to turn turtle at any moment. This was their second attempt to drive their pig to market and they were four months into it. The first vessel had gone down under them in a storm and this time they had prudently negotiated payment in advance and were not in the least averse to seeing this loathed ship go to the bottom as the *Emden* used her for target practice.

"You wouldn't let me have just one shot at her I suppose?

No? Thought not."

The British crew watched and cheered as the hated dredger turned over, pointed its red bottom rudely at them and disappeared with a slurping noise. They settled cosily into the *Buresk* and luxuriated in the unaccustomed fags and booze stripped from other, larger prizes. Several more ships went down over the next few days for, in an attempt to frustrate them, the allied shipping routes had been conveniently shifted to precisely where they now were and British vessels virtually queued up to be sunk. Then they stopped the *Troilus*, a Blue Funnel liner, packed with strategic metals, rubber – and passengers.

"Hallo, Julius." A small woman, short hair, mid-forties, fashionably dressed in a manner somewhat too young for her years. "I'm sure you remember me ... that night on the *Kraetke*."

"Er ..." He looked round wildly. None of the crew were within earshot.

"Oh. Don't worry. My husband's not here, busy dumping the brats at school in Shangers and making more money in Singers. Rodney only earns, never seems to get time to *spend* ... I've been off in Honkers and Rangers and now I'm here." She smiled and preened. "I've never been ravished by a pirate ... before."

"Er ..." Neat body. A mouth used to laughter. Nice condition for her age. In peacetime she would have been nothing special but now, with the war, the world was on sexual short rations. She was not, even on closer examination, just some rancid old tuna boat. Mmm.

"This is the third time you've blocked my passage, you naughty boy. Every time I get on a ship, they make us get off it again because the *Emden*'s been up to its old tricks." She fiddled with a diamond brooch pinned over her right breast. "I was lucky with the *Troilus*, brand new ... maiden voyage." She lit a Black Cat, blew and flicked the match. Very bold that. She was poised and assured. Clearly a total bitch. "They say your commander's quite dishy. Where is he?" She sucked on the cigarette – blatant red lipstick circled the stub – and threw back her head, exhaling hot smoke and showing to advantage the line of her throat. Too much gold gleamed a trifle indiscreetly at neck and ear. There was a pale line on her finger where a ring, normally worn, had just been removed. She flashed him the smile with which Eve beguiled Adam and the serpent rose within him.

"What? Who? Von Mueller? No, no. Small, ugly, totally bald. Anyway a monk." Who the hell was she? Had he already boarded her on the Shanghai run? She pirouetted and her skirt flounced up as if by chance. Good legs. Peach silk shift flapped against her calves. Action stations trumpeted in his brain. Eyes goggled. She patted coquettishly at his arm and pouted little-girlishly. "So what are you going to do with me, captain," she gasped huskily. "Make me walk your beastly long plank?"

That was it. Any more whispering and she'd begin to remind him of cock-crinkling von Mueller. Lauterbach ran up the battle flag and rang up full speed ahead. He smirked cheesily and offered a gallantly crooked elbow. "Perhaps, madam, at the risk of bringing comfort to an enemy, you would honour me by having a little drink in my cabin before we part? For old times sake."

She slid her hand confidently into it and squeezed. "Oh how kind. And then, perhaps you might take me on a tour of the less public parts of your vessel, what you might call your private parts. I should just adore to have a look at your torpedo tubes ..."

Ah. So he *had* ... "Lieutenant Fikentscher," he beckoned the young man across. "My compliments to Lieutenant von Muecke. Please report that I am obliged to remain on duty here this evening to ensure the security of this prize and take an inventory of her cargo." His ordinance was primed and ready to fire. He had the range. Now where the hell was the captain's cabin on this ship?

Lauterbach stood stark naked and ready-soaped staring at von Mueller's silhouette up in the wheelhouse. The captain sat tightly buttoned in his baking deckchair, shuffling manifests, maps, shipping-lists, marking, penciling and tutting- the world reduced to a manageable thing of paper. Pigeons preened and cooed in a loft attached to the masthead and tethered cattle examined in puzzlement the green anti-slip paint of the prow as if it were some new and unsatisfactory kind of grass. But von Mueller ignored them and stared purposefully out ahead, deliberately unaware that around him was not a ship of fools but of nudists. A mood of truancy had descended over the vessel.

To the left of Lauterbach, burly, tattooed stokers disrobed and displayed hirsutely on the forecastle, while Two, Three and Four cowered coyly behind a sheeted screen on the afterdeck that reduced them to a public display of bony ankles. Apart from von Muecke, who was on duty on the bridge, all the other officers congregated in bashful nakedness on the poop, gripping Elysium soap before their privities. Lauterbach was sure that von Muecke considered physical processes a military inefficiency while to von Mueller they were simply vulgar.

Von Muecke's job was to chase the tropical thunderbursts so that the men could refill the tanks of drinking water and benefit from the rare treat of a fresh shower. Salt water dried and cracked the skin. Over time, seeping wounds like chilblains formed under the armpits and festered between the shoulders and toes. Heels gaped with raw flesh. Boils nested and suppurated between the buttocks. Lauterbach posed in the posture of a classical statue against the sun, an unplinthed satyr amongst hairless fauns, big-bellied and shameless, a thing to frighten schoolgirls in a herbaceous border. Fikentscher nudged von Guerard.

"So it's true about the Lauterbach torpedo," he whispered in awe, nodding. Dr Schwabe, ears ever-pricked for innuendo, edged closer, fumbling at his left nipple for the pencil he usually kept- in his top pocket, peered through his glasses against the lens-flashing glare. "Mein Gott!" There was a Freudian crash of thunder and sudden warm, clean rainwater hosed down on their gasping, searing skins like a blessing. Salt water formed no lather but this rain gushed instant white foam. They cheered and frotted and groaned and danced on the spot orgiastically, desperately washing, afraid that they would emerge from the cloud's rainshadow before they could rinse. But this was a good downpour not one that left you soaped and sticky. Time to wash the hair, to let the sweet rain slosh down your face and into your mouth, to grow chill and shiver and rush laughing and towelling for shelter. They wrapped themselves in bathrobes, filched from their twenty-two victims, emblazoned with names such as *Diplomat*, *King Lud*, and *Clan Grant* and played rough boyish games of tag in blood heated by the burden of seed that had gone too long unspilled, undischarged lightning looking for any rod. Von Guerard laughed and danced in the outpouring of a benevolent Nature, his eyes sparkling with pure joy. But Lauterbach, classically clad in white towelette *Troilus*, was not laughing. He contemplated them with unsolaced sadness as he wrung grey water from his pubes. Earlier they had deliberately steered away from any new prey they sighted. He had been told to set a southerly course towards the Island of Penang, off the coast of Malaya. The shower, the change of clothes. It was standard preparation for battle and meant some of them were about to die. For him the stench of death overpowered even the thick and sickly perfume of Elysium brand toilet soap.

At two in the morning, there was no sound except the regular thwack of waves against the bow and the acidic hiss as seawater dissolved into foam. They were alone, the colliers *Buresk* and the more recently captured *Exford* were elsewhere, steaming slowly towards the next rendezvous.

"Lighthouse sighted, sir."

The men were still burping over their morning meal of milk soup, followed by ghastly British tinned sausages and Indian coffee but wide awake. Von Mueller scanned the horizon through British naval glasses.

"Rig the fourth funnel, Number One."

Lauterbach was sweating. Damn von Mueller and his military ambition. Merchant vessels were too easy for him, he had to go after warships, into the lion's den armed with nothing but a peashooter. This was not a repeat of Madras, a civilian port with its broad seafront. Lauterbach, feigning enthusiasm, had examined the chart of Penang harbour earlier that night. This was a military base built for defence. The entrance was a narrow tube from the north. The southern exit was too shallow for them so they would have to make a tight turn to escape back up it. Officially there were no modern fortifications but it still looked like a deathtrap, a narrow throat to get stuck in like a fishbone. There would be heavy warships in there with good thick armour they could not hope to hurt with their own small bore weapons. Only a torpedo would do and that could only be relied upon at close range. They would be like, like ... a duck quacked from the menagerie outside, neatly providing the image Lauterbach was searching for.

At 4.30 the men were called to attention and the speed increased to 18 knots as they ran for the inner harbour, ignoring the waiting pilot boat. Like Madras, the whole port was all lit up invitingly. The first dawn light probed the horizon. Somewhere on shore a bird sang with heart-wrenching beauty and then suddenly there was a huge target right in front of them, crisp in morning light. Von Muecke was furiously thumbing through a book of naval silhouettes, hissing excitedly through his teeth.

"Russian, I think, a cruiser, light probably. Wait. One of three possibles." He flipped pages wildy.

"*Zhemteg*," pronounced Lauterbach tiredly, eyeing the cyrillic letters swarming over the bow. "We're close enough now to *read* the bloody name." He had got hospitably drunk on her once in Vladivostock on raw vodka, danced, sung and vomited over the rail. The captain was a good egg. Now he was about to repay his hospitality.

At three hundred, Franz Josef was at last allowed to let loose one of his pampered torpedoes. In the coffin-like bay beneath the deck the dials glowed, the electric contacts crackled and the needles danced behind their celluloid screens as the glorious word "Fire" flashed up as he had so often seen it in his dreams. He completed the contact and tore up to the deck to see the effect, fixing the trail as it shot across the gap between the two vessels and clutching the rail, trembling, like a boy finally losing his virginity.

Von Mueller was all crisply starched authority. "Starboard guns open fire. Rapid salvoes." The guns blazed fire and thunder as the torpedo struck the Russian aft, more or less where Lauterbach had voided his stomach, detonating mightily and somehow lifting the whole vessel. He watched with the horrified relish of fear as the great guns swivelled and bore down on them but no answering fire came from the Russian. Their own shells riddled the superstructure and raked the decks, starting fires and explosions till her sides swiftly glowed red hot. Their captain was ashore with a lady friend and many of the crew promptly abandoned ship and sought to join him, swimming, grasping their caps in their hands. In the Russian navy there was no charge for losing your entire ship but they fined you a whole month's pay if you lost your hat. While in port, their own torpedoes had been disarmed and only a dozen rounds were available for the guns and, then, when the sleeping Russians finally got one of them working, it simply strafed the friendly merchant vessels around her. But now other shells were flying overhead. There were French warships in there with a proper watch being kept and plenty of ordinance. Now that they should be smartly running off, the *Emden*'s response was to stop dead and begin to turn and manoeuvre with painfully slow engines and whirring screws. As the prow came round, the port side guns opened up and another of Franz Josef's torpedoes swirled off towards the Russian foe. At first it seemed that nothing had happened.

"A bloody dud," hissed Lauterbach, clenching his hands about his head.

Then a blaze of flame ripped abruptly through the ship, engulfing her in a pall of choking yellow and black smoke. Huge chunks of iron rained down, clanging onto their decks and skidding into the sea. They must have hit a magazine. A gust of wind cut through the billows of smog and she was revealed in naked agony, sliced in half. Only mastheads remained above the water.

"Flippin 'eck."

"Open fire on the merchantmen, sir?"

Von Mueller wheeled round, aghast. "Certainly not, Number One, we cannot be entirely assured of their nationality or the destination of their cargoes." Lauterbach howled silently and gibbered at the sky. He life was in the hands of fools who wanted only to kill him.

"Torpedo boat at harbour entrance, sir." Sure enough, there she was, small, grey-painted, billowing smoke and coming at them fast with menace. In the narrow space there would be no possibility of avoiding a torpedo. It would be lethal. Lauterbach had marked down the nearest lifebuoy. Now he began edging towards it. The *Emden*'s guns swivelled and fired as they charged. The torpedo boat scuttled out of their way, being, after all, only an unarmed vessel of the harbourmaster. But now they were already heading out of port at speed and did not dare turn yet again and sail towards a battle-ready, superior enemy. Cursing his ill fortune in passionate whispers, von Mueller ordered them to run for the open sea.

"Oh what bad luck, sir." Lauterbach consoled cheerfully. His heart laughed. He was alive!

"Ship off the starboard bow, could be an auxiliary cruiser, sir." Damn and Blast! No not an auxiliary – thank God – the *Glenturret* carrying explosives. Lauterbach set off, smirking, with a prize crew. This would make a very big bang indeed which would calm his nerves. Wait, no. Hold everything. Another ship out there. A French warship, the destroyer *Mousquet*. Lauterbach was called back as he was about to step into the boat, von Muecke cheerily waving from the bridge.

"Quick Lauterbach. A scrap at last. You wouldn't want to miss this to save your life!"

The *Emden* opened fire at 4,700 yards and the French made their first and last mistake. Instead of attacking frontally, they turned to port, presenting their whole side to be raked with devastating fire. A hit on the boiler room and she was dead in the water, to be destroyed at leisure. After a dozen salvoes, her guns were silenced but no obvious attempt was made to surrender. Another ten were pumped into her and she sank, laying further concerns about her battle-readiness to rest.

Having tried to kill the French, they now sought to save them The men had never seen the horror of naval wounds before, the terrible burns, the limbs blasted off, the great holes that steel shrapnel would tear in soft human flesh so that a man's entrails were tipped out hot into his hands. At last Schwabe had something useful to do, dressing crushed stumps and festering wounds agonised by immersion in seawater. Some of the younger ratings wept. They had never meant to do this. They had not known. They, mumblingly, brought humble gifts of chocolate and cigarettes to undo the harm done by shredding metal. Meanwhile the Frenchmen tried to escape their efforts to rescue them, swimming desperately away from their boats. They had been told the Germans massacred prisoners. Only one swimmer made it back to shore Many others drowned. Over the next days, von Muecke busied himself with honourable burials, heel-clicking, flags, trumpets, nice neat little ceremonies, speeches and three cheers for the Kaiser that reassured the men about the honourability and decorum of war. Military pomp and circumstance, Lauterbach saw, were simply something both sides put in place of an avoided issue. A little later, they took another British ship, unsinkable for its neutral cargo, and unloaded the prisoners and wounded Frenchmen into her for prompt hospital treatment. Their officer asked for an *Emden* hatband as a memento and was given one. Normally these were the souvenirs bestowed upon ladies.

"It seems that the French captain lost both his legs to one of our shells," von Muecke explained lustily over dinner, eyes shining, to Lauterbach and eating with good appetite. "But had himself gallantly strapped to the bridge so he could go down with his ship rather than live with the dishonour of having seen some of his men dive over the side to save themselves. What a fine officer! And it was magnificent the way those men fought on and joyfully embraced death long after all hope of victory had been lost, simply for the glory of their nation. Pity, in a way, we came out of it untouched. There is nothing improves a fellow's looks so much as a good, deep duelling scar." He ran his fingertips lightly along the groove that scored along his own left cheek. "It is a sign,

Lauterbach, that a man has honourably engaged the world."

Lauterbach looked down and saw that his hands had begun to shake. He dropped knife and fork and gripped his own knees until the spasm passed. Again they had escaped death but it was moving ever closer, attracted towards them by the likes of von Muecke. He could *feel* it, see its shadow on the stairs. He saw not just the obscenity of torn bodies but, in the crew, a whole vision of those who died unwived, the unbegotten, the bereaved, the hole ripped by their deaths in the close-stitched fabric of history. As he took the potatoes, Lauterbach began to wonder seriously at just what point in an engagement he would be obliged to shoot Number One. Henceforth he would make sure to wear sidearms at action stations. He could pretend it was to save time in case of being ordered to form a boarding party.

"The only thing that puzzles me is that they mistook us till the very end for a British vessel, even allowing for all the confusion, the dark and so on." Von Mueller chewed happily, sipped wine, swallowed, rapped militarily with his fork handle. "That shows bad seamanship. They could have sunk us if they'd gone about it in proper fashion and not exposed their starboard side. One or two of their men even swore it happened because we were flying the white ensign, which is clearly not the case." He threw his head back and sniggered. "As if we would!"

Lauterbach looked up and bit his lip. Ah yes. Another thing. That reminded him. He must get that damned flag back from Number Two Washboy, chop – bloody – chop.

The Cocos Keeling Islands only existed as a series of accumulated mistakes and misunderstandings in history. They lay well off the northwest coast of Australia in an otherwise determinedly blank, blue bit of the chart. In the early 19th century, an extraordinary and uxorious follower of Stamford Raffles, Alexander Hare, had used the coral atoll to dump his large polychrome collection of ladies and children before being – almost certainly – murdered by his own business partner. Over the years, the people had attuned themselves to the realities of an enforced servitude to the rapacious trading company that ran the plantations. Previously, the British had assumed overall responsibility for the place by mistake, having despatched a naval lieutenant to plant their flag on the *other* Cocos Islands strategically located off the coast of Siam. Afterwards, they were too embarrassed to admit their confusion and repudiate such a pointless and isolated possession of sand and rock. Yet, out of this mix of arrogance and error had emerged an unlikely convenience, for the Cocos Keeling Islands were the junction point of the undersea communication cables that held the whole British empire together – one to Mauritius, one to the Dutch East Indies and a third to Australia, the lot topped off with a powerful radio station central to the co-ordination of allied shipping.

Another coaling from the *Buresk* brought them to the Cocos where they were to meet the *Exford*, a captive British collier. From radio, they were comically amused to learn that the might of Portugal had declared war on them. Only Franz Josef was concerned at this development. After all, the Queen of Portugal was his sister.

"Mr Lauterbach, " whispered von Mueller, sipping tea. "I have a special favour to ask of you. I imagine you know what it is?" The captain looked terrible. He had lost weight.

Dark circles ringed his haggard eyes and the cheekbones were of almost oriental prominence. He had not left the bridge for days and half the shades were pulled down against a beating sun. No wonder the foreign Press liked to speak of him as Germany's Flying Dutchman. A favour? Oh no. He knew at once. A suicidal attack on the British radio station. Even the British would not be so arrogant and stupid as to leave such a vital installation undefended. God knew how many troops they would have garrisoned there, dug in, well-armed, snug behind their machine guns, concrete bunkers and mines, aiming at a nice, big target like Lauterbach.

"No idea, sir." He stood to attention, face locked.

"I have it in my mind that there is to be a real fight here and I know you are a man of determination and initiative and it is precisely for these qualities that I wish to ask of you the ultimate sacrifice."

"Sir." Suicide it was, then. He began to sweat. What should he do? Fall over the side and break a leg. No, shoot himself in the foot while handling unaccustomed weapons of land offence. Christ! That would hurt. With Schwabe as doctor, he could easily lose a leg. With gangrene in this climate he could die. Food poisoning, then He had some tincture of cloves in his cabin. Drink the whole bottle and he would go down with the runs and a fever. No. Best try half a bottle first, the other half he could do with acting.

"I have to ask you to leave the *Emden* for a civilian vessel, the *Exford*. You are aware how completely we are dependent on her coal out here in this part of the world. I need a man I can trust absolutely to survive, in command of that vessel, a man with the full *weight* of a captain's experience and used to handling a Chinese crew. I know you are good with

Chinese."

Lauterbach exhaled in relief then seemed to catch something in the captain's eye. Just what did he know? You always thought von Mueller knew everything, could look straight into your soul. Those eyes were mesmerising. Speech was always the most cumbrous and imprecise form of communication.

"Sir."

"You will take her to a rendezvous off Socotra and wait until the end of November. If at the end of that time we do not appear, then it will mean ... you are to surrender yourself at a Dutch port for internment." It began to sink in.

"You mean, sir, I'm going to miss the whole show?" He couldn't believe it. He was being sentenced to life. He stifled a laugh.

"I'm afraid so." Von Mueller looked suddenly stern and irritated. "This is war Mr Lauterbach. We must all make sacrifices," he murmered almost angrily. The tea trembled in his hand. Miniature waves crashed into the saucer. "Sail as soon as possible." He turned away, back to his world of paper. The interview was over. Lauterbach was to go to the far end of the Indian Ocean and sail in peaceful circles and keep safe for the glory of the Fatherland.

"Sir." He would have to move fast to get his comfy chairs aboard before they sailed.

To land from the sea on a tropical island is to repeat a primordial act of discovery. An island is a perfect world, complete in itself. It bears within it the theoretical possibility that, here, the laws of the universe are simply different, that they are benign and that innocent peace and enjoyment are the sum total of human experience. Diego Garcia had been the proof of it. Direction Island, in the Cocos-Keeling group, was to be the refutation.

The *Emden* had depended on luck and now that stock of luck was exhausted. It began badly. There was a large convoy of troopships on the way to Europe bringing men, horses and supplies from New Zealand to be shovelled into the great military furnace that was the Western front. A cargo of such vulnerability and strategic value required a warship escort and the British, Australian and Japanese navies had pooled resources to supply it. The *Emden* had monitored their coded Morse traffic all day. A skilled listener could tell a Marconi from a Telefunken transmitter, a military from a civilian operator and the strength of the signal could be used to estimate distance. The little ship operated in the knowledge that the allied fleet was a good 250 miles away, at the very least ten hours' steaming. They did not know that HMS *Sydney*, faster and more heavily armoured and gunned than themselves, was a mere two hours distant and using its faulty radio transmitter at reduced power.

A squad of fifty men was mustered, drawn from the most experienced sailors. This land outing was regarded, after all, as something of a treat for old sweats, a relief from incarceration in a small vessel, a bit of a jaunt. The four machineguns were dug out and assembled. All the gunlayers were included in the landing party, making the ship particularly vulnerable during their absence An assault at night was judged too dangerous, given the rocks, but at first light, the ship manoeuvred into the harbour entrance, dropped anchor and released the boats. Since the weather was so calm, it was an opportunity, not to be missed, for coaling. The *Buresk* was summoned by radio from over the horizon, bringing a puzzled enquiry from Direction Island as to who was transmitting. Then the operator turned and looked out of his window and saw the great, white cruiser, lying still in the water with its guns pointing at him.

They could not believe that the station was completely undefended. Every shadow under the palm trees was a machinegun nest, every coconut lying on the sand a potential mine. But totally undefended is what it was. Nevertheless, while the Germans were planning and executing the military assault of the tranquil beach, the British operator had time to identify the *Emden* and transmit a cry for help to the world both by wireless and cable. They might have prevented this by shelling the installation from the sea but von Mueller had forbidden an unannounced attack on a civilian installation as ungentlemanly behaviour.

"The *Emden* is here! The *Emden* is …" And then the Germans really *were* there.

Von Muecke was sadly deprived of the hoped-for swashbuckling and derring-do. There was no passionate charge ashore under a hail of fire. The steam launch pulled the boats quietly into the lagoon and they tied up at the jetty as on a municipal boating pond. The thirty-odd Brits shrugged on their kit and wandered down in canvas shoes, pipes gripped in their teeth, smiling and waving. They simply refused to behave like enemies being invaded by superior forces.

"Hallo, there. You don't mind if I take a quick snap do you? Hold it. Oh do smile. Thanks awfully."

"That machinegun looks frightfully heavy, can I give you a hand with it ashore? Would it help if I held the boat for you while you climb out? Careful now. Never do to fall in, not with Cecil and his camera.there."

Some sort of manager stepped forward, hand outstretched for shaking. He had a beard tended with the care some would have devoted to a flower border. "Welcome ashore. Lovely weather, isn't it? We've been sort of expecting you. Oh by the way congratulations."

Von Muecke was nonplussed. The men had their rifles waving about at nothing in particular or pointed at the ground. They were standing around not knowing what to do when they should be flat on their stomachs taking resolute aim. There could be snipers in those trees. One or two were accepting a drink of water. It could be poisoned.

"What? Who?" He looked around wildly. "Congratulations for what?"

"Your Iron Cross. Came over the blower yesterday. All you chaps on the *Emden* have been awarded the Iron Cross by Kaiser Bill. Oh, sorry, where are my manners? I'm Farrant, Head of Station." He smiled self-deprecatingly. "Not that we stand on ceremony much round here. All the chaps sort of just muck in, don't yer know."

Von Muecke shook his head to dispel this terrible matiness, stood to attention and started screaming in German.

"This station is now under the occupation of His Imperial Majesty's forces and subject to military discipline ..." He paused. "What class was the Iron Cross? One or Two?"

"Sorry, old man. Haven't a clue."

Von Muecke started screaming again. "Any disobedience to my instructions will be punishable by summary execution in accordance with military regulations ..."

"Jolly good," said Farrant. "Will you come inside? Have you had breakfast, by the way?"

"All firearms are to be immediately surrendered to His Imperial Majesty's forces. All foreign aliens will assemble in the square. Failure to comply at once with these orders will be counted an offence against military discip—"

"Do excuse my interrupting," said a bony man in round glasses. "Most of the fellows here don't speak German, you see. Would it help if I lent a hand and tried to translate a bit? I did some German at school. Now. We've got a few shotguns for keeping the animals in order – monkeys and squirrels and so on. Would you like us to go and get the old guns scattered about the place first, or would it be best if we all turned up at the square so we can be properly introduced? What do you think?"

Von Muecke was hot and flustered. This was not going at all the way he had intended. He felt panic rise in his throat and switched to English.

"You will forthwith surrender all keys to strategic installations. Demolition will commence immediately. Failure to comply at once with these orders will be counted an offence against …"

"Righty-ho. Be back with the keys in a jiffy, then." Farrant wandered slowly off.

Von Mueckc began shouting orders at his men, telling off a detail to demolish the radio mast, another to set charges in an old schooner down by the jetty, leading a third, himself, to the offices where they seized fire-axes and set about the furniture, the Morse equipment and anything else with wires coming out of it. Last they turned over the huge jars of printer's ink.

"Oh, I say, couldn't they do that outside? Frightful mess." Farrant mouthed distaste, having returned with the keys, redundant now, because any locked doors had been booted in in best soldierly fashion. They seized all papers and bagged them for transport to the ship. Von Mueller liked papers. Then they moved on to the outhouses, smashed generators, switchgear, the maze of condensors and transformers, gratuitously poked in the glass at the windows with their rifle butts. One steel door remained locked. It would take explosives to shift it. A Chinese voice called indignantly from inside.

"You fluck off. No belong lectic. Belong makee ice."

Farrant was there, square-mouthed in apology. "How terribly awkward. Our technician. He's right I'm afraid. Very proud of his ice-plant. Built it himself from a sketch plan in an encyclopedia. Frightfully clever fellow. Could you possibly …?"

They moved on to the radio mast, surrounded by crouching sailors in pith helmets, where no progress seemed to have been made. This was all taking much longer than had been allowed for. The first detonation had achieved nothing at all. The mast was unmoved. They had set new charges but the structure was deep-rooted in the coral rock to withstand typhoons. It swayed a little but still stood proud.

"Ah yes," said Farrant. "Our Chinese technician again. He drilled right down into bedrock. Frightfully clever fellow. I wonder, if I might make a suggestion. Just over there," he pointed with wet pipestem, "Is the tennis court, you see. We're a bit short of level ground round here so that's just about the only place on the island we can put it. If we put it on the beach the bounce is no good and we lose too many balls and it's quite a hike to a tennis ball shop, as you can imagine. Now, if you make the mast fall towards the court, it'll be a

frightful bore. We're half way through the club tournament."
He leant forward confidingly. "Now some – no names, no
pack drill – might argue that the change of surface would
invalidate the previous rounds, you see. Might have to start
the whole tournament over from the beginning and frankly
I've been doing rather well this year. We should be most
awfully obliged if you could topple it the other way into the
undergrowth there. Then things would be just tickety-boo"

Von Muecke was stunned. These people were mad –
tickety-boo? – but complied. The mast fell with a great crash
and lay there, a tangle of twisted girders.

"Oh good shot," Tarrant popped his pipe in his mouth
and clapped both hands together lightly. At the sound of the
explosion a Chinese face appeared round the steel door and
surveyed the mess ruefully.

"You fluck off," the same voice called simply, as if
confirmed in its first opinion, waved a fist and slammed the
door again. Bolts could be heard clanging back into place.
Farrant shrugged, mimed more elaborate regret.

"I say," he offered, removing the pipe again excitedly
from his mouth, "Do any of your chaps play? We could have
a quick game. Doubles, perhaps?"

"Mr Farrant. We are not here to play tennis." Von
Muecke, scrupulously belligerent, strode off down the neat
path towards the beach. These people *were* mad.

"The cables," he ordered. The plan was simple, they
would use hooks to grapple up the undersea cables where
they touched land, cut them and tow the ends out to deep
water, to make repairs more difficult.

"Ah," nodded Farrant. "I see. A bit like in croquet
where you knock the opponent's ball off into the rough.

Jolly good."

There were problems. First there seemed far too many cables. They were all over the place. They did not know that Farrant had laid phony cables, trailing them off a few hundred yards into the sea to confuse the enemy. Then, they had pictured them as simple wires to be lightly snipped with pliers. But they were huge serpents and actually consisted of many layers of insulation and protection, steel, pitch, copper, even stout brown paper that all had to be hacked through laboriously. The sailors worked like dogs in the hot sun, sawing and chopping with axes and chisels under the amused gaze of the British who sat, fanning themselves. They regretted now demolishing the workshops – there would surely have been something useful there. Then, once cut, the slimy cables were horribly heavy and unco-operative, refusing to be disturbed and snapping back into place once the ends were released.

Farrant scratched his chin sympathetically, sucking on his still unlit pipe. "Pity. You haven't got the right equipment, you see. Damned awkward blighters, undersea cables, if you're not used to them. I say, would you mind if my chaps moved off the square and into the boatshed? Getting a bit hot and some of them didn't bring their boaters, it being first thing. Or perhaps I could get the servants to serve us all some lemonade?"

It was true. The heat was building unbearably. They had been here hours longer than intended. Von Muecke had a sudden flash of insight. These stupid, ponderous, silly-arse Englishmen – was this not all some elaborate ploy to keep him here, a trap to waste his time? He looked round at those red, big-nosed, smiling faces and felt bright hatred flare inside him like magnesium. He opened his mouth to speak when short blasts from the *Emden*'s siren rang out, recalling him to urgency – the signal to return to the vessel immediately. He screamed orders, counted the men, ran down to the boats, embarked the weapons. The bags of papers were desperately dragged down to the jetty and they set out for the ship, bathed in sweat, hearts pounding. But it was clear they would never make it. A large A was already being flown at half mast. The *Emden* was weighing anchor. Her screws churned and she moved off, gathering speed. She was leaving without them. They were castaways on a foreign island full of madmen.

The *Emden* had sighted smoke on the horizon. North, the direction the *Buresk* would be coming from. An officer went to the lookout post and confirmed the identification. It was true that there was rather a lot of smoke but it was known that the collier's coal was damp and that could affect the combustion, so the *Emden* swiftly prepared for coaling according to the routine they had practised so often. Fifteen minutes later, the other ship turned and it was suddenly clear that she had two masts and four funnels – one of those foreign warships they had so often imitated – from the look of her, a cruiser and coming on at over twenty knots, ready for battle. This was the fight they had all known would come one day, the fight for their very lives, and adrenalin surged through the ship like an electric charge. Orders rang out – steam up in all boilers – action stations – full speed ahead. Wallowing heavily from lack of power, they steered hastily out of the narrow entrance, running for deep water, the stokers working like demons to raise pressure, shells already clanking up the electric hoists to feed the guns.

By the time the *Emden* opened fire both ships were heading

north, on parallel courses. They slammed away at each other with screaming shells like two bullies in a shin-kicking contest. By the implacable logic of naval engagements, all the *Sydney* had to do was keep out of range and use her bigger guns. But she foolishly got too close and the *Emden*'s crew had the better aim though the gunlayers were all stranded on Direction Island. A quick lucky shot was desperately needed and they got one off and blew away the enemy's firing controls. Had all their shells detonated, a major explosion of ammunition might have decided the day, but they didn't. That apparently inexhaustible pool of good fortune was now at an end and its tide had turned against them. They would never be lucky again. An Australian rating seized blazing cordite from amongst his own ordinance, carried it in his arms and dumped it in a washtub. He got the VC and scars he would wear all his life but the *Sydney* was saved. Most of the hits from the *Emden*'s smaller guns only dented her opponent's thick armour plating before simply bouncing off harmlessly into the sea.

It took the Australians, now firing manually, a full twenty minutes to score a hit of their own. Pulling, back to 7,000 yards, the *Sidney* now began to coolly pour fire into the German vessel, knocking out communications, the radio room, fire control, one by one and with impunity. Lethal shrapnel zithered along the decks, slashing and eviscerating wherever it encountered human flesh. The stern of the ship was ablaze. Any attempt to close with the enemy was thwarted. Then the steering was shot away. Below decks the torpedo men, in smoke bandages, were fighting the pounding of inrushing seawater and poisonous fumes as they desperately held the tubes in readiness for one last attack, choking like Jonah in the whale's belly. They had to release compressed air from the tanks just to be able to breathe. But the range was still too great and they still had not got up full steam in all boilers, so that the *Sydney* could outpace them with ease. Soon the men were forced out on deck, rolling on the hot plating, gasping and choking, hands and arms blistered from contact with the sizzling metal. The funnels had not been locked in place, released ready for coaling, and now they collapsed onto the decks further suffocating the crew in smoke, coating the gunsights with soot and reducing speed because the boilers would not draw. One by one, the *Emden*'s guns were blasted to pieces or fell silent from lack of ammunition and after an hour and a half, it was all over. The *Emden* was a punctured wreck of tortured metal, glowing red hot from the fires that raged below decks and, everywhere a shell had hit, men had died. Bodies were torn and ripped into meat and bloodspray by blast and shrapnel or lay still, mysteriously untouched in death. Many had simply disappeared, blown to pieces or flung high over the side. A bosun's mate, with one arm shot clean off, doggedly kept up fire for a while on a lone gun.

Von Mueller descended from the bridge, minutes before it too was shot away. Von Guerard's slim body lay pitifully crushed by the toppled foremast, a trickle of blood from the mouth already crusting over, the eyes wide in innocence, the youthful immortality and lustrous beauty snuffed out contemptuously like a fag end crushed beneath a heel.

"Set course for North Keeling. Aim for the reef," he whispered.

Despite the din of battle, the hoarse instructions seemed to fill the echoing body of the ship as he called steering directions down through a hatchway and grimly manoeuvred by throttling back one or other of the engines. The prow glided relentlessly toward the line of surf and they grounded slowly. Abruptly he ordered "Full Ahead" one last time to drive her screaming and protesting down on the rock. It would prevent the vessel falling into enemy hands and save more of his men than sinking her, since there were no usable boats left on board and the cruising sharks were voracious. It was a decision that would ruin his career. To the admirals in Berlin it looked like the impulse to vandalism overcoming the urge to proper heroism. A finished ship belonged discreetly on the sea bottom not blatantly displayed on a rock and its captain should be dead. They went through further rituals of destruction – the magazines were flooded, secret documents burnt, torpedo-aiming equipment dumped overboard. The *Sydney* gave her a couple more broadsides and hastened off to capture the *Buresk* that had inadvertently blundered into the conflict. Too late. She was scuttled and now her crew too must be rescued.

On the *Emden*, the wounded had been assembled on deck. Many had terrible injuries or burns. They were running out of morphine to quieten the screams of the dying and – worse – there was no drinking water for those who might still live. And now another horror. As they lay there exposed to wind and sky, they were dive-bombed by huge, razor-beaked birds that swooped down to attack their eyes and faces and feed on their wounds. They had to be beaten off, squawking, with clubs and revolvers. Some of the crew had tried to swim to the island with its tantalising hope of water and coconuts, a mere hundred yards away, but the treacherous currents dragged down most to their deaths. Dr Schwabe would perish in this way. Some of the carnivorous birds were caught and lines attached to them in the hope that they would fly to the island so that a Breech's Buoy could be rigged. They plunged into the water and also drowned. The men searched the various compartments of the ship, often having to break open the buckled hatches with crowbars, to release the trapped and wounded screaming and beating against the metal. Down there, lay the bodies of three Chinamen collapsed over wet washing, hands still gripping Elysium soap. The fourth washboy, Number One, certified on the manifest, had mysteriously disappeared and would never be found.

The *Sydney* returned. They prepared to be rescued but, to their surprise and dismay, the enemy cruiser kept her distance and opened fire again. The Germans had not replied appropriately to signals asking them to surrender. Captain Glossop of the *Sydney* sat down and wrote von Mueller a formal letter inviting him to do so. On the *Emden* they hauled down their colours, raised a white flag and the firing stopped. By now, half the crew were dead or badly wounded but rescue was still not imminent and instead, Fikentscher, saved from the *Buresk*, was sent on board with water and medical supplies. The *Sydney* 's priority was to establish what had become of von Muecke and his men. She sailed off again.

At Direction Island, the Australian ship cruised up and down all night at the entrance to the bay. Then, as soon as dawn broke, several boats were sent, crammed with armed hands, flying a flag of truce. Like von Muecke before them, they expected to storm on land beneath a hail of machinegun fire. Like von Muecke before them, they were disappointed.

"Gone," said Farrant, finally lighting his pipe and puffing smoke. "Sailed off last night in the *Ayesha*, our old schooner. Hauled up their flag and made a big speech about her now being the smallest man-of-war in the German navy. Got to admire their guts but they took all our dashed record papers with them and we use them in the loos. Shouldn't think they'll get far though. We've had no use for the old *Ayesha* since the new ship so she's just lain there, rotting. The old girl's got a dodgy bottom. Odd. If you'd come a bit later they'd have blown her up. If you'd come sooner, you'd have bagged the lot. Just shows. Still, they were jolly decent, split the stores and water with us fifty-fifty and promised to drop a line to Cold Storage, Singapore, to let them know we were running low on condensed milk. We lent them some togs and a few wrote letters home to wives and sweethearts but frankly most were so young the letters were to their parents and they asked us to send them on. Got some ripping snaps. Cecil's just running them through the darkroom. And they were absolute gentlemen about the tennis court. I say. Any of your chaps fancy a game?"

Finally, the *Sydney* returned to the wreck and took off the crew. Von Mueller came last, haggard and silent, piped honourably aboard despite his appearance, dyed in the colours of the German flag – black from soot, white from explosive and red from the blood of more than half his men.

CHAPTER FIVE

There were only twenty potato-eaters aboard the *Exford*, including himself. Yet they had loaded enough sacks of gritty, grey potato powder to sink a battleship. Lauterbach was sure all would be well till the rice ran out. He did not yet know that Lieutenant Gropius, whom he had replaced as captain of this rust bucket, had leapt to his death from the stricken *Emden* with three cheers for the Kaiser. As an old Asia hand, he *did* know that Gropius had not insisted on the provision of enough rice to feed a mainly Chinese crew. So instead of rice, they had this cement-like potato powder and nuts of Cardiff coal coming out of their ears. And when the rice ran out the Chinese would mutiny. They always did. Then he would have to shoot someone.

They had installed a radio post, filched from one of their victims, and Hagendurst was down there struggling to apply a one-day radio familiarisation course in Tsingtao to the state-of-the-art British apparatus hot from Cambridge. The ether yodelled with a hundred Morse voices, all in code, except for the occasional word *Emden* that came through the fug with the clarity of one's own name whispered in a crowded room. It could mean only one thing, the destruction of the vessel, yet Lauterbach's orders were to preserve himself at all costs – which was a duty dear to his heart – and to wait, so that's just what he would do. He would wait away from all shipping and away from the war and turn in stately circles up this remote north-western end of the Indian Ocean until the rice ran out and the crew mutinied and he shot someone.

"Damn and blast these bloody British dials." In the absence of von Muecke, the *Exford* had resumed a more civilian air. Hagendurst, a dumpy, unshaven petty officer with ten years' service, was sweating through a torn singlet, fag pluming smoke, a beer bottle open on the table. There would be no problem from the potato-eaters till the beer ran out and they would be harder for him to shoot. Hagendurst was surrounded by squat black boxes that he thumped occasionally and snaking wires looped together with string. It was unbearably hot though the door was propped open with a large lump of coal. His hands on the knobs were slick with sweat.

"Juli-bumm, what's 400 meters in feet?" He flicked ash and mouthed at the soggy fag-end.

"Don't even the British use meters for broadcasting?"

"Do they?" His hand dropped from the switch he had been twisting and his mouth gaped open, the fag staying glued to his bottom lip. "Bugger. That explains a lot, then."

"Just do the best you can, Hagendurst." Captains, he realised, said stupid things like that all the time – most captains – von Mueller was the exception, never saying a word that was not strictly necessary. Most captains showered words over their commands as a sign of their authority while proper radio-operators were silent creatures with permanently cocked ears. But Hagendurst was not a real operator and his conversation was all chatter and static.

"Can I have a go at transmitting? It's a British set so

they'd all think we were some poxy British vessel – which we are. I could ask for war news, ask about the location of the *Emden*." Eagerness shone in his eyes.

"Best not." Lauterbach put fat regret on his face. "Our orders are quite precise, to preserve ourselves, whatever the sacrifice, for the mother ship. Carry on Hagendurst." Everyone was bored. It hurt him to admit it but von Muecke was right. You had to keep them busy. He must think of something.

A rash of bleeps fought through the hiss of the loudspeaker. Hagendurst grabbed a pad and pencilled away furiously, crossing out and revising, then froze, looked up and held the tip to his lips as the transmission died. Schwabe would have liked that.

"It's Tsingtao," he said, puffing sternly. "That was a British merchant vessel. The place has been shot to hell but the siege is over and the city's surrendered to Japan. The British gave them a hand. So that's that and all about it." He slammed down the pencil. There were real tears in his eyes.

Lauterbach sighed. In his innocence, never having seen a major land battle, he did not think immediately of destruction, carnage and suffering – no cliches of smoking ruins, blasted flesh and violated maids peopled his imagination. Instead he pictured the absurdity of Japanese officers in British uniforms and shiny boots sitting there stiffly in their Bavarian landhouses, ruling over Chinese in *Dirndl* dresses and *Lederhosen*. They would be busy changing all the street names as their first priority. There would be some keen, humourless Japanese who looked just like von Muecke in charge of that. One day they would have a word for such nonsense. Anyway, he knew the Chinese. Those *Dirndl* and *Lederhosen* would be slipped off and *kimonos* shrugged lightly on. The shopkeepers would quietly take down the framed portrait of the German Kaiser, put up that of the Japanese Emperor, hung from the same nail, and indifferently reopen their shutters for business the next day. Maybe they would have time to put the prices up a little. He liked Chinese.

Lauterbach plodded back to the captain's cabin, heavily and frowsily furnished in dark wood, its one comfort a fat man's bed with a frilly counterpane. It came ready equipped with tinted photographs of a large and ugly wife and two vacuous children with buck teeth and as he lay there at night, he found himself slipping into the skin of his predecessor, inventing stories about them. Her name was Blodwyn. They lived in Cardiff. Sexually unresponsive, she had yet been viciously unfaithful with a rippling muscular Lascar stoker. When he got back he'd give her what for. In this blistering heat, he often fell asleep thinking about giving her what for.

As he opened the door a big rat stood up on its hind legs, looked at him with brief surprise and sneered before darting away under the bed. Inspiration flashed into his head like Morse. Of course, now there was the answer to the boredom! They could no longer hunt British ships so they would hunt British rats. In the morning, he would set the men to clearing the ship of them.

There were no cats on the *Exford* but even if there had been, the rats were more than big enough to take them on and win. The bored ratings threw themselves delightedly into the hunt as into a new sport, called up old sea-dog skills in knotwork to make elaborate traps of stout wire that would snare and choke and draped the gangways with them but succeeded only in wounding each other nastily about the ankles. But Genscher, one of the machinists and a big, slow straw-haired country lad, had his family firm-rooted in poaching and the lore of country life. His hands still recalled landlubberly, ancestral craft that he now applied, humming quietly to himself, in dark corners, twisting wire and string and knocking great nails into the woodwork. Lauterbach let him be. They would not be discussing with any landlord the wear and tear on the decor. And bait? What about cheese? Genscher laughed. "Chocolate, captain," he said with quiet emphasis. "For rats, chocolate." They plundered the stores for sickly English dairy milk, a sweetmeat that the rats would appreciate more than the men and the use of chocolate somehow lent Lauterbach's mission a dimension of moral retribution. For days Genscher stalked the ship, a smirking executioner, clutching fat bunches of garotted rats, their faces clotted with blood and cream chocolate.

The giggling Chinese sailors preferred more active, communal methods, driving the pests like hungry ghosts, from one end of the ship to the other with firecrackers and hellish symphonies beaten out on the bottoms of saucepans. Perhaps ghosts would be frightened away too, so, after the rat-cleansing, they would be twice-blessed. At the other end of the drive, crouched the leering Chinese cooks, their trouserlegs tied up with string, hidden behind the sacks. At last they had found a use for the dried potato. They were all adept in the handling of wicked steel choppers that they swung indifferently to whittle firewood, dice cabbage or trim their toenails and as the rats dashed past, they leapt out, stamped out a fandango dance among them, swiped, sliced and eviscerated with cries of glee, to such effect that many rats died and one cook's assistant lost a finger. That evening, the Germans were appalled by the delicious smell of fresh-cooked meat that suddenly wafted from their quarters and engulfed the entire ship. They sat on deck, arms crossed across their chests, desperately puffing cigarettes to overcome the growling of stomachs simultaneously attracted and repelled.

Lauterbach lay in the stagnant heat of his cabin, resisting the smell for hours, then rose, lumbering, at midnight from his bed and crept, both dribbling and nauseous, to the big, ugly sideboard that he opened with slow hands. Inside, gleamed a great stack of ancient cans, mostly nostalgic English treats such as bloated steak and kidney pudding, left by the former master, though with the occasional oriental novelty of crickets in brine or sago grubs in vinegar to trap the unwary. The tins were dappled with rust and the labels had long unwound in the damp air and been lost. To dine here was a gastronomic lottery. Lauterbach seized a great tubular tin and sloshed it by his ear, appraising the heft, the liquidity of the contents. Whatever was inside was big and mobile but could, with equal possibility, be pilchards in tomato sauce or toads in syrup. He seized the tin opener from the top of the sideboard and hammered through the lid, sliced through the metal in great tears and prised it up carefully. Tins were dangerous. You could cut yourself. Apricot halves. He fingered one out and let it drool down his throat. Then another. Then another. Enough. It was time to set a new course for Padang in the Dutch East Indies, a week's sailing time away, but an agreeable place to either draw new supplies or be snugly interned for the rest of the war. There they would finally be safe.

The rain gushed down as if from some cosmic drainpipe. They had long since sluiced away their accumulated stench and grime in it and profited from the chance to refill their fresh water tanks but there was just no end to the downpour that filled sky and sea, obliterating the small space in between. It was no longer a blessing but a curse. Lauterbach had always been wisely modest about his skills as a navigator and now visibility was nil and all he had been given as a chart was an old school atlas in alphabetical order whose end pages were flaking away. He could no longer take them to Zululand. And the compass was four points off true anyway. For all he knew they could already be ten miles inland.

"Dead slow ahead." A little native boat with sails of brown matting had tacked to avoid them and disappeared back into the hissing curtain of water with a cheery wave. It was thinning a little, out over the prow. There was land out there somewhere. Soon he would have to risk using the radio to try to contact the nearest harbourmaster, asking for a pilot and hoping he was already in the protection of Dutch waters. And then, all at once, they sailed into the stillnesss of a small sunlit glade in the forest of rain ... and there, in their path, was a huge ship flying the English white ensign, an armed auxiliary of the Royal Navy. With the *Exford*'s wallowing pace there was no chance of ducking back into hiding, so now they were on the receiving end of what they had so often handed out. A crump and a puff of smoke and a live round was put across their bows.

"Stop engines. Do not use wireless."

Lauterbach obeyed and watched appalled as, in a dream, a boat was swung out to bring an armed boarding party over to them, taking an oddly detached and professional interest in the niceties of the proceedings. In a matter of minutes, they were there, no English Lauterbach at their head but a trim, golden-haired child of twenty in a sparkling lieutenant's uniform. There would be no three cheers from the German crew.

He saluted. "In the name of His Britannic Majesty I take command of this ship and declare you and your men prisoners of war." He made it sound like some sort of congratulations.

Lauterbach looked down at the old-fashioned rifles, clutched awkwardly in the hands of the British sailors, unused to this manoeuvre, and up at the huge guns trained on them from what was – he now saw – the *Empress of Japan*. They were nervous. They had never done this before. Try bluster. You could never tell.

"We are in Dutch territorial waters. This is an outrage. I protest. You will please leave my ship immediately"

The waif shrugged and grinned, waggled his ears, an old party trick. He had a big schoolboy spot full of pus on his chin.

"Not according to our reckoning, old cock. You're slap bang in international waters. Not that it matters much anyway. My commander's given his orders and you're nicked. May as well make the best of it, old socks. "

Cocks? Socks? What was all this? Did he know, then, that he was dealing with Lauterbach of the socks song fame?

"I shall protest to the highest authorities. I shall ..." Oh what the hell. Grease. It was like cleaning boots, there was a moment to switch from stiff bristle to smarmy grease. "I bear you no personal grudge, lieutenant. You are only obeying orders, which is the right thing for a military man to do. You will have noticed that I have a largely Chinese crew. I trust you will honour their neutrality and put them ashore in the nearest Dutch territory? Do you like Chinese food by the way?" Lauterbach slipped a paternal arm around him and guided him towards the mess room. "I have an excellent cook who would be glad to offer you some lunch, something really special, very fresh."

The lieutenant disengaged himself. "Sorry chum. No time for that now and as for the other, we're bound for Singapore. Me for rest and recreation. You for a prison camp, unless I'm very much mistaken. I dare say your Chinese crew will be released, though. Would you tell your chaps to lay down any arms they may be bearing and I'll take a quick shufty round the ship and we can all get under way again." He saluted, formal again. "Please be ready to leave the ship immediately with all other naval personnel. Personal effects may be taken."

Lauterbach stiffened. His money was down there, locked in a trunk, subject, no doubt, to seizure by some light-fingered British official. He must get it safely stuffed in the cummerbund pocket double quick. What was this child waffling on about and smirking?

"What?"

"I said that it was not all bad news. In special recognition of your gallantry, the First Sea Lord has exceptionally decreed that members of the *Emden* may retain their swords." Lauterbach was speechless. He made a face like a man who has silently broken wind on a crowded omnibus and wants to pretend it was one of the horses.

"A sword?" What the hell was he to do with a sword? Were there more rats to be killed on the English ship?

"But you may as well tell me right now where the others are hiding and save us all a lot of trouble. You can't hope to keep them hidden for long." The child did a sort of comic yawn and stretch routine and waggled his ears again.

Now Lauterbach was totally perplexed. "Others? What others?" His mouth gaped clownishly. His piggy eyes half glimpsed an opportunity here to be exploited.

"Oh come on." The boy was picking at his spot and making it bleed. Lauterbach had a terrible urge to smack his hand away. "The landing party from Cocos Keeling, three officers and forty-five men, the First Officer of the *Emden* and the rest."

"The landing ... You mean von Muecke?" Lauterbach felt suddenly unbearably weary, a terrible, unfaceable truth was about to be confirmed. Smothering in a blanket of fatigue and frustration, he leant against the rail and took a deep breath. It was one of those situations you got into with women, where your total ignorance of what it was you had done was the ultimate proof that your offence was unforgiveable. "Perhaps, lieutenant," he hissed through clenched teeth, "you had better fill me in. I have, you see, no idea what happened to either my ship or my men ..."

Book Two

The Sepoy Mutiny

CHAPTER SIX

"Lauterbach, Lauterbach, the best mate a bloke ever had." Lauterbach was glad to be back in Singapore again, a steaming, teeming town where all the races and religions on earth poured their essence into a single malodorous pool. He breathed in the pungent city air where the smells of Klings and Chinese and Malays and Buginese jostled and warred on each other, as they spoke their different tongues, sang their different songs to their different gods and made a good living hating each other under the British flag. In the harbour, across from the little Malay houses built out over the water on poles, lay the *Pontoporos*, her status currently undergoing ill-natured legal investigation in several other languages. Lauterbach hoped to be called as a witness and would lie gloriously in whatever fashion would cause most trouble for everyone. He felt truly himself again, a foreigner, an alien, all his senses heightened. Not far from there, the *Exford* rested on the rocks, the bottom torn out of her by the embarrassed young lieutenant. Lauterbach had forgotten to mention the matter of the faulty compass to him. It was a shame really. He had been nice enough, even asked schoolboyishly for an *Emden* cap badge as a souvenir for his girl. Still, a sensible sailor would have checked. Now he would never make captain. The wreck was a vast monument to Lauterbach's own sheer bloody-mindedness.

They had been driven through town in a rattling open truck, guarded by two stick-legged Tommies, with terrible teeth, in baggy shorts. As the biggest British military base East of Suez, Singapore normally wore a pall of khaki and grey and so had changed relatively little from the place he had known before the war. Indeed most of the troops had been called away to the West so there were, if anything, fewer of them about and almost all Indians. Here were the scenes he remembered from a dozen peacetime shore leaves – the Esplanade, the cricket club, St. Andrew's Cathedral. All inculcated in the natives a caricature of village-green Englishness under tropical skies. He caught a tantalising glimpse of the white facade of the Raffles Hotel and its fanned traveller's palms and was assailed by a terrible thirst for the haven of the bar with its ancient 'boys' and yarning expats. But it was snatched away from him in a swirl of honking traffic. Orchard Road bustled with all its accustomed flocks of memsahibs in hats and gloves followed by troops of parcel-carrying servants. It was the dance of life from which he was, it seemed, to be banished for an indefinite future.

"Lauterbach, Lauterbach, the best mate a bloke ever had." A beardstubbled madman in a torn Tsingtao captain's army uniform rushed up, hugged Lauterbach, looked round smirkingly at the onlookers through crazed grey eyes, basking in reflected glory. Lauterbach did not recognise him and paused nonplussed as Sikh guards seized Schulz and slashed him to the ground with practised elegant strokes of their bamboo batons. "Best bloke a mate ..." he muttered and succumbed.

In the absence of von Mueller – imprisoned in Malta – and

von Muecke – God knew where on the high seas – Lauterbach alone inherited the chivalrous mantle of *Emden*'s glory in arms. Soon he was installed in the old Tanglin Barracks in a spare but spacious bungalow that echoed to dripping taps and his further reward was to be allowed unrestricted visitors and electricity after the normal ten o'clock lights-out. Abruptly, he was a man of substance. For the first time in his life Lauterbach was famous, feted by rude soldiery and camp followers alike, indeed for the first few days a permanent guard was necessary to protect him from their excessive enthusiasm. The German ratings from the *Pontoporos* were in the same compound and cheered him as their leader. Their reputation, too, rode so high that a considerable black-market currency had now developed in *Emden* cap badges within the city. Lauterbach swiftly arranged to have more made by a clever Chinese tailor and found them useful for the purchase of food, drink and sexual favours but, as a man of the world, knew it was only a matter of time before the tailor, like any self-respecting Chinese, went into business on his own account and spoiled the market.

The camp was a series of bleak wooden barracks, surrounded by barbed wire and with sentry posts every hundred yards, manned exorbitantly by twenty British officers, six hundred Indians and apparently numberless Malays. That, in turn, was encompassed by an electrified fence and beyond that a deep ditch as though for the trapping of tigers. Lauterbach felt finally *safe*. No one, it seemed, could get at him here. It had been explained that if he gave his word as an officer and a gentleman not to try to escape he might install himself more commodiously in a hotel in town. He could have his own batman there if he cared to. And who would pay for all that? They had shrugged. As a gentleman he naturally must pay for it himself from his private means. Not bloody likely. He would rather sit in the camp than fritter away his hard-earned cash on trivia such as daily food and board. Since joining the merchant marine, he had never paid for either and did not intend to start now. King George had put him in jail and King George would pay the bill.

"Our chief concern," said Herr Feldschwein, mopping his domed brow with a large snowy handkerchief that exuded the scent of frangipani, "is to continue the war by other means and, of course, we look to you not simply to inspire us but to direct us in our struggle to support the fatherland." Lauterbach had felt safe. He had been wrong. The enemy was already lying in wait for him inside the camp. There were half a dozen of them – Lauterbach knew the type – elderly patriots of the dentured classes, cosily civilian but eager to spill the blood of younger men, German nationals interned by the British for the duration of the war. They were business men, Hamburg merchants, shippers, condemned to live here in hot, stuffy barracks while their cool, white mansions just down the road were requisitioned by tippling British officers who put their dirty boots up on the tables. They still insisted on the propriety of the white linen suits and ties of commerce even in the professional void of this prison camp. Many were part of that shadowy force, the German *Etappe*, a network set up to secretly buy supplies and illegally communicate with German naval vessels through neutral ports and so overcome the dreadful handicap of not having a world empire in a world war. It operated, inconspicuously as they thought, out of a fake Rhenish castle up the road called the Teutonia

Club. The only thing that could have made it more obvious was singing mermaids posted on rocks outside. They loved the whole glamorous business of Berlin intrigues, rustling nocturnal rendezvous in the Esplanade shrubbery and secret despatches written in invisible ink and stamped with imperial eagles, since it transformed their mundane acts of sterile trade into a national crusade. Also they had made a great deal of money out of it. Now they were obliged to limit their activities to directing a stream of strategic supplies into Lauterbach's own kitchen. Out there he had crates of beer and hams stacked up to the ceiling. The table was littered with the debris of tinkling teacups and rich chocolate cake. Lauterbach's stomach growled and gurgled like a contented baby.

"As senior officer here, Oberleutnant, we look to you to put a bit of backbone into the men and we look forward to hearing your detailed plans for resistance as soon as possible. There's been a frightful slackness around the camp with a deal too much fraternising. There has even been an outbreak of cricket." They nodded solemnly, speaking with the arrogance common to all financial backers. Feldschwein of Meyer and Co. had put a slight edge in his voice, just a tiny hint perhaps, that Lauterbach was part of that slackness.

But Lauterbach was all smiles. These men were a pain in the arse but necessary for his creature comforts, a little like the women in his life and as needful of shameless flattery. He looked down on his Iron Cross, newly forwarded by the British and fingered it casually. He had gone out and bought the formal sword that British deference permitted him and clanked it now as token of his superior status and military expertise. Since fame had come upon him, he had found it easy to assume a pose of approachable greatness but it was just as pleasurable, from time to time, to slam the green baize door on the fingers of mere tradesmen.

"You may be assured, gentlemen, that, as a military man, I have already conceived several ideas as to how we may best proceed ... Drawing on my experience in the *Emden* where we destroyed for all time the myth of British supremacy at sea ... Security forbids a fuller account at this stage ...You will be aware yourselves, as men of responsibility and discretion of the absolute necessity for silence on all details at this point ... I beg you therefore to follow your usual patterns of behaviour ... Above all let us not be seen together too often lest it arouse the suspicion of the enemy whose spies are everywhere ... I must give out the air of a man who regards himself as retired from combat ... We must do nothing precipitate until we are certain of the current situation." His mouth flapped glibly, the empty words flowing with generous ease. The less he told them, the more exciting they would find it. They nodded earnestly. He yawned, his mind elsewhere. Tomorrow, he would start the men doing some pointless physical drills to impress and confuse them. He could get the gymnastics team training themselves up to form human pyramids sufficiently high to get over the perimeter fence. His mistress was coming at three. It would be nice to get a cat to share his quarters, a big complacent tabby perhaps. He missed the cats of the *Emden* and wondered briefly whether they had all died in the conflict. Maybe the English, a sentimental race, would have been less free with their lobbing of shells if they had known there were innocent pets on board. He shook his head. He was nodding off. His visitors rose to go, searched fussily for hats and sticks and he waved them wearily away. They crept through the door in one's and two's, making off hurriedly in opposite directions with the brims of their hats ostentatiously pulled down. That would be *Etappe* training.

"We must do nothing precipitate," said Colonel Martin, "until we are certain of the current situation. It could unsteady the men."

Captain Hall looked out through the open door where chubby Jemedar Khan of the Fifth Light Infantry stared in total absorption at a buff form, picked up a pencil and began to write industriously. Hall opened his eyes wide and nodded back over his shoulder, warning Martin that they were not alone.

"What? Oh don't be silly, Hall, Khan's all right." He sat down in his creaking chair, creaked his Sam Browne belt and cracked his knuckles. "This isn't the first time there have been rumours of disaffection in the ranks." He pouted petulantly. "Not enough goat's meat and milk? Men don't mutiny over that. I don't believe a word of it. It's traditional to belly-ache about rations. It's like boys complaining about school dinners. You should know that."

"There is also," Captain Hall dropped his voice, "the more serious matter of the Muslim connection."

"What? Speak up man. Don't mumble. The Muslim 'connection', as you term it has been grossly exaggerated. So Christi Khan holds a few meetings telling the men not fight fellow Muslims in Turkey. They're not going to Turkey. We've been slated for Hong Kong, as you very well know. He'll be a laughing stock when we're in Kowloon." He was getting irritable again. It was all becoming Hall's fault. From the outer office, Jemedar Khan made a foul gurgling noise with the thick snot far up his nose and scraped his chair on the floor as he lent back, aimed, swirled and spat. Hall paused, waiting for the *Ping* as it hit the cuspidor. Prudence dictated he should call it a day. Never mind. He had come this far. He would see it through.

"I think I mentioned, sir, that my friend in Intelligence warned us to expect some sort of demonstration on the 19th, co-ordinated by those Indian Nationalists funded out of Berlin. They picked up a couple more of their agents in Johore Bahru last week and down at the mosque in Kampong Java the *imam*'s been stirring them up again. With the Chinese New Year coming up and crowds in the streets, we can expect trouble."

Something in Martin snapped. Hall could almost hear the sound of it, like the wishbone of a chicken. Beneath the tight collar his neck coursed with a sudden gush of throbbing blood. His nostrils dilated. Spittle flecked the corner of his mouth.

"You're just like all the rest aren't you, Hall. You want me out of here so you can petition the War Office for service in the West again and get yourself some quick medals. Fancy yourself as CO here don't you? You've never forgiven me for telling them the men just aren't ready, that we need a tour of duty back in India. Don't think I don't know what you all say about me in the Mess, how you try to poison their minds against me. The men tell me all about it. They know whose side I'm on. You'll never understand the Muslim mind, Hall. You're too pig-headed." He stopped, sniggered at his own joke, then snarled, "Oh get out."

Hall stiffened, choked back the rage and bit down hard on it. He saluted icily and strode through the door, pulling it hard so that it slammed behind him. As the reverberations died away by Khan's desk, he stopped and stared down at the top of his glossy, bobbing head.

"You may fool him, Khan, but you don't fool me."

The Indian did not look up but pencilled quietly away with gentle hands. "Sahib?"

"I've got my eye on you Khan, don't you forget that."

Khan turned towards him a face of ineffable sweetness and innocence. The lips parted over white, smiling teeth almost in the gesture of a kiss. "Yes sahib. Thank you sahib. Oh, and happy Chinese New Year, sahib."

CHAPTER SEVEN

Lauterbach groaned and belched. He turned on his stomach so that a hand dangled heavily over the edge of the bed, encountered empty bottles and sent them rolling and crashing like skittles. Light penetrated the grubby curtains and seared his pupils. His eyes, when he rubbed them, ground in crystals like powdered glass. A small furry animal had crawled into his mouth, vomited, voided its bowels and then died. He cursed, reached under the bed with shaking deliberation and found a gin bottle full of tepid water whose contents he sucked down gratefully, then fought stomach convulsions and a terrible sense of suffocation that ended in a coughing fit. On that table there, somewhere, was a fag. He groped, found, struck a lucifer and swallowed smoke blindly. "Himmel, Arsch und Wolkenbruch." This could not go on much longer. The mix of outrage and boredom in this camp and limitless beer were a combination that would be the death of him. Too much free time led to brooding over the meaning of life and for Lauterbach the meaning of life had always been to be too busy to have time to think about it.

Naked, he struggled to his feet, the bed groaning with relief, and headed, panting, for the bathroom. Bare feet padded over damp concrete. Thank God this was the cool, wet season. Thank God he was excused the morning roll call.

Lauterbach grasped the great wooden ladle, dipped it in the standing jar of cold water and basted his head with scoop after healing scoop, shaking like a dog. "Oooaarghscheisse!" Then he gave up and just leant forward to plunge his whole face directly in the jar. "Whoarbloobloob." As he raised his eyes from a swimming world of blur and water, he encountered the trim, prim, disapproving rectangle of Elysium toilet soap. The sight depressed him for some reason. And when he turned round, there stood Taj Mohammed, grinning from ear to ear, holding out his cup of tea and openly ogling the Lauterbach torpedo. Lauterbach growled, seized towel and cup in either hand and slapped him away fiercely.

Taj Mohammed was theoretically the refuse-cart handler of the camp but had determined, for his own unclear reasons, to attach himself to Lauterbach as a sort of freelance helper. His official batman, Private Schmerz, had not taken to this arrangement and now sulked, making only intermittant appearances where he complained with incessant bitterness, like a wronged wife, of his rival. Mohammed was not, Lauterbach suspected, very bright, but he was cheery and willing, unlike joyless and literalist Schmerz, and it pleased him to spin endless fantasies to the boy, rather as he had to Privett and Rose on Diego Garcia. To one who had spent his life in creative mendacity, such flights of fantasy, free as a bird, were liberating. He could shift the pinch and press of reality like gas with a belch. When once he had embarked on such a trail of the imagination, there was no wire, no ditch. He could wander where he would. Anyway, he loved the sound of the boy's Indian-accented English that rumbled and throbbed like a fart in his rainbarrel. Lauterbach had resumed his former extravagant 'full set' of facial hair but was badly in need of a trim so he slipped on his faded *Troilus* bathrobe, sat on a hard chair and prepared to be soaped and shaved.

"You will know," Lauterbach assured Mohammed through thick lather, "that all Germans have secretly converted to Islam."

The boy stopped in mid strop, stared, his jaw dropped. "Is true?"

"Indeed. The latest secret orders have just been delivered from Berlin. You will have heard that Germany has formed an alliance with Muslim Turkey against the British infidels. A holy war has been declared. Even the British papers could not conceal it. I always receive the latest papers since friends send me parcels from the outside. The British foolishly inspect the contents but never think to read the wrapping. The Turks, as you know, are staunch Muslims like the Germans and yourself. You can always tell a good Muslim by his beard."

The boy broke into a delighted grin and breathed benevolent curry fumes over him.

"Then we go to mosque together. We friend."

"Ah no" Lauterbach headshaking. "This is a very great secret, Mohammed. If the British knew they would become very angry and do terrible things to all the innocent Muslims under their rule in India. For their sake – for *your* sake – we must say nothing."

Mohammed executed a firm calligraphic razorstroke the length of Lauterbach's cheek, above the line of his beard. "I no afraid," he sneered and flicked whiskery foam boldly to the floor in proof of it. "You see. We go mosque together, you me."

"The mosque? No. We can do better than that. One day we shall go to Mecca, together. We shall go on my ship the

Emden which the English claim falsely to have sunk. She still sails the Indian Ocean exacting a terrible revenge on their shipping. One day, you will see, she will come to the harbour in Singapore and then we shall go aboard her and sail to Mecca."

Mohammed clutched the shaving cup to his chest in delight, threw back his head and laughed at the ceiling, scaring the gecko lizards that lived there.

"Mecca!" he cried, slopping ecstatic suds. "We go Mecca together. I become *Haji* Mohammed."

Lauterbach proffered his other cheek for scraping. "A fine and godly name. His Imperial Majesty, the German Kaiser, too, has already completed his pilgrimage and similarly taken the title of Haji Mohammed Guiliano. The Empress has become Fatima and assumed the veil and my old friend Prince Franz Josef has been formally circumcised with great ceremony and amidst public rejoicing in what was formerly the state opera house in Berlin."

Mohammed, having begun trimming the broad wings of the moustache, waved the gleaming razor under his nose. "You want circumcise too?"

"Er no. It is not deemed strictly necessary in the case of converts, a certain liberalism in the interpretation of the Koran by the arch-*imam* of Berlin. Moreover, to confuse the enemy, I shall perform my devotions only in the strictest privacy."

"Is not good to pray the way you do, like a Hindu, in that polluted place." He gestured towards the bathroom. "Sometimes I hear you praying in there. You saying, 'Ten, twenty, thirty …'"

Mohammed stepped back to assess the Islamic symmetry

of his work and found it good. "You stop drink beer too?" he reproved. "Is bad. Muslim no drink beer."

"You will be aware from your studies that it is not the act of drinking but the state of drunkenness that is prohibited by the Prophet. Those unaccustomed to beer become easily drunk. I shall therefore continue to maintain my resistance to wicked drunkenness by constant drinking."

Mohammed shook his head in awe. "You clever man. Very learned, very holy."

Jemedar Khan shook his head fiercely. "My friend is a clever man." His voice reached out to the back of the barracks and caught the attention of the few men still lying on their rope beds. "Very learned, very holy. Is he not a postman? Does he not need his great learning for the reading of addresses? Is his position not one of trust where, like us, he wears the uniform of the King Emperor? Yet because he is a Rajput man like ourselves, he is constantly harrassed and persecuted by the other races. Not just the white men of whom nothing better is to be expected but also the Chinese and the Malays who are their servants – yes – and by other Indians like the Pathans, just as we are persecuted by them here in our own regiment."

He looked round at the circle of eager, nodding turbans. He knew he held them by the beard. "You will not have forgotten the recent vacancy for jemedar that should rightly have gone to Imtiaz Ali, also a clever and learned man, a Rajput man, but was given instead to an ignorant Pathan." A low growl rose from the men. "Everywhere we are surrounded by a sea of injustice." The sea hissed in his mouth.

"My friend the postman was thrown recently in jail

unjustly for a matter of missing funds. Many people are sending money by the post office, just as you are sending money home to your mothers and wives and sisters. Allah knows it is little enough. Just enough so they do not starve." He wiped his forehead at the misery of it. "And the people, being ignorant people, cannot sign their names so they just make a mark with their thumbs in ink when they receive that money. It seems that although the receipts are there in the post office with their thumbprints, these people are now saying that they did not have that money. So who took it? And who do they accuse?" Another low growl from the men. "My friend, the Rajput man, always the Rajput man.

So they threw him in jail, a terrible place, and sent a fat white man to take his thumbprints in the jail. 'This wicked deed,' he said, 'was not done by a little person. No Malay or Chinese could have made a great thumbprint like this. This is an Indian hand for though a white man has thumbs big enough, no white man could bend low enough to do such a deed. And you are the only Indian postman in this area, so it must be you.' This is what they call cleverness. But when they compared the prints with those on the papers what do you think?" You could hear them holding their breath in the taut silence. "They did not match. Those thumbprints were not my friend's thumbprints." They exhaled Aah as one. "He is innocent."

"The fat white man was very stupid. He did not know what to do. He sighed and rolled his eyes and held his many chins." Jemedar Khan did all three to roars of laughter. "'It *must* be you,' he kept saying foolishly to my friend. 'I cannot work out how you did it but it *must* be you.' But my friend is a very clever man like all Rajput men. 'Call together all the postmen,' he said calmly 'and I will prove to you who it is.' So they called them all together in one place and the fat white man came and sat down and they brought my friend from the jail. He walked along the line of postmen and looked them, like a man, in the eye and he knew who his enemy was amongst them. It was a very small, very old Chinese." Jemedar Khan hunched his back and screwed up his face to catcalls from the men.

"'This,' said my friend, pointing him out, 'is the villain who has done this terrible thing.' Everyone was amazed. 'How can this be? You are mad. He is only a tiny man' But my friend bent down and tore off his sandal and there on his big toe was *ink*.'" Cheers, applause.

"So it must always be with injustice. We will not suffer it any longer just as the Rajputs of Singapore will not suffer it any longer. They will rise with us," he shouted. "Postmen and soldiers shall be as one. Prepare yourselves! Injustice is at an end!"

Mohammed shook his head in awe. "You clever man. Very learned, very holy."

"Indeed," Lauterbach assented and stroked his moustache. "That is why I am developing an Islamic garden, a vision of paradise in flowers and shrubs."

It was almost true. Out there, across from the front door of the bungalow, something blossomed where once had been a mere heap of rubble. It was not Lauterbach himself who did the work of course, especially the troublesome watering, but he directed it from the verandah, lent – as von Muecke would have said – his vision. Various sailors had seeded and trimmed a formal garden, a series of horticultural tattoos really, anchors and knotwork, even an Iron Cross, executed in peonies and box. Experimentation had led to certain subjects being excluded. After a series of unfortunate acned caricatures due to the unpredictable activities of aphids, the face of the Kaiser had been excised. Maps of the fatherland had been vetoed on the grounds that they might give useful geographical information to the enemy and the German flag had only been permitted after some hesitation by the British authorities, though not all parts of it could be made to bloom at the same moment and the black strip was a constant headache for Nature did not favour black plants. At the rear of the bed, a topiary cruiser of the *Emden* class had had her keel laid and a little more rain would grow in the rest of her superstructure. But this constant shifting of images disguised one fact that the British did not notice.- that the mound itself was growing daily larger. It was the dumping ground for dirt from the tunnel. And once the cruiser was complete, her shadow would entirely conceal the tunnel entrance, hidden under a square of turf, from the searchlights that ranged the camp at night.

The tunnel had been a reluctant gesture by Lauterbach towards the grim-jawed *Etappe* members, a bone for them to gnaw on. Just as every nation must have its flag and its army, so, it seemed, every prisoner-of-war camp must have its tunnel. In its way, it had worked excellently, sopped up their excess of patriotic energy and kept them off his back. Moreover, in this separate compound, the only source of wood for shoring up the roof was the empty beer crates, carried in full under the eyes of the guards. Lauterbach was drinking to support his nation, drinking to keep pace with the diggers. There had been a long discussion of possible starting-points and trajectories in which Lauterbach had favoured opening the shaft inside one of the deep latrine pits, since that would certainly slow down the digging – but this had not found favour. And he was far from pleased to have it so close to his own quarters since, if discovered, it would certainly be laid at his door with attendant loss of comforts and privileges. Already, the British had staged a dawn search of his bungalow but, fortunately, his little nest-egg had been well hidden. In the interests of security, he had insisted that no tools be imported but that all works be effected with a spoon and fork filched from the canteen. It would take them another three months at least to make any substantial progress like that and then he would sadly discover either that it was too narrow for him to accompany the escapers or that it must be greatly enlarged, which would put off the evil day still longer. Lauterbach insisted on a patriotic pause in tunnel construction on national holidays and on the birthdays of the German royal family and those of ally Austria and had an uncanny ability to fix those of even the least members of both royal houses. He had bought a little time but not enough. It was clear that once the diggers had free access to the tunnel mouth the rate of progress would be doubled. He sidled across to the garden, bent to sniff appreciatively at a flower and looked furtively around. The guards were leaning out of their watchtower in the other direction. A group of prisoners were staring out through the wire towards the main road and pointing at something. He reached forward to the topiary *Emden* and snapped off what amounted to about fifty feet of glossy, green keel and stuffed it up his tunic. That would hold them for a bit.

The Chinese New Year was a non-digging day. "Too many people about. Too much disruption to the normal timetable," Lauterbach explained to the confused *Etappe*. Down in Chinatown, crowds were thronging the streets, shopping, getting new year haircuts, eating carp and oranges and dancing dragons in token of good fortune as they watched flames climbing, coughing and farting like old men, up the great strings of firecrackers that hung down from the tenement buildings. In the prisoner-of-war camp, the strutting, shouting Indian troops had been replaced by shy Malays who flitted like pale shadows about the fences. With the departure of his rival, orderly Schmerz had flounced back to his duties, determined to be seen as indispensable. But Lauterbach missed the innocent credulity of Taj Mohammed. It had lent freshness to his world.

For the British, the noise and disorder of Chinese New Year was just another imperial inconvenience of living amongst natives who were in thrall to percussion and superstition and it had to be borne with condescending good humour. Without the Chinese, there was no business to be done so it would be a day of outings to the beach or golf or tennis, or aimless motoring, picnicking and tea on the lawn. In their nearby barracks, the officers of the 5th Light Infantry were taking leisurely tiffin, packing their things, preparing to embark for Hong Kong, when it occurred to some of them that the Chinese firecrackers sounded awfully like rifle fire. In fact, it was rifle fire. At the last minute a rumour had circulated – that the regiment was bound for the Western Front where it would face Turkish troops, fellow Muslims and half their regiment, the Rajput half, had mutinied. The other half, it would later appear, had not mutinied, but since they had neither ammunition nor the will to fight their fellows, they either hid or fled. The result was that Indian troops were wandering about the island in identical uniforms, some shooting down every European in sight and even Chinese when their attention wandered, while others, 'true to their salt', shamefacedly remained loyal. The British military responded with sluggish disbelief and then panicked. Singapore had been stripped of all European troops for the war and the sepoys could do much as they wanted. Colonel Martin sulked in his bungalow, while many of his officers lay dead and decomposing in the sun. At nightfall – he knew -the sepoys would come for him. The General Officer Commanding was unavailable over the telephone but his wife answered happily and freely offered tactical advice, counselling one besieged officer just to hang on till relief came. There was a bang and the line went dead. Probably not very helpful advice then. It remained to be clearly defined who was actually involved in this odd fighting and the very rules of engagement were yet fluid and instinctive. Non-participants outnumbered those committed to either bloodshed or active opposition. European office workers and senile pensioners were hastily summoned to the reserve and issued ancient weapons they did not know how to use. Captain Hall was heard drilling the volunteers. "Load weapons! Now, what you do is pull down that sticking out bit on the side and push a bullet in the hole. No the bullet faces with sharp end pointing the other way round." They were ordered to set up roadblocks to deny the mutineers access to the metropolitan area so they milled about pointlessly in the road in a nice group waiting to be shot down. Everyone settled nervously to wait for someone else to make a decision about what was to be done. There was no public broadcasting. The one thought of the newspapers was to hush things up and they declared that there was absolutely no cause for alarm. The public at large had no idea what was going on and what exactly it was they were not supposed to be alarmed about. Rumours flew wildly round the European community and then the government started evacuating white women and children, sending them out to baking, overcrowded ships in the harbour, where *mems* called into play all the base arts of snobbery and influence. Servants took over the city and enjoyed a time of blissful peace and quiet, drank their employers' gin, lazed in their soft beds, laughingly tried on their clothes in mirrors. Meanwhile the mutineers wandered about in aimless mayhem.

To the military's surprise, one of their immediate targets was the prisoner-of-war camp where Lauterbach lay unpeacefully on his belly in a hail of bullets and cursed, after all, that the tunnel had not been made big enough to accommodate him. That was the place to be. The shots outside could only mean one thing, that those fools from the *Etappe* had persuaded some poor sod to make a break for it and now they were all paying the price. He raised his head over the parapet of his fragile bungalow and watched amazed as Indian sepoys cut down, not German prisoners, but the Malay guards from their watchposts. Now they were firing erratically in all directions. He noted that the Germans, milling panic-stricken all over the parade ground in their distinctive naval outfits, were largely immune. It was clear, then, that the Indians' target was Malay and British officers but it was far from obvious that they were well versed in the discrimination of uniforms at a distance. He heard shots and saw a couple of khaki-clad German prisoners stumble and fall and ducked down again. Most of the sepoys, fortunately, were terrible shots. It occurred to him that maybe they were all short-sighted.

The safest place above ground was perhaps the chapel. No wait. These were Muslims. Memories of the Indian Mutiny flooded in, with Europeans shot down before Christian altars by leering Lascars. The hospital. Hospitals had a more convincingly cross-cultural sacred status. He tucked a bottle of water and a hunk of *Etappe* sausage in his haversack and set off at a fast waddle, cutting behind the main buildings. When he arrived at the sickbay via the back door, the patients were all gathered round the front windows, offering excellent targets. This would not do at all.

"Get back to your beds!" he roared from behind. Some leapt a foot in the air, others dashed blindly for cover. A man with a broken leg rolled in agony on the floor. Bray, the attendant, stood dithering. He was a 'conchie', a man opposed on principle to any bloodletting other than the purely medical, and therefore treated universally by British and German alike as a mass murderer

"If I were you," Lauterbach remarked to him with a calm he did not feel and stowing his food securely under a table, "I would get out of British uniform and into a white coat."

He went around the ward, arranging it to look more like a hospital, scattering charts on the desk, tastefully displaying the instruments of medical emergency on bedside tables. When, a few minutes later, the sepoys clattered in with their hobnail boots, rifles nervously poking at the occupants, he was standing behind a big steel box with a red cross on it and taking the temperature of a protesting patient while talking loudly in authoritative German.

A bearded soldier in a turban, clearly the leader, tugged the bedclothes down off the first patient and asked if he were English. Lauterbach recognised Schulz, now revealed in comical Charlie Chaplin pyjamas, washed too often and far too small.

"German," he declared roundly. "We are all German here." Schulz grabbed back the sheets in offended modesty and clutched them up around his breasts. They looked around suspiciously, eyes resting on Bray. Lauterbach addressed him firmly in a child's German tongue-twister.

"Die Katze tritt die Treppe krumm in Ulm, um Ulm und um Ulm herum."

"Ja," nodded Bray wisely. "Ja." and executed what was not a bad heelclick for a civilian in sandals.

The Indians laughed, shouldered their arms and marched out the way they had come, one fist in the air.

"Long live the Kaiser! Long live Enver Pasha!"

Further shots, shouts and a scream came from outside.

"I think," said Lauterbach to Bray, "You should prepare for more casualties."

There was a sudden noisy melee around the main gate. He peered cautiously round the doorframe to see what was happening. More Indian troops had arrived and were smashing off the lock. But what kind of Indians were these? Loyal? Mutineers? In the heat and dust there seemed to be a general scrum. The Germans were being attacked. No. Wait. They were being embraced by ecstatic Indians, pressing hairy, bearded kisses upon their shocked, squirming faces, gesturing at the gates now thrown wide, virtually pushing them out. "Free," they shouted, "free." A group of them spotted Lauterbach and ran over

"You see? I come for you. We friend." At their head, under the turban, in immaculate military dress, was the face of Taj Mohammed.

"But how ...? What ...?"

"You are free. We make you our leader. Our brother in Islam. Tell us what to do. We will take the forts, kill all the English."

Brown men rushed up and seized Lauterbach, slapped a soldier's turban on his head, hefted him on their shoulders and bore him, laughing and clapping around the parade ground, stamping rhythmically and grunting in some dark, native chorus normally used for the manhandling of fieldgun barrels over obstacle courses. The leader tripped and buckled under his weight but they recovered and laughed and swung him from shoulder to shoulder like some great Hindu god. Lauterbach choked, sweated, pulled the turban from over his eyes, laughed too and then abruptly froze as he raised his gaze to see intrigued British officers, crouched on the brow of the nearby hill, watching the whole thing, with impunity, through field glasses as if in the dress circle of a theatre. A terrible shivering gripped him. His bowels loosened. Incitement to mutiny, assuming command of rebel troops, murder, mayhem, treachery, wearing British uniform – the charges extended the length of a corridor that led to death at the end of a swinging rope. Perhaps, he thought vainly, they would not be able to identify him, would not know his name.

"Lauterbach! Lauterbach!" the troops began to chant obligingly. A British officer frowned and made a note.

"For Christ's sake why don't you spell it for them?"

"L-A-U-T—" Mohammed drew proudly on his mastery of the name on Lauterbach's door, demonstrating his own learning by shouting it to the world.

"Put me down!" screamed Lauterbach in mental agony. Mohammed looked puzzled and released his grasp, unbalancing the load so that Lauterbach tumbled in the soft dirt under a pile of malodorous Indian bodies. A knee struck him in the mouth. Someone trampolined painfully off his stomach.

"I cannot join you," he gasped, struggling to rise. "It is not possible."

Mohammed frowned. "Then you are our enemy too."

"No, no. We wish you well. But we have no weapons. We are mere sailors, unused to land fighting. We would be a handicap to you. We are not army men." He thought briefly of giving them Schulz as leader but it would confuse them. "It is not as if the port was full of German ships. Then we could do something."

"German ships," someone shouted from the rear. "The port is full of German ships. Lauterbach has promised German ships." They hugged each other, resumed their dancing, raised him aloft again and chanted his name and his promise in excellent English for all to hear. Finally, they gave him three cheers and left shouting loudly their resolve to return later with guns for all the prisoners and marching away to English patriotic songs, the only ones they knew how to march to.

"Well done, Lauterbach, quite magnificent." It was Feldschwein and the rest of the *Etappe*, creeping out from hiding, smirking. "A splendid brave gesture. Germany can be proud of you. How long do you think you will be able to hold out once the English mobilise their forces? Shall we get the other chaps organised? No point in your staying here, though. Will you make your final stand in one of the forts or take to the hills for a long guerrilla campaign and wear them down?"

Lauterbach shook his head. "You don't understand. The whole thing is hopeless. The British can call on some fifty ships in this area alone to put down the rebellion. They can bring in troops from the mainland, or use the big gun emplacements out in the islands to blast them to pieces. In the long run, the Indians haven't a hope in hell."

Feldschwein gripped his shoulder in a wizened claw. Tears started to his eyes. "Quite so, Lauterbach. We fully appreciate the glorious futility of your gesture. You may be assured that Berlin will hear of the way you have laid down your life for the fatherland. As long as there are prisoners here, we will maintain the shrubbery model of the *Emden* as a fitting monument to you. You know, there was a time when I had my doubts about you, Lauterbach. It seemed to me you were lacking in team spirit with a nasty streak of tolerance. I'm glad I was wrong."

Lauterbach's mouth gaped. Of course, he was doing this all wrong, speaking the wrong language. These people spoke the same weird tongue as von Mueller.

"Herr Muell— I mean Feldschwein," he snapped grimly and moustache-twirling. "You surely do not think that an officer and a gentleman, a member of His Imperial Majesty's forces, could really collaborate with mutineers? Men who have broken their sacred oath of loyalty to their command? You are aware that hot-blooded troops of colour, when out of control, are gripped by but a single passion – lust – their only thought is the rape and ravishment of white virgins, the dashing out of the brains of innocent children. Where do you imagine the rest of the sepoys are at this moment? What forbidden pleasures are they enjoying? Are you prepared to accept responsibility for all that? Do not some of you have wives and children still in the colony?" He glared in simulated outrage, hands on hips, making his bulk an unanswerable argument. There was a terrible brooding silence as dire images flared across the minds of the audience as from a cinematograph. Feldschwein began to look doubtful. "Er well … If you put it that way …" He began browmopping with the handkerchief again.

"He's right," came a voice from the back, loud with instant outrage. "Lauterbach's right. My missus is up in town. Let's get guns and go and fight the Indians. Shoot the raping bastards down like dogs, I say. Teach them to touch our women." The men started cheering. It was beginning to get dark. Darkness always favours the forming of a mob.

Lauterbach groaned and clutched his head. "No, no, no," he cried weakly. "We must keep out of this. Whatever we do we will be damned, don't you see that? If we attack the Indians, the British will attack *us*. Our only hope lies in extravagantly doing absolutely nothing.

Look. How do you think the British will explain all this? Will they seek to find how they came to alienate the loyalty of brave men? No. They will speak of irrational natives running amok. That is how they always explain everything that happens in their colonies. It is a very useful explanation because it asserts that there is nothing to be explained. Natives are just like that, they run amok and there is nothing to be done about it but shoot them like elephants in must. It is a fact of nature. But if we are seen to be involved – no matter how slightly – on either side, this will all become our fault and we too will be shot down – that is – it will reflect gravely on the honour of Germany. I would suggest we gather the dead honourably in one place, German and British together, relock the gate and go to bed."

The men slunk away like curs, snarling, feeling cheated. To do nothing was asking too much. To go to bed was scarcely an act of manly courage. So they got out some old German flags and marched around, waving clenched fists and impotently singing "Die Wacht am Rhein."

Lauterbach lay awake, hour after hour, sweating and jumping at every sound. Whenever his stomach rumbled it made him start. It was the sepoys coming to drag him off to fling him against the impregnable British forts. It was the British coming to bind him hand and foot, drive him away and hang him after a chortling parody of a trial. It was the *Etappe* coming to chase him into the hills to suffer and starve till his pointless and miserable death. At midnight, he rose, put on full uniform, slipped an *Etappe* sausage in his pocket and walked out of the camp, knowing he would never come back. On the moonlit road he met six others similarly wandering off, less a bunch of desperadoes bent on escape than abandoned orphans resigned to seeking their fortunes in a wider world. No agreement was made to travel together. It just happened. In the velvet magic of the moonlight they somehow knew that all the decisions were making themselves and that, for the moment, they were safe.

The moonlight lasted until three o'clock when a sudden chill wind blew cloud in from the sea and then the lashing rain began. It soaked and wearied their bodies and frightened their minds with the shadows conjured up by the splittering lightning. In the distance they saw lights moving and left the road since either loyal or mutinous troops could prove equally fatal. Miserably, they picked their way through ranks of rubber trees. In the dark they too looked like soldiers. Lauterbach knew the thick undergrowth was the haunt of lethal snakes and that every stumbling footfall in the hissing rain risked death. They wandered for hours in circles till at dawn they reached a Chinese settlement.

What the Chinese thought as Lauterbach, streaked with mud and rain, wild-eyed and gesticulating, surged into their hut from the darkness will never be known. The riches of Chinese folklore offered a wealth of mythological beings to give him a name. But a dozen pairs of eyes flew up from their mah-jong in terror, chairs were flung back and the table toppled as they screamed and fled. Lauterbach surveyed the damage and then stooped and pocketed up the Straits Settlement dollars scattered on the ground. You never knew when they would come in handy. Then he fished into another hut and extracted a tiny, whimpering Chinese, set him on the ground and said loudly, "Beach, *pantai*." A plan had formed in his mind – to find a Malay village with boats and hop across the short sea passage to Dutch territory. The Chinese pointed with a trembling arm but Lauterbach, drove him implacably before them with threats and growls. After ten minutes, they pushed through waist-high razor grass onto a beach of golden sand and crashing surf with little houses and canoes at a distance. Fishermen, then, maybe even smugglers in a small way of business. Lauterbach extracted some of his new-found dollars, pressed them into their guide's hand, did an imitation of a pouncing tiger, slit his own throat in lurid gesture with his hand and chased the man off wailing. He took great pleasure in being generous in money that was not his own, an act combining as it did all the Protestant virtues.

The wind was blowing sea-spray in their faces as they crunched over broken coral to the ladders that led up to the houses where phlegmatic Malays were already afoot, gathering their sarongs about their shivering bodies and dousing themselves in cold water. They nodded and smiled as if an early morning visit by a gang of Germans was an everyday occurrence and waved them in to sit on the worn floorplanks. The little house shook in each gust of wind and everything smelled of fish. Tiny, naked children were crawling about inside and they smelled of fish too. To make friends with a man, first make friends with his dog, thought Lauterbach. Since Malays didn't have dogs, he seized a gurgling child and dandled it approximately on his knee. An old woman with a quid of *sirih* tucked under her lip came and cackled at him, dripping red saliva like blood. But she came back and offered coffee. The coffee smelled of fish too. The Germans bestowed cigarettes in exchange. It was the first time Lauterbach had really seen his companions of the night.

There was Diehn, a shipping agent, big and blond, in his early forties and his wiry assistant, Schoenberg. Dedicated to business, Diehn had made money early and a lot of it and had no reason to love either Feldschwein or Lauterbach, for the *Etappe* and the *Emden* had been his undoing. At the beginning of the war, the British had left the international businessmen who were the backbone of Singapore largely alone. In those days, wealth bestowed a sort of honorary Britishness. Anyway, Diehn knew most of the important Brits by their first names, rubbed shoulders with them in their own clubs. Since he was the local agent for the British Blue Funnel Line, most of them had business dealings with him too. He it was, who had booked some of the most expensive cargo aboard the *Troilus*, one of the vessels that Lauterbach had sent to the bottom. Diehn had unwisely made a joke to the customer. "Maybe the *Emden* will get your cargo." When it did, a complaint was laid by the insurers, Diehn's office was searched, accusations of *Etappe* links were made. Nothing was found for there was nothing to find since Diehn let nothing interfere with business. Then they searched his house and discovered in triumph that his washing line was made of steel wire. It could be used, they alleged, as a wireless aerial for communicating with enemy agents or submarines, though no transmitter was ever found. It was never mentioned that all Diehn's British neighbours had similar metal washing lines that aroused no adverse comment. But despite his protests he was interned and sent to the camp alongside Lauterbach.

Then there was Hahn, a tall, easy-going merchant of nothing in particular, the sort who fit well into a war because they have no distinctive shape of their own and like things organised for them. He had tried his luck in all the riches of the islands, bird-nests, gums, rubber, but always found himself hopelessly outmatched by sharp Chinese competition. Instead of ranting of racial injustice he had settled comfortably into the firm of an ancient Chinese *towkay* and quickly married his plain daughter. Early to bed, early to rise. Then three strapping sailors, Johan, Jensen and Reinhart, all muscle and tattoos. Even their eyebrows had muscles. Last was Thompson, a waif of a lad, just eighteen, who spoke like a stoker but looked like a phtisic poet.

The headman of the settlement, appeared, flicking wet hair out of his eyes and knotting his sarong, settled quietly on the floor, daintily accepted a proferred cigarette that he lit with a flint and began chatting with Lauterbach in Malay. He spoke very quietly and without gesture in tones of extreme politeness. He might only be a fisherman but he knew courtly etiquette and Lauterbach was moved by the instinctive good manners. He had heard that there were strangers here and he had come to greet them. He hoped Tuan's coffee was acceptable but this was a poor house. Tuan must forgive the simple welcome. Could he perhaps do something else for Tuan?

Lauterbach declared that he sought nothing but the pleasure of seeing this place and meeting these fine people and their great leader. The headman smiled and bowed. But there was indeed, one matter – a very small matter – that he might perhaps make bold to mention in case his new friend knew someone who might be able to help with this difficulty.

Indeed Tuan should not be shy, for – who knew? The headman smiled and looked coyly away into a corner with his soft brown eyes. It would bring great joy to help Tuan in any reasonable way.

Then he *would* mention it. These Dutch gentlemen required, for complicated reasons, to pass to the Dutch side of the water, to Great Karimon Island. There was a slight irregularity of papers. The British made such a fuss about these small matters but between sensible people such things surely could be arranged.

The headman nodded and exhaled smoke, thinking hard. Yes he too suffered in this matter of papers. It was the same for everyone. Did fish carry papers? No. Why then should fishermen? Perhaps he knew a man who might help Tuan but a certain risk was involved. The British made life difficult for everyone because of the war. If these gentlemen were found in his boat, it would be confiscated and how then might he earn his living? They would be punished and times were already hard. He had a wife and children to take care of. He was sure Tuan understood.

Lauterbach dug in his pocket and straightened out the tangled notes of Straits dollars he had seized in the Chinese hut and turned them into a fat wad. The Lord giveth and the Lord taketh away. He passed it over, politely, with both hands. He had no idea whether this was a fortune or a paltry sum to a Malay fisherman but the man nodded simply, pocketed it up without counting or comment and despatched a snot-nosed child to fetch someone else. A few minutes later they were back under the house in the sea-mist with another young Malay, packing themselves among nets and tarpaulins into two black sailing canoes with outriggers. Lauterbach splashed out into the sloshing waves and clambered aboard, nearly upsetting them with his bulk. He jammed his body in so tightly between the gunwales that he could scarcely move. Whenever he breathed the sides creaked. The boats were shoved off to bob high in the water and then there came a shout from the child who slid down the house-ladder excitedly and waded out to whisper through the mist into his father's ear. The headman looked at them without bitterness and coiled the line fixed to his anchor.

"You German," he said laughing, allowing a wave to lift him and drop him back on the sand. So the British were looking for them and the news of their flight had already reached this far. Would he turn them in? Perhaps soldiers were already on their way. Should they make a fight of it right now and just take the boats by force? There were seven of them and only two small Malays to stop them. They were unarmed, at most they would have the odd knife tucked away in their sarongs. Lauterbach could see the sailors had grasped the situation and were ready for anything. He cast an eye around for a weapon but there was nothing to hand in the boat. It would have to be a rock. That one there with the rough edge. The headman came closer and Lauterbach stiffened and let his arm drop casually towards the rock.

"You German," he said again quietly. "Very dangerous. Much trouble in town. But I promise you and so I keep my promise. One thing only. You give me that." He gestured towards Lauterbach's *Emden* cap badge, as a crackle of distant gunfire echoed across from the town. "You give me that."

BOOK THREE

WANTED
DEAD OR ALIVE

CHAPTER EIGHT

Your Excellency,

This is just a card to let you know that we have arrived safely in Padang (Sumatra – but perhaps you know that having been to an excellent school) after a superb and refreshing cruise amongst these beautiful islands. You need have no further concern for our wellbeing. Thank you for looking after us and putting us up in your large and luxurious residence in Singapore. Our only regret is that we remained as guests on your hands for so long but we are now to be considered permanently non-resident members of the Tanglin Barracks Club. Be assured that whenever circumstances permit we shall be delighted to return the favour and are assured that we shall offer you our hospitality in the near future when Singapore comes under German rule after the war. Please thank our attendants, the 5th Light Infantry, for all their kindnesses and the truly excellent and unforgettable send-off they gave us. In the rush, certain items of laundry were left behind. Would it be too much trouble for you to take them into your care until we meet again?

With warm affection,

Lieutenant Julius Lauterbach

The card bore a hand-coloured picture of the main street of Padang, in the Dutch East Indies, showing a peaceful mix of strolling natives in sarongs and *mems* in high feathery hats. It was a lesson to the messy British in Dutch neatness. He turned the card over and wrote the address in a large, slightly clumsy hand, "His Excellency the Governor, Sir Arthur Young, Government House, Singapore."

He shouldn't have done it of course. It was certainly a mistake, childish but also irresistible. Some mistakes were too much fun to make only once and, God knows, he had had little enough fun of late. It was too much to hope that the card would arrive uncensored on a silver salver at the breakfast table of Sir Arthur and cause an apoplectic besmirching of the gubernatorial white tunic with coughed-up toast and marmalade. Yet it *would* reach him finally and it would rankle like a starched collar. Lauterbach knew all about rankling. There, on the table was something that rankled and would go on rankling. It was a poster bearing his picture, or rather an artist's impression of Lauterbach. It had little piggy eyes, jowls which he was sure he did not have and a fat smear of facial hair about a leering mouth. The overall effect was of a mentally impaired sexual delinquent. But what really rankled was underneath. "Wanted dead or alive, for treacherously fomenting disaffection amongst His Majesty's troops. Reward £10,000." He had encountered it in Padang and copies were posted everywhere. So, it was as he had predicted. The British had settled on the version of events most convenient to themselves, blaming everything on foreign intrigue and now he was safe nowhere in the East. There would always be someone after him, keen to lay hands on that reward. After all, £10,000 was a lot of money. He was almost tempted to hand himself in and claim it. Now every British sea-captain and trader, every warship and merchant vessel would see him as their walking pension till the end of his days. He gummed the stamp gloomily in place, frankly not bothered if they had to pay an extra charge at the other end because of inadequate postage. He was doomed.

It had not been the pleasant cruise he had claimed to H.E. Governor Singapore, in fact, it had been a right pig of a journey that often found him longing for the comfort and safety of the prisoner-of-war camp where three square meals a day and a soft bed were guaranteed. The first stage in the canoe had been well enough. They were all so tired that sleep had come easily. Lauterbach had been dimly aware of being splashed by bow waves and disturbed by the constant retching of Schoenberg but as long as the retching and the splashing were separate things they were not unduly troublesome. He had turned over to feel the comforting, hugging pressure of his money pocket against his paunch and slept. Discomfort came the next day with the empty heat and lack of water as he gnawed surreptitiously, under the tarpaulin, on his *Etappe* sausage. It was not until sunset that day that they finally reached the safety of Dutch territory but freedom did not look, at first sight, very attractive. The shore was an unrelieved dark green, a stinking tangle of malarial swamps and mangrove roots that snuffed out all life. Dark green, Lauterbach saw at once, was the colour of despair. After an hour's splashing knee-deep in diarrhoeal mud they had finally found a miserable fisherman's house where the owner's dismay was converted into joy by the sight of silver dollars.

"Where is the town?" inquired Lauterbach, pointing

east, west, opening his hands in enquiry. The owner looked puzzled. "*This* is the town," he said. They dined on rice eaten with unwashed hands straight from the pan before collapsing again in sleep.

"Should we post a guard and take turns?" Diehn asked him, yawning, already semi-comatose. Diehn was a fusspot. Did he think they were still at war here? As far as Lauterbach was concerned, the war lay behind him in Singapore.

"What's the worst that can happen? We might get our throats cut in our sleep but can you think of a more comfortable place to get your throat cut?" There was a protruding knothole sticking into his back. They did not bother with a guard.

The next day brought more rice, but now they had established that the main settlement lay on the other side of the island. The others were keen to be rid of the boats – anything was better than another day on board – and decided to walk across. Lauterbach had seen something of jungle paths before, roots to trip you, snakes to bite you, thorns to rip your flesh. No thank you. He would go by boat. He was comfily enjoying his third glass of gin with the Dutch chief of police when they arrived, bloodied and exhausted, digging leeches out of their boots, to find the gin was finished. Dumpy, beaming Mr Herman rattled out orders over one shoulder to his Malay servant.

"I was just explaining," he sighed, "that the District Officer is away on a tour of duty and will not return for several days. There is a case in one of the interior villages involving smuggling and women – alway here it is smuggling and women, sometimes smuggling *of* women. In the meantime, I can settle you in the resthouse. I cannot, as I explained to your leader ..." they transferred their sour gazes from the glasses of tepid water being set before them to Lauterbach's face "I cannot deal with such a major matter in his absence, but I can assure you you will find the resthouse quite comfortable."

Surprisingly it was, a long cool thatched building in a leafy garden with a verandah over the sea and a quiet and competent Malay manservant, Yusuf, who tweaked away dirty clothes, provided bathwater, sarongs, Malay jackets and slippers and then tucked up proferred dollars into his waistband to slip into town and find gin while his wife composed a pungent curry that seared out all fatigue and pain. By the end of the evening, gathered in light around the oil lamp, they were human again – which meant that Diehn began to boast of his wealth, Schoenberg of his travels and Jessen of his ability to split a coconut with his bare hands.

Lauterbach rose, movements made oddly elegant by Malay dress, and sidled into the kitchen, letting himself down cross-legged beside bony-bodied Yusuf. He smiled, lay his cigarettes gently down on the black floorboards between them.

"*Mari, rokok sama-sama.* Let us smoke a little together."

In half an hour he knew most of the scandal of the little town. He knew that the Mr Herman had not come to this backwater seeking either the power to make decisions nor the hard work to engage his free time. The absent District Officer detested Germans, having made the mistake of marrying one, a sour widow, whose alleged fortune had proved illusory. He would be away not for days but for weeks, enjoying a rest from her tongue. They would do well to be gone before his return. There was a comparatively reliable Chinese skipper in the harbour who planned to sail for the Kangsar river in Sumatra the next day. All these facts added together made a plan. Lauterbach bestowed more dollars, shared more cigarettes …

At dawn the next day a large junk stole out of harbour bearing six passengers in freshly-laundered clothes. Lauterbach almost expected to find four dollars in his top pocket. This time they took fruit and water with them and sarongs to wear against daytime heat and nightime cold. Yusuf waved them a warm goodbye.

"How long catchee Kangsar?"

The Chinese captain shrugged thin shoulders, spat, scratched. "Bye bye. Depend." He shouted orders to the crew, four obvious mass murderers and two tiny, terrified lads who looked about twelve so were probably in their twenties.

"Where map?" As a navigation officer he could work it out for himself.

"No map. Me already knowee way. Ship knowee way." He pointed vaguely at the eyes Chinese paint either side of the bow so that their vessels do not get lost. Perhaps it did know the way but not, it seemed, the tides. The vast daily surge of green water linking the two great oceans of the world was flowing against them. It was hopeless to continue until the tide changed. They put in at one of the small uninhabited islands, ducking into the bleak mangrove trees, and settled down patiently to play cards and feed the mosquitoes. The captain, a gambler like many Chinese, nodded in approval.

"Me play you for passage money," offered Lauterbach insinuatingly. The captain tittered and waved the offer away, settled an opium pipe in his mouth and lay back to doze while the boys set lines for fish.

It was not a boring afternoon. The sea was alive with British ships, cruising aimlessly round the islands, snuffling gently in the bays and inlets. The finer points of territoriality were clearly set in abeyance in their eagerness to capture mutineers – and Lauterbach. The Germans took time off to bathe at the mouth of a stream that flowed down from the interior.

"Are there sharks?" inquired Lauterbach anxiously. He had always worried about sharks.

"No shark," the captain yawned.

"You sure?"

"Die-die I sure".

They swam langourously, splashed each other in a grotesque mockery of exuberance they were far from feeling, luxuriated in cool, deep water. When they were back on the boat, Lauterbach asked again.

"Why no shark?"

The captain pointed at the bank. "I tellee. Here no shark. You safe. Here plenty big crocodile, big teeth, big tail, plenty hungry, chasee shark away."

At dusk the tide changed and the British ships grew tired and went home. As soon as the coast was clear they clapped on all sail and dashed straight for Sumatra. They awoke in a chill dawn to explosions. The British sending shots across their bows? No. The Chinese crew letting off firecrackers to chase away devils that might impede their progress up the great river and leave them fast on the bar. They had clearly arrived in Sumatra.

They river itself was broad and powerful, the colour of cocoa, so they hugged the muddy banks to take advantage of the slack water and soon a settlement of neat white bungalows appeared through the great trees that reached out over the main stream. Diehn shouted to the captain to go ashore. The captain argued heatedly with him and looked at Lauterbach seeking support. This was not, he knew, the moment to defend his leadership so Lauterbach withdrew to peacefully admire the boys' catch of fish and let them be, railing at each other in mutual incomprehension. Finally Diehn leapt in irritation from the boat and splashed arrogantly towards the shore. He paused for a moment, then plunged into the thick reeds by the river's edge, crashing through with great sweeps of his arms. After a couple of minutes he reappeared on the bank, looked about with hands on hips, climbed a bit further and called out. Then he disappeared. The Chinese master settled to his pipe and laughed like a cat. Lauterbach looked at him curiously. Then suddenly Diehn reappeared, an expression of indescribable terror over his face as he flailed at the reeds and ran panic-stricken back towards the water, plunged into the mud and wallowed, panting and swallowing back to the water and the boat, shouting now for them to put out further from the bank. As he lay on deck, whimpering and looking fearfully over one shoulder, the reeds by the water parted again and a sinister head emerged, wearing the peaked hood of a Seville penitent and surveyed them through holes hacked in the fabric. Then it slowly pulled off the hood to display a face that was no face, unfleshed bone and rotted cheeks. As they stared in horror, there emerged a band of the most appallingly filthy and diseased humanity, some lacking fingers, others toes, others whole limbs. Lepers. This was a leper colony. They waved their seeping deformities cackling at the boat, beckoned them back, though whether in supplication or mockery was hard to tell. A horrible fecal stench engulfed them all. The captain threw back his head and roared with unchecked laughter. Lauterbach turned away.

"Poor souls," he said, and smiled to himself.

A steady needling rain set in as they sailed on up a river that seemed to despair of further settlement until, at dusk, they rounded a bend and saw before them a desolate village with a tattered Dutch flag and a large, seagoing junk, a three-master, moored by a jetty.

"Perhaps we should land here," Lauterbach suggested mildly to Diehn. No reply was necessary for a sudden squall picked them up and rammed them up hard against the ironwood stern of the junk, toppling most of the crew into the water. The master laughed again.

A figure surveyed them from the landing stage, not it appeared, a District Officer but a lowly customs official, the usual half-caste of these backwoods settlements, his golden beauty mocked by the contempt of both Dutch and Sumatrans. He greeted them with a handful of fanned-out forms in Dutch.

"Welcome to Pulu Mudra." The smile was flawless. "Your papers?"

Diehn thrust out his chin, brushed the forms aside. "Never mind all that nonsense. We have no papers. We are German nationals and demand to be forwarded to the German consul in Padang."

The little brown man drew on a cheroot carefully. He had built up a good three inches of ash, poised delicately to fall, and he considered it with absorption. Lauterbach knew he could make all this last as long as he liked. Grossly underpaid, like all Dutch officials, he expected remuneration either to do his job or to fail to do it as regulations required.

He slipped the cheroot back between his lips and puffed truculence. "Demand is it? Without papers you are illegal immigrants, belligerants in time of war, and must return promptly to your point of entry to the Dutch East Indies to await proper procedures." He abruptly tapped off the ash, ground it viciously underfoot and turned as if to go.

Lauterbach sighed and dug in the cummerbund pocket and laid a hand gently on his arm. "Mynheer," he urged softly. "My friend has perhaps not made our case entirely clear." With both hands, he proferred old-dog-eared papers wrapped in oilskin. "My seaman's papers. We are, you see, shipwrecked sailors, in distress, cast upon your compassion. Pray examine the details and satisfy yourself as to our status."

The official opened the package with clumsy ill-temper and a large banknote fluttered to the floor. He bent without shame, still reading, and slipped it into his side pocket as if not looking at it made it invisible to everyone else.

"It seems to me," he inclined his head and returned the papers, "that your case exceeds my own low powers. I have no choice, therefore, but to forward you on to Padang immediately, to competent authorities who will decide what is the appropriate action to take." With a brisk salute he stalked away jauntily, pluming smoke, his hand in his pocket.

Padang was a mere four hundred miles away, the other side of the island, through a complicated and hostile geography of jungle and mountains and rivers. To go by sea involved a circuitous journey around the whole of Sumatra, some two thousand hazardous miles, during which they would be at risk of detection by the British. The only viable route was to follow the river as far as possible and then engage the long, onerous trek overland.

They set off the very next morning in two light dugout canoes that bobbed on the water like corks. Lauterbach drove them mercilessly. He knew that time was against them. In the enervating heat, they would soon have neither the willpower nor the energy to undertake such a trip. Each had within him an accumulated stock of goodness that was running down, bled by the tension and exertion, and young Thompson's would be the first to give way. They had to be got rapidly to the point where it was easier to go forward than back or they would be stuck in this god-forsaken nest for ever.

Four cheerful Malay paddlers came with the boats, singing back and forth in four-lined *pantun* verses, extemporised question and answer as they went. The best, those so clever that they disrupted the paddling by an explosion of guffaws, would be remembered for use at weddings where the two sides celebrated their union by battling verbally across the marriage feast. Once they were clear of the settlement, the river tired of bravado and refined itself to a narrow rivulet over gravel, with occasional rocks standing adamant in mid-course. The trees crept down on either hand, purple and red with flowers, and lianas even reached across from side to side to serve as bridges for the troops of solemn-faced monkeys who cooed their resentment at this incursion into their domain. On the banks, the eyes of occasional crocodiles glittered with cold malice. The boatmen delighted in splashing them, whooping, to drive them – hissing and snapping – zigzagging away. Lauterbach sat very still, his gaze fixed on theirs, hanging on to the rocking boat for dear life as the laughing Malays had their fun. Later still, they surprised little bears, wild boar, even a midget rhinoceros, come down to the river to drink and the air danced with a million fireflies that flitted over the water like tiny golden flames. Thompson, already sickening, recited German poetry, wet-eyed. Diehn loudly regretted the absence of a gun. Lauterbach fell asleep and dreamed bitterly of sausage and chewy dishes cooked from thick, stringy tripe.

After five sunburnt days they reached Pulu Lawan, home to a sultan of great piety and power, who turned out to be an unassuming little man who lived in a simple thatched house much like those of his little subjects. A Lilliputian air reigned over the whole town and the Germans felt themselves to be clumsy well-natured giants who put their feet through bamboo floors, crashed into low doorways and snapped any piece of furniture they sat on. Even the svelte Malay paddlers seemed huge. By some mystery a shipment of American denim overalls, cut to fit children, had recently arrived up-river and made a sensation in the town so that all persons of fashion and quality were dressed in them.

The etiquette in the palace was long and tedious, made yet more irksome by the fact that the sultan was quite innocent of the very existence of Germany, the fact of a war or the nature of a warship so that every explanation required another ten. But his smallness and Lauterbach's girth spoke to each other and the little man hugged him ecstatically and offered the use of the rest house, built to Dutch dimensions, for the night.

"Only you must be careful." He wagged his finger "The last person to stay there was eaten by grandfather ..."

Lauterbach laughed and dismissed the words, thinking he must have misunderstood owing to the odd local accent. Could cannibalism still be endemic in this backjungle and tolerated as a mere eccentricity in an endearing elderly relative – and all this so close to a Dutch station? Surely not. But when they arrived at the clean, decent building, escorted by most of the town, the guardian pointed out with great pride deep clawmarks shredding one end of the verandah and the hole ripped in the sidescreen through which a tiger had entered to tear apart and eat the last guest. "A local man of the lower class only. Fortunately," he comforted. Lauterbach remembered then that the Malays often referred to the tiger with the respect name of "Grandfather." Members of the crowd stepped forward and showed wounds they too had incurred from the tigers of the area who not only lurked in the forest but came into their homes and bore away their children. One displayed a brown back scored with pink slashes like pork crackling. But what had these people done? Had they shot the tigers? They all shook their heads and looked shocked. That would bring great bad luck. There was only one thing to do, give the tiger gifts, address it most respectfully and ask it to leave. Now Lauterbach joined Diehn in regretting the lack of a gun.

"Lauterbach. Lauterbach." He was being carried around on the shoulders of a pack of Indians. Very black skin. Very white teeth. The teeth became long and sprouted pointed incisors and the faces bunched and whorled into those of striped tigers and roared at him. He woke with a start, sweat flowing down his chest. There was something rattling at the door.

"Lauterbach. Lauterbach."

If it spoke it could not be a tiger. The voice came from out there in the moonlight, where the tigers lived. It was still dark. His internal clock said it was about two in the morning and no time for social calls. He rose, wrapped his sarong tighter and peered out through the shutters. A glittering eye peered back at him.

"Oberleutnant Lauterbach? I am Distict Officer Filet. My man at Pulu Mudra sent word that you were an escaped German officer and travelling in this direction. Although Holland is neutral I have always had many German friends and I should like to help you."

The barricades of furniture, erected against tigers, were dragged away from the doorway. Sleeping forms were slapped back to wakefulness. Schoenberg stood terrified in a corner and dithered as Lauterbach flung wide the door and grandly beckoned Filet into what was, after all, his own house. He entered, looked around at the soldierly disorder and smiled, hooked a foot round a chair and dragged it forward to sit and look down on the men still on the floor. As he sat, he let out a long sigh.

"I always wondered why my parents sighed when they sat down," he smiled. "Now I am old enough to know." He rubbed sore legs. Filet was a dapper little man in his early fifties, blond moustache, cropped hair, wearing a travel-stained colonial uniform. The sun had dried and creased his skin as though from too much squinting into a bright light but his movements were spare and tight so that he exuded a cool sense of control. "I have chased you all the way from Pulu Mudra in my launch. Thing is, you can carry on the way you are but frankly you'll find it pretty tough going. Not a regular route you see. What I suggest is you all come back to PM with me and we can try to get you the steamer connection to Padang. If not, I invent some emergency that takes me up to Siak by boat and from there you can save a good ten days' trekking time over the mountains to Padang. Much easier going too. What do you think? Got any gin there?"

A glass was pressed into his hand that he sank in one swallow, followed by a belch. Perhaps he used to wonder why his parents did that too. Diehn was already there fussing, sticking his chin out and his nose into things that did not concern him.

"Impossible!" he snorted. "Why go back? We have come too far to go back now. There is the question of morale amongst the men. To turn back would prove fatal."

It was true. It had been Lauterbach's intention to get them quickly beyond the point of no return and he thought he had done it. Young Thompson was lying there, spent, in a fever. He had eaten nothing all day. But then there was also the awkward matter of man-eating tigers already licking their chops at the thought of Lauterbach and there was the chance of cutting ten days off that damned trek if they went back with Filet. He could not see himself hauling his bulk up sheer rockfaces by his fingernails in this stinking climate. With the District Officer on their side, they should have no more annoying local problems. He would make their ways smooth, a doddle.

"I absolutely agree," he nodded gravely. "We must at all costs press on. But ... there is poor young Thompson there to consider. I can neither commit him to such a course nor abandon him to fend for himself. An officer's first duty is to his men. I shall return to PM with him and take my chances. It is a matter of honour. The rest of you must of course go on."

They collapsed into argument. No, no he could not make such a sacrifice. This was not the moment for solitary heroics. But Lauterbach was immovable in his virtue and finally it was agreed that Schoenberg would accompany them so that he should not entirely lack for adult company. As they strode off towards the river the darkness reverberated with the roar of a hungry tiger, away up there in the hills. Bold Lauterbach pushed his way to the front and led down the path, apparently heedless of danger, leaving Thompson to bring up the rear. After many years in the East, he knew as a sure and certain fact that tigers lying in ambush always went for the last in a line of men.

PM had not improved greatly in the few days they had been away but with Filet as their host, it offered soft beds and beer. Thompson gathered strength. The steamer connection to Padang was unsure and a glance at the passenger lists revealed a sudden and inexplicable rise in the proportion of unattached English 'traders', come from Singapore, unexpectedly flooding into this area at the time of year when there was no trade to speak of – and asking questions about strangers. Ah no. Siak it would have to be then.

"There is the matter of administrative costs," mused Filet over lamplit dinner. "This is not a rich district you see and I can't just take it into my head to wander off to Siak, which is outside my area, in the launch without due cause. The paperwork would be hell. The commissioner has an eye for these things and once he gets his teeth into administrative costs ... A nice little riot in the market there, with me assisting, is the sort of thing we need." He reached absent-mindedly for another of beer. Several had already been taken in the course of a long, slow, bibulous evening. It slipped from his grasp, smashed on the table edge as he unthinkingly lunged for it.

"Damn and blast!" He had a nasty, oozing cut and a big grin on his face. "There we are then," licking fresh blood.

"A badly cut finger risking turning poisonous and on my account-signing hand too, rendering me unfit for duty. The only hospital is at Siak. QED."

Siak did not exactly bustle but at least it twitched with intermittant commercial and government activity. It was basically the usual collection of wooden huts stood on poles out over the mud, but had, in addition, a church, several stores and two miles of navigable road that had encouraged the importation, by a wealthy Chinese, of a single motor car. Above all, it swarmed with children and when Lauterbach looked on the local ladies, waving to him bare-breasted from the riverside he could see why. Thompson was back on his feet, staring goggle-eyed. He would have to arrange something for the lad.

They settled into one of the eating houses by the jetty, forking in fried rice in token fashion, while Filet went off to have his finger dressed and do the usual administrative rounds. He arrived back a couple of hours later, flushed and with his wound elaborately bandaged into a boxer's hand in token of alibi, demanding beer, with two grinning native policemen in tow.

"Now then," he sat and sighed, flung his hat wearily on the table. "Let me explain. The DO for here is not happy. The fact is he's from too near the German border and doesn't greatly care for your chaps, Lauterbach. Up this end of the Indies most people are scared to death of upsetting the British in case they just walk in one day and take over and then we're all out of a job. But he'll turn a blind eye as long as you move on straight away. So *these* two," he indicated the policemen, "just happen to be here from the next district along and have agreed to take you back with them to Tratabula where the

DO, my old friend Dahler, will take care of you. He's German-born you see. If I were you I'd get out of town fast."

And so it was. There was to be no escape from walking across Sumatra. They trekked every day from five in the morning till ten, then rested until the heat cooled off and set out again from four till ten at night. In the morning, they waded through steam, in the evening through swooping swallows. Around them everything smelled of rot and decay. The policemen, heavily laden as they were, streaked away and would pause, polite and uncomplaining, to wait for them at every junction of the path or river crossing. Whoever had done the calculations of time from one village to another had used supermen like these. Four days' march stretched into over a week, then two. Whenever the policemen were asked how far they had yet to go they would smile, make a limp stone-throwing gesture and say "little bit yet." They lived on fruit bought at the roadside and rice begged from villagers, slept where they could and tried not to give way to despair.

"Lauterbach, what will you do when we get to Padang?" Schoenberg did not usually ask questions like that. It was one of the things that made him an acceptable travelling companion.

"I will have a bath, a shave, drink a beer and have a woman. I contemplate the prospect with abated breadth."

"No, no." Schoenberg frowning, shaking his head. "I don't mean that. I mean will you stay there? I know the others are planning to settle in Padang or Batavia rather than risk trying to get back to Germany through the English fleet. For myself I am a trader in an international house. I can always get work wherever I am. Thompson can get another merchant ship, even a Dutch one. But you know there is talk of Holland coming into the war on the British side. If they do, they might just let me be or intern me in some nice house, or – if things go badly – put me in a prison again but you – I think – they would give back to the British to hang."

"Thank you Schoenberg. You have given me pleasant thoughts to keep me going and make me walk faster."

Dahler, when they finally arrived, was a bit of a disappointment, shrugging, unenthusiastic, steeped in tropical tropor, unwilling to make their problems his own. After a few days' rest on short rations they set off again.

If the previous stretch had once seemed difficult, it now became an easy stroll through a noble park compared to this. Here, the mountainous backbone of the island towered up to over three thousand steaming feet and they lay in its full rainshadow. Every day it poured down and sometimes the rain felt warm and sometimes cold but always there was just too much of it. The earth was slippery clay, the rocks brittle meringue, crumbling between their fingers and under their feet. Lethal precipices lay on either hand, tricking eyes full of water and sweat. The tracks had been made by small men and for small men so that the steps they had cut into the rocks on the really dangerous sections were too tight for clumsy Western feet and invited disaster while the branches they had cleared to their own head height poked Westerners in the eyes and stabbed them in the mouth. They were charged by buffalo, taunted by monkeys. The peak of felicity was to arrive trembling from fatigue in an astonished settlement and collapse as a giggling Malay sent his pet monkey scampering up into the trees to rain down coconuts on their heads. Scorpions and snakes were abundant but worst of all were the innumerable insects that made war on them day and night, mosquitoes, ticks and leeches, that burrowed and gorged on their flesh, leaving wounds that festered and turned septic. Soon they were afraid to take their boots off at night. Putting them back on bleeding, blistered feet was torture. Fungus sprouted rapidly between their toes and then swarmed all over them in a suppurating itch that could only be called 'athlete's body.' Worse yet, from sleeping on old mats, in abandoned huts, they were invaded by lice that crabbed and devilled into their pubes, itching and flaring their private parts like chilli.

"Look, Lauterbach, look!" They had scrambled to the crest of another rise, knowing, as always, that there would be yet another on the other side, and another after that. But instead there was a view of two smoking volcanic cones, Merapi and Singgalang, an apron of land that dropped away before them with a distant view of sea and hazy city, with pointed-roofed Minang houses in between. Schoenberg and Thompson wept and hugged each other weakly. The guides grinned, "little bit further" and pointed to the countless miles ahead.

"Moses," thought Lauterbach, his head giddy. "I feel like Moses looking at the promised land."

It was Padang on the west coast of the island. They had made it clear across. Lauterbach bent forward, admiring the rich, tended landscape, sucking it in through his eyes. Better yet, cutting straight through the lush plantations, he had spotted a railway line down there, just a couple of miles away. Unlike Moses, he could catch the train straight to the heart of the promised land – first class.

Lauterbach sat cosily on the cane settee, extravagantly cushioned on all sides, elegantly clad in fresh white linen, while the electric fans worked away overhead with the combined power of a dozen demented punkah-wallahs. He was preened, purged, purified and lightly perfumed. On the table before him stood a glass of cold beer, a new hat, a smoking ashtray. He looked for all the world like a prosperous member of the *Etappe*. His paunch had been restocked by the German consul, yielding to his cries of desperate poverty. His salary would be ticking up nicely, untouched, in Germany. Across his knees lay the latest Singapore newspapers and he was mildly irritated by the ruffling draught of the fans. Urban colonial gentlemen, he found, could be irritated by very small discomforts indeed.

There was an article on the Singapore mutiny which was declared finally and officially "put down." French, Russian and Japanese warships had converged on the harbour and debarked contingents of battle-tried marines. The 'trim' Japanese troops had particularly distinguished themselves while Japanese civilians had been sworn in as special constables to patrol the streets of the colony. So, the British Empire was saved by the rising sons of Japan. Lauterbach laughed aloud. Wars made strange bedfellows, not that he had had many of those lately himself.

Some sepoys had got across the causeway to the mainland but not to make hay with civil order, only to surrender with due formality to the astonished Muslim Sultan of Johore. It had been a holiday with a little homicide thrown in rather than a coherent attempt to take and hold a military objective. Over 400 were now in captivity while a prominent Muslim civilian had been briskly hanged and some fifty sepoys shot by firing squad – almost the same number as the British civilians killed in the rising. A grainy picture showed crumpled bodies in British uniform lying against a long line of stakes with an officer administering a coup de grace to one of the sprawled figures with a revolver. Poor innocent Taj Mohammed! He would surely be among them. Born to be hanged for the best of motives. Lauterbach could see that it was all being tidied up and hidden away nicely. The documents would be neatly bundled up with string to be shipped home, stuck in the archives and declared secret for fifty years so that everyone could go on with the serious military business of declaring European superiority while quietly getting their promotions, medals and pensions. There had already been a number of strategic retirements and reshuffles and a certain Captain Hall seemed to have done rather well for himself out of the business.

Still, he had given the British a good scare. They had feared not only for the future of Singapore but the whole of Muslim India. Troop convoys had been disrupted. Self-confidence had been destroyed and a fatal wedge had been driven in the trust between the British and their Indian Empire. Now they would not be sending any more white troops back from the East to the Western front, at least not for a while. No, instead, they would hunt him down like a dog. He looked down at the bloated faces of the dead and abruptly felt his collar tighten around his throat as his bowels loosened. Shaking, he slackened his tie and popped his top button and gulped in gasps of air. The article ended by reminding readers that several dangerous German collaborators were still on the run and that all householders should remain vigilant.

Lauterbach too would remain vigilant. There was a European across the room, sitting in the corner, waiting idly, fanning himself with his hat and staring into space, watching the dust motes dancing. The other hand twitched rhythmically. In the sunlight, Lauterbach could see the unmistakable shape of a small bullet, a little jewel of lead, copper and brass, that he tumbled compulsively, base over tip, like a Muslim telling his beads. He had been at the restaurant last night and the draper's shop this morning. When Lauterbach had come out of the cigar shop and abruptly turned left, he had nearly cannoned into him standing in a side street. From his complexion, he was fresh out East, maybe English. He wore old lady's lavender cologne and only the English did that. The smell of it had transported him immediately back to his childhood – Lauterbach, six years old, sniffing a bar of Old English Lavender soap sent by a distant Manchester cousin.

Lauterbach shook his freshly-barbered head and turned to the Batavian papers. Von Muecke had created a sensation a few months before by himself appearing, out of the blue, in Padang in that old schooner he had stolen from the Cocos-Keeling islands, dodging lurking British gunboats and sailing off again to war like a romantic pirate of old. There was continued Dutch speculation as to his whereabouts and intentions. Lauterbach thanked his lucky stars he had missed that happy reunification or he would now be god-knows-where on the open sea, in a leaky boat, directly under the orders of von Muecke, probably planning the lone conquest of Australia. He himself had dropped from the headlines but the belated arrival of Diehn and the others in Padang was being made much of. Most of them had tried to march into town and ended up in hospital. Diehn would be furious to have a much smaller price set on his head by the British than Lauterbach.

"Oh. Herr Thompson. You poor lamb. You are so brave

and so young."

Lauterbach swiftly raised the newspaper like an armoured visor. It was the sound of cooing female enthusiasm that he had got to know so well in Padang and, though it had served him well enough initially, he was now heartily sickened by it. For Thompson it was all new and wonderful – food, drink, smart clothes, sexual initiation. You couldn't blame the boy. He lowered the newssheet and peered cautiously over the edge like a submariner. Middle-aged merchants' wives, faces hot and shiny with maternal lust, weevily enough hard tack for a boy to cut his teeth on but, once he had got his foot in their door, they would have more tender daughters for him back at the house.

"Tell me, my dear young boy, how you fought that tiger with nothing but your bare hands and your young courage and what happened when you were attacked by cannibals with blowpipes, like you told that man from the papers."

Lauterbach snorted behind the personal column and forced his eyes to concentrate on the print. A young Batavian gentleman was looking for partners for tennis mixed doubles. A respectable, "almost white", lady – fresh from the country – offered breast-feeding. Thompson cleared his throat and began his heavily embroidered yarn in a new, deep, confident, manly voice. Lauterbach smiled to himself. The lad was growing up, giving them what they wanted to hear. Better yet he had given him an idea.

"All his fellow countrymen will be saddened to hear that Oberleutnant Lauterbach, ex-officer of the *Emden*, is suffering from a bad attack of the fever as a result of the exertions made during his recent famous crossing of Sumatra.

As soon as his condition permits, he plans a journey into the Sumatra highlands for his health. Let us all wish him a pleasant journey."

It appeared in the Padang German-language paper the next day. But Lauterbach was very far from lying on his sickbed. Instead, he was in the rear seat of the publisher's car, bucking and roaring along the motor road south to Bengkulu, where he would pick up the steamer to Batavia, the capital, and arrive before the news of his disappearance could reach a British ship. Arrived at the harbour, on the passenger manifest, there was, of course, no Lauterbach. But there was a portly and goatee-wearing Belgian, Eugene Gilbert by name, a gentleman who declared his luggage mysteriously and irritatingly lost at Bengkulu and was therefore treated by the shipping line with the greatest consideration and generosity. Monsieur Gilbert spent a great deal of his time on deck and was particularly interested in the British warships that cruised around the Sunda Straits, the narrow waterway that divides Sumatra and Java, always waving a friendly greeting to the sailors on board and executing a sort of exuberant and abbreviated nautical hornpipe to their departing sterns.

CHAPTER NINE

Batavia was the most modern and cosmopolitan city in South East Asia, at least the European quarter, Weltevreden, was. The native suburbs boiled in tropical heat and disease and steeped in foul water, but Weltevreden spoke of the optimism of pre-war years with bright new trams gliding along the tree-lined avenues and sparkling canals built by the Dutch to bring coolness and soothing motion to their crisp, white, residential areas. In the commercial quarter, the stiff, narrow fronts of Amsterdam had been preserved but out here in the suburbs there was enough space for the Dutch *Landhaus* to take their place. Fat dwellings sat securely in large grounds, pruned and watered by copious gardeners who fought a relentless battle against tropical exuberance, just as their owners waged war on the manic disorder of the whole, vast colonial archipelago.

Lauterbach moved into the sprawled gingerbread villa of one of the *Etappe* merchants where the man lived with his pale wife and three big-boned daughters but he spent much of his own time in the gentlemanly atmosphere of the *Harmonie*, the famous club on the corner of the noisesome main boulevard where carriages, horsed and horseless, rattled up and down around the clock. In the early 19th century, the *Harmonie* had been completed by Stamford Raffles, under the British interregnum, so that Dutch and British should mix socially and they were still doing it. Its cool white pillars and luxurious clubrooms were one of the wonders of the East, panelled with every exotic oriental wood and paved with foot-smoothed flagstones that called softly but insistently to Lauterbach. The bar, dotted with potted palms, bore that sense of unchanging and well-patinated perfection otherwise found only in heaven. Oleaginous Javanese boys, with headcloths like flames, pattered deferentially among the drinkers while, in the leather armchairs, lounged the men who ruled this great swarming empire of millions of brown souls, mostly red-faced and foolish but certainly not evil. And mostly Lauterbach liked them as they did him and they brought him shelter from the burden of cosmic loneliness that nested like ice in his breast. Of an evening, his entrance roused a cheer and calls for a drink for good old Juli-bumm from German and Dutchman alike. Even some of the British joined in so that he preferred to sit in the main concourse rather than what was known jocularly as "the German lines."

This morning he settled himself opposite the great tented lap of Potter, an English planter with a big spread of rubber up in Probolingo. Potter's ghostly palour was odd for a man whose occupation should involve an active outdoor life but probably told sad truths about his style of management. It was only about eleven but there was already a sprinkling of dedicated drinkers round the room, complaining as always about the heat and the servants.

"How's the price?" It was the other unchanging subject, a universal greeting for merchants and administrators alike. The fortunes of everyone in the club rode more or less directly on the rocky price of rubber and the price of rubber depended on the war in the wider world which was beyond their control. The corner of Potter's mouth turned down. He was fat, unlined, like a great soft-fleshed baby.

"Not so good. The Brits have just brought in another twenty thousand acres of plantation in Malaya. We can't compete with their quality for the Australian factories."

He reached, gulped gin, swilled it round as if to cure toothache, did not belch. Lauterbach scowled sympathy. A boy pattered over and smiled. "Tuan?"

"Satu Bintang besar."

He bowed and slithered away deftly to fetch beer. Potter swigged dutifully.

"Learning a bit of the lingo, I see. No harm in that. It's all this talk of Holland entering the war on the British side, makes people nervous. If they do, we lose the German war market and what will become of us?"

"What will become of Germany?"

"That too." But said, Lauterbach noted, without much conviction. Moreover, Germany was a large mass of rock and soil that would always survive but, if Holland entered the war, what would become of poor fragile Lauterbach dangling at the end of a British rope? He felt gloom descend on him and gloom, for him, was more usually a thing of the small, morning hours. An elegant, pared figure slid into the chair beside him, ordering drink nautically with both hands, at long distance, in sign language, and dug in a heavy leather document case.

"Herr Lauterbach. Herr Potter."

"Hallo Kessel." Lauterbach flashed him a smile of genuine warmth.

Kessel extended a sheaf of crisp documents with the letterhead of the German Ministry of Supply. "Sorry to keep you waiting Mr Potter. I hope I haven't delayed you too long. Paperwork always takes longer than you expect. The permits for the next shipment from the embassy. Payment on the usual terms."

Potter grimaced and stuffed them all crumpled in his breast pocket. "Thank God for one steady customer. Been busy?"

Kessel pouted, accepted a beer from a boy and slurped through the pout.

"Busy, busy," he sighed. "H.E. who must be obeyed has got a bee in his bonnet about unrestricted submarine warfare. The Crown Prince – God bless him – has been making speeches in America again and put everyone's back up. Their newspapers are full of it. So muggins has to do a position paper that has to be sent off to Berlin by tonight. Otherwise they won't be able to start sinking neutral vessels on Monday."

Potter gaped and staggered heavy-gutted to his feet, reached down to the table for his glass and drained it. Lauterbach could not keep his eyes off Potter's stomach. On himself such a paunch would contain at least ten thousand dollars. Unrestricted talk of unrestricted submarine warfare upset Potter perhaps, made him a party to things he did not wish to know, smacked a little too much of collaboration. The British authorities were said to be getting interested in such things and he couldn't get out of the room fast enough.

"Thanks for the papers, Herr Kessel. Sorry I can't stay. Got to go and get back to the plantation. Got to keep at them. The minute my back's turned the lazy sods all sling their hammocks and go to sleep till they hear the sound of the car coming back up the road."

"Quite so. It is the same at the embassy. I keep a hammock there myself. Good journey back to Probolingo. Keep the rubber flowing." Kessel smiled coolly. The old white man tottered wearily away on flushed and chubby legs.

Kessel arranged his cuffs. And so to business. "I shouldn't taunt him I know but I just can't seem to resist it. It tickles my fancy and – as you know – I have a highly ticklable fancy. It is nice to have the English working for us, in a manner of speaking, and for those of us attuned to an ironic resonance the war provides some deeply affecting moments. A wonderful thing commercial neutrality, Juli-bumm, but not for the likes of you and me. I am a faithful servant of the state and you are – let me see – a war hero."

"Perhaps so, perhaps not." Lauterbach liked Kessel, a man with a lightness of touch and an elegant sense of detachment, a taste for sheer deliberate badness that matched his own. Those sparkling cuffs would never be stained with the gravy of the war though the hands had dipped into it often enough. A southerner, he was as sincere as one of those rococo altarpieces – all fat cherubs and barley sugar – that they did you in Bavarian churches.

"Tell me." Kessel leaned his seal-like, brilliantined head closer to Lauterbach's ear. "What does order 87/562 mean to you?"

"Absolutely nothing – except of course that 562 is the code for the *Emden*."

"Quite so. I don't think the order ever got to the ship but it got through to all *Etappe* posts out East in October and had them running round like headless chickens. The Admiralty were doing a favour for the Foreign Office. Two old chums must have had lunch in Berlin and decided that the *Emden* should make a landing on the Andaman Islands at Port Blair where the British have their penal settlement. Apparently there are 1,500 Indian revolutionaries interned there all dying to work for German victory. You were to take the prison, arm the revolutionaries and release them on the Indian coast." He grinned. "Sounds good eh? What do you think?"

"Bloody nonsense," growled Lauterbach, exacting bitter revenge on his beer. "A cruiser is hardly the best vehicle to take a prison. You can be sure that all the intelligence would be wrong – just as it was on Cocos-Keeling. I'd give you even money the revolutionaries aren't even there, that they were moved two years ago to some other hellhole. And what are Indian revolutionaries, anyway? Skinny blokes who write hot newspaper articles about not paying taxes, like as not, and don't know one end of a rifle from the other. The Brits would round them up in a couple of days and it would be all for nothing. With intellectuals even the natives would be falling over themselves to hand them in."

Kessel threw back his head and roared with laughter. "Quite so. I knew you'd see it my way. I got the order squashed. After all, you were doing more important things on your own. It would have been stupid to distract you."

He semaphored energetically to the bar for more drink, pointed at Lauterbach's glass, signalled some more, saluted and grinned. Message received and understood by the giggling barman.

"But now it has come up again and they're after a chap who could take it on. No warship this time – it's being done on the cheap – just a shipment of old arms from San Francisco and the revolutionaries would have to do their own fighting."

Lauterbach collapsed across the table and groaned just as the drink arrived. The boy, disconcerted, started to take it away again. Kessel leapt lithely from his chair and seized it with both hands.

"Think what a price the Brits would put on your head this time," he grinned innocently, pressing a glass into Lauterbach's paw and clinking against it. "Think of the honour."

Lauterbach drew himself together and rose unwillingly like a bear awaking from hibernation. "As a serving officer, my duty is to report back for active service as soon as possible. I cannot go West through the British blockade, so I must go East through China, avoid Hong Kong and Japan and get to America. To steer for India would be simply to head in the wrong direction."

Kessel laughed again and applauded. "Well done, Julibumm. I knew you'd have a reason not to get mixed up in such tomfoolery. So I've fixed it all with H.E. You're to be sent East and asked to carry urgent secret despatches to Shanghai on your way home, all costs paid. I don't know what the despatches are, I haven't invented that bit yet. Anyway, I think you owe me the next drink but that'll have to be some other time. Got to get that paper out to a panting world." He typed a quick sentence with his fingers in the air. "Bye Julibumm ..."

Lauterbach felt a great weight slip from his shoulders. He must get out of Dutch territory fast. He dare not fall into British or Japanese hands. China was home, even if Tsingtao was now an enemy land. A government postman? It would do. The gloom had lifted. He shrugged happily and looked up to beckon the boy for the bill, then suddenly saw a familiar figure, sitting by the door. It was the lavender man from

Padang, fanning himself with his hat and staring off into space.

Lauterbach rose and slowly crossed the bar, strolling down the corridor towards the cloakroom with a feigned planter's insouciance, a man for whom time was measured not in minutes but in seasons. From the other side of the door, despite the best efforts of the servants, there seeped an acrid whiff of *petai*, the soft, bitter bean that was newly in season and scented a man's pee like asparagus. Not pausing to ease the contents of a full bladder, he crept back to the corridor and leapt up the stairs to the first floor where sleeping accommodation was available for out-of-town members at reasonable rates, hastened to the end of the long verandah that fronted all the rooms and rattled down the second spiral staircase that led to the side of the building. A few strides brought him to the pavement. He turned right and moved swiftly towards the Governor General's palace with its odious pink hydrangeas in pots. They always made him think of the sagging breasts of old women. There was heavy traffic. Everything from motorcars to rickshaws wove in and out of the sunshine and shade and the pavement was full of bustling traders and self-important officials with folders of papers. Outside the square white facade, Dutch soldiers stood on guard in businesslike khaki, not fancy ceremonial uniforms, a sort of token recognition of the war that ravaged the wider world. He turned right again down a sidestreet and made his way purposefully to the huge square that marks the centre of the city, stepped back into one of the shrubbery arbours and sat on the bony seat, leaning back into shade to wait.

A white woman went past in noisy, clomping shoes, walking a fat dog with lots of ears. After a few minutes a chocolate-coloured car turned gently into the square, drew up opposite, then set off slowly again with a crunching of gears. A small brown child with its finger in its mouth stole round the edge of the arbour and stared at him with enormous eyes of wonder. He made a pig's face and it ran away laughing. Several minutes crept by on tiptoe. The chocolate-coloured car reappeared, cruised round the square and drove past again. At the wheel was a tiny man with his hat well pulled down *Etappe* fashion. Who else wore a hat *inside* a car? It stopped, pulled over to the kerb out of sight and Lauterbach heard the slam of a door and the scuffle of approaching feet. When he came round the corner of the arbour he was Japanese, sharp lapels, sharp nose, sharp little parti-coloured shoes, thin moustache, a tie so loud it shouted and socks with clockfaces on them. The wire glasses strapped to his delicate ears seemed like an instrument of torture. He must have dropped the hat on the seat before climbing out. His clothes looked as if they had been sent from abroad by different wellwishers, each in total ignorance of the others. Something about his movements suggested a dancer. He walked with odd precision over to the bench, dusted it off fastidiously with the folded newspaper he was carrying and sat. Lauterbach, feeling he was getting the hang of this, fanned himself with his hat and stared into space. In such a public place he had no need to fear a knife slid between his ribs.

The little man cleared his throat. "Captain Lauterbach I presume?"

Lauterbach stared back in silence. In his mind he deleted the little moustache, added a beard, restyled the hair. Nothing. "Have we met before?"

The Japanese grinned and hissed, turned lost-dog eyes on

him. "No, Captain Lauterbach. I have not had that honour. But your face is known to me from the newspapers." And the wanted poster with the reward on it, thought Lauterbach. The voice was low-pitched, silky. "My name is Katsura. I apologise to trouble you like this but it is a matter of mutual advantage. I am lowly employee at the Japanese embassy, in the consular section. I understand you wish to leave Java and regain your native land. Though our nations are at war, I have always had high regard for Germans and an umbrella may shield a man from sunshine as well as from rain. After all, both our nations seek only the recognition of their proper place in the world. Consider how well we treat your prisoners of war, yes please."

Lauterbach felt a flare of outrage. He was meeting all the high-principled diplomats today. "In Tsingtao for example?" What prisoners of war? The Japanese and Brits had blown it to bits. For Lauterbach war had never been about abstract principles but about the detonation of friends. That made it both alien to his nature and deeply personal.

The little man detected no irony. "Precisely. But this is a neutral place where we are free to pursue our own interests, yes please. I wish to warn you. Do not travel again under the name of Gilbert. It has been marked down and will be immediately reported if you book onto any of the ships in that identity ..."

He broke off as the woman with the fat dog came back the other way. The dog looked at them, dug in its heels, crouched and laid a long turd carefully on the pavement, watching them intently the while as if seeking a reaction. Then it stuck out its tongue and frisked off. Its product was not the usual twirled meringue affair but a long straight line, skilfully executed by the dog's advancing at a rate precisely commensurate with its exit. They both contemplated the turd in Zen silence.

"If you will look inside the newspaper you will find something there I believe to be of interest to you."

With some trepidation, Lauterbach reached down and took the newspaper that lay between them, riffling its pages with his fingertips. No turd inside but a Dutch passport, apparently genuine, made out to Dr Blaamo. He examined the particulars. Age, height, weight of the personal description were all about right for him. He could certainly travel on it without fear of detection, with a little doctoring. Blaamo suggested someone moon-faced and clean-shaven. That could be arranged. But why was a Japanese helping him in this way? He looked again at the turd. It seemed to be trying to tell him something.

"You will be wondering Captain Lauterbach just why a son of Japan should help a German sailor in this way?" Katsura tittered.

He smiled back stiffly. "Well ... it had crossed my mind Mr Katsura."

"It is very simple, yes please." Katsura nodded and grinned. "First you will please give me one hundred American dollar. I am not well paid and the money is needed for an urgent purpose. Also, at the very beginning of the war, you may remember that your own ship, the *Emden* encountered a Japanese passenger ship off Sumatra and spared her. My wife and child were on that vessel. It was a very gentlemanly act. I feel for them both melty love." His eyes swam behind the thick lenses.

Of course, *that* passenger ship. They had not known that they were at war and cursed their luck at having to let her pass. They would much rather have looted her, blown a hole in her and sent her to the bottom. Melty love? The expression ricocheted round his brain – a brief image of a block of Swiss hazelnut the instant before it gushed sweetness over his tongue. Lauterbach smiled and covered his teeth with the passport. As the edge of it passed over his moustache, he caught a slight but unmistakable whiff of lavender, like a memory borne on a distant Provencal breeze. An odd way to smell a rat. This was clearly a trap, then. By selling him this excellent passport they were encouraging him to flee from this limited safety of Batavia to a spot where they might more easily lay hands on both him and the reward. They would simply have to watch the shipping manifests and when Blaamo came up, the vessel would be neatly intercepted in international waters and goodbye to Lauterbach. They must think him very stupid, which was good. Well two could play at that game.

"Very well, Mr Katsura. I agree to your proposition. I thank you. You are doing me a great personal service." He did not have a hundred dollars in his wallet. "Excuse me."

To Katsura's obvious horror, he rose, walked to the back of the arbour and relieved his bladder over the grateful hibiscus with loud manly splashing, emitting grunts of satisfaction and digging the while in the cummerbund pocket till he fished out an appropriate denomination. Katsura averted his eyes and stared red-faced at the turd, less embarrassing, it seemed, than the sounds of micturation. Having wiped his fingers politely on the seat of his trousers, Lauterbach reached over from behind, scooped up newspaper and parcel and deposited the note smoothly in Katsura's top pocket.

"My regards to your honourable wife and child."

Katsura leapt to his feet grinning and bowing, reversing

out onto the pavement with a hiss as of wet tyres. "Thank you. Thank you, yes please." As he gave one last reverential bow, he set his foot squarely in the turd.

CHAPTER TEN

"Purely officially, you're on your way to Hong Kong," Kessell executed a complicated foot manoeuvre on the pedals, like a man playing a Bach flourish on a cathedral organ, and kneed Lauterbach in the face. "Sorry old man, not the best place to be lying I know." Lauterbach was rolled up on the floor of the Mercedes as they roared at high speed along the main road to the north. Indignity was a price he was willing to pay for a little more security. "I think you might as well come out now. If you are going to be spotted by any spies that's already happened long ago."

"Hong Kong?" He emerged and clambered up onto the seat like some unruly crotch-sniffing dog. Red-faced and panting, hair spiked into a madman's halo and soaked in sweat. Even at this hour the furnace of Java was being stoked He was nervous, excited, loth to move on, cursing the world that would not leave him in peace, that lashed him to this eternal desperate nomadism. Why not stay here, settle down, take a wife, raise little Lauterbaecher? He had never dreamed of such a thing when shackled to a steamship. Now domesticity seemed abruptly a beguiling prospect. As he steamed around the east, he had not realised the importance of that unchanging cabin as his only security, his anchor. Even tribal nomads when they moved from place to place, pitched the same tent with the same known and familiar objects in the same arrangement, wherever that might be on the face of the planet. He did not just hang his hat on the back of the cabin door, he realised, but his whole identity that was carved into the fabric of the room like the lines on his face. The marks scored into the headboard of the bed recalled a raucous fling with a long-taloned *ronggeng* dancer off Java. The burn on the tea table was from a cigar left too long unpuffed during an unaccustomed ejaculatory difficulty off Shanghai. The cracked glass marked a bout of fisticuffs with a stroppy first mate whose skull he had similarly split. And now they were gone and the tale of his life had gone with them.

Kessel grinned in cheerful innocence and swerved to avoid a buffalo cart, honking after the event. For him this was all a big joke. "We sent one of our traders along with that passport to book a passage in the name of Pieter Blaamo, direct to Hong Kong, non-stop and a load of luggage with that name has been delivered to the ship. At the last minute, our man will use the ticket for one of his company employees so it's no loss. It doesn't have to go on anyone's balance sheet – sorry." He bit his tongue and took his eyes off the road to perform facial melodrama for Lauterbach who had eyes for nothing *but* the road. "You see? They've already got me thinking like some blasted bureaucrat. Anyway, with a bit of luck the Brits and the Japs've crammed the ship with their own men and arranged a reception offshore. They won't be worrying about sailings from Surabaya now. They'll be thinking how to spend the reward money. Teach them a lesson. As we say here in Java, it's not over till someone bangs the big gong. So when you get to Surabaya our chaps will look after you.

Since they're all interned they've got nothing else to do but sit around polishing their navigational instruments."

They advanced thunderously down the centre of the road in a plume of dust, most local forms of life scattering to either side. Only chickens were stupid enough to avoid a car by running *down* the road instead of across it. At this hour, the flow of the traffic was against them into the heart of the city, a mix of pedestrians, bicycles and lumbering carts that occasionally threatened to prevent their passage entirely. As it thickened, Kessel cursed and honked but did not slow, merely reduced the margin of safety. "Mustn't miss that train," he urged, as if intending to smack into it and looked at his watch.

Through the windscreen, Lauterbach saw terrified faces and leaping bodies and closed his own eyes in desperate self-protection. With a great wrench of the wheel and a squeal of brakes, Kessel brought the vehicle to a skidding stop. The engine rumbled on in the silence.

"Quick. You've just got time." He reached into the back seat, threw a tiny bag at Lauterbach who stood waif-like. "Run man, run. The train's about to leave."

Tears in his eyes he turned and stumbled across gravel for the ticket office, slapped down money, slithered back the ticket and was pushed, blind, aboard by kind brown hands. A Javanese conductor led him to the first class compartment, indicated a reclining chair, bowed and withdrew, leaving him entirely alone in a luxury of leather, polished wood and crystal. He threw himself into it in misery.

Two beers later, he had revived a little. Of course, he suddenly realised, the chair was like those on the *Emden* and on his own ship before that and the attendant had packed him round with cushions as though he were a Meissen shepherdess likely to be broken in transit. One hand rested comfortably on the swollen money paunch, the other grasped the silken stem of the beer glass. Through the windows, it was suddenly a beautiful world.

The train hunched its shoulders and began the long, winding climb from the coastal heat to the cool uplands where copious rain and volcanic soils coaxed coffee, tea and other rich export crops from the slopes. It was this that had brought cold northerners here in the first place. Bananas and melons hung out over the narrow railway track like gold-embossed invitations to stay. Gorges crammed with wild forest scored the plantations, crossed, back and forth, by bridges that looked in the distance like matchstick models. Below them, on the plain, lay open fields where men and women, all slim and comely, smiled as they worked the rich grey mud and tiny children drove huge pacific buffalo that were the same size as the baleful tanks that would soon churn up the battlefields of Europe to raise a less happy crop. There is no green so intense and full of life as that of germinating rice shoots and Lauterbach let the colour wash over him like sunshine.

Soon they came to a wilder area of primeval forest and dark-stemmed bamboo where the Javanese lodged the humble gods that were important in their everyday lives. Here the villages were like islands in a green sea and the occasional felled trees lrose up like great beached vessels. Lauterbach glided effortlessly by, looking benignly down into their simple lives and moving on like some huge airborne albatross. When he raised his eyes, a range of great, conical volcanoes towered up into a blue sky, some smudged with smoke as before in Pagan, where, he imagined, the villagers were now wrestling with their Japanese grammar books. As he watched and sipped, an attendant came and knelt, polishing his soft civilian shoes, applying the polish with bare hands so that it became an act both of massage and of worship.

At the hill station of Bandung, they served him lunch, a thing of many small and delicious courses on a lacquer tray, fired with chilli and softened by luscious fruit. The waiter cleared and soothed and brought fresh coffee and a single beautiful orchid before he climbed down with his boxes at the next stop to return to Bandung by road and repeat his service the following day.

Yet another attendant appeared and showed the many unsuspected tricks the chair would yet perform, like some great wooden work of origami. All afternoon Lauterbach dozed in its extended, reswivelled comfort to the tympanic rattle and sway of the train and when darkness arrived, his contented cigar echoed the glow of the distant volcanoes and the chuffing engine until they drew into a station and stopped with a final clank and an extended sigh. Here they would all disembark and spend the night as at some medieval coaching inn.

This was the point at which the train from Surabaya to Batavia also stopped for the night and all the passngers, their minds pointing in opposite directions, slept in the same mock-Germanic Valhalla of a hotel, while the trains nested nose-to-tail outside. Lauterbach bathed by hissing lamplight under great beams, throwing gouts of water over his body with a giant's wooden ladel. What would he be tonight at dinner, Belgian, Dutch, French?

"German," said the woman across the table with a smile. "I would have said you were German not Dutch." At this altitude the evening was quite fresh. The Dutch often built their houses with huge baronial fireplaces, even in the torrid swamps – being perhaps mentally unable to arrange furniture in a room without a hearth – but here it was a functional item and great logs crackled companionably, pouring out heat and nostalgic forest scents. Outside, moonbeams ghosted through pine trees like pale wolves.

Lauterbach mimed astonishment over the mashed potatoes, sticking firmly to Dutch. "From my childhood perhaps. I spent many holidays there, in Germany, just across the border." He had constructed an elaborate tale of being the representative of a Dutch printing house travelling on business, specialising in visiting cards. No alas, he had no card on him having left all in his room. To more important things. She had huge dark eyes and golden skin. After three hundred years in the islands, many of the Dutch had blood spiced with exotic infusions. It had been a while since he had touched female flesh and several glasses of wine and dramatic firelight lent enchantment.

"You are travelling alone, madam?" His expression disapproved of her loneliness. Her loneliness was an affliction he could dispel.

She nodded. "I am joining my husband in Weltevreden. He is," she locked her gaze with his "considerably older than myself and finds it hard to manage alone. My name is Anna." The door had opened a crack. Lauterbach thrust his foot into it.

"He is a very lucky man, Anna. I should think any man would find it hard to manage without you. You should not have to travel alone." There. He had smacked his stake down on the table. He watched the dice roll behind her eyes.

"What a sweet thing to say." She tossed her hair. "I must be careful. I am unused to gallantry. It might sweep me off my feet. But I hope you are not telling me what to do."

He smirked, rounded, hot eyes openly ogling. "I think you already know what to do."

She swilled wine, the nasty, flavourless Sumatran vintage that the waiter had thrust on them. Her glugging oesophagus was delightfully physical, showed his number had come up, she was gulping down the bait with the wine. He was in.

He smirked and simpered, cooed and oleaginated. It ended, as it must, quite early in her room where, it was alleged, she had a little brandy that would help two overtired travellers to sleep. She poured, offered, sprawled back, all rustling invitation, on the bed and then suddenly, as he rose to accept that invitation, her face and eyes hardened.

"And now, if you please," she snapped, "you will give me two hundred dollars or I shall call the manager and accuse you of forcing your way in here and attacking me. Be warned," she swigged brandy and hardened further, "I can be very convincing. Everyone says so. With a little effort on my part, it can even become a case of rape. I could rip the dress. I don't want to. It's a very good dress."

Lauterbach was poleaxed. He sank back on his chair, mouth gaping, puffing air. Like all men, it had occasionally happened to him in the past that some women were immune to his charm. He could live with that. Not everyone had good taste. But this was a matter where, for the first time, something important was really impugned. There were many paths to shame and fortune but this one she had chosen was just not nice. The world, it seemed, was a worse place than even he had imagined. He was genuinely shocked. Bitterness flooded his simple heart. Like most habitual liars, he expected other people to be honest.

"Tell me," he said deadpan, "If I pay you the money do I still get what I came here for?"

She threw back her head and laughed, a nice laugh, a little girl laugh. "My dear, you put it so sweetly. You are a man who keeps his eye on the ball. I think I might manage that. We shall see."

"The husband," he was stalling for time, trying to think, "in Weltevreden, all that was a lie?"

"Oh he's real enough." She turned and looked at him with the blatant self-confidence of a dog looking at a bone. "Now where's the money?"

"The money," he articulated carefully, "Is in my room. Would you like me to go and get it?"

She laughed again but this time it had a little more grit stirred into it and she did not bother to have a facial expression. "Like hell. We'll go together. You're not getting out of my sight till I get paid. I deserve it for those corny lines you made me listen to all evening. Jesus."

They set off, he leading, she staying close as a wart, down the long, creaking corridor, lined with anonymous doors. This should have been a stirring place, dark, full of flickering shadows from the oil lamps, redolent of hot, adulterous, nocturnal paddings and pantings. Now he felt like a five year old being marched to school by a grim-faced mother. In the sudden silence, his unruly digestion gurgled and throbbed like steam in an old boiler.

"My God!" She poked him in the ribs. "Is that you? You should get that seen to."

He would try to lure her into one of the communal rooms

where she could not make a scene, sit down with the men, wait her out. He could not afford to do anything that would attract attention to himself. If the worst came to the worst he would have to pay.

"Oh no you don't. Try to slip away and I scream the place down right now. I have a very loud scream. Everyone says so."

There was a loud click and one of the doors was flung wide, casting a great square of light on the floor, framing the huge black shadow of a superman. The shape moved slowly out into the corridor and turned so that the light fell on its face.

"Potter!"

"Lauterbach!"

Potter strode forward, hand extended. "What are you doing here? Everyone said you were in Hong Kong." He peered. "Ah. I see you've met Anna. Virtually a fixture on the Surabaya line. She has her own summer timetable, our Anna. Don't worry she doesn't speak English."

"What? Who?" Lauterbach stood becalmed, eyes popping.

Potter seized Anna by both shoulders and pecked her familiarly on the cheek, turned her round in avuncular fashion and smacked her bottom in fluent Dutch. "Off you go my dear. There's lots more in the bar just waiting for you. Big, rich planters."

She pouted, hissed something that was a curse maybe in low Javanese but left with a little regretful flutter of the fingers and, as she turned the corner, was laughing.

"Hope I didn't spoil anything. I take it you didn't ... weren't going to ...? Thought not. She doesn't usually deliver.

That's not her style. Everyone knows Anna. Been at it for years, the dear old thing. She's getting a little heavy in the thigh these days but can still pull the less discriminating punter. Sometimes ..." he leaned forward confidingly, "she pulls the old Indian rape trick, you know, screams the place down, but only when she's met a real stinker."

"But Potter what are you doing here?" Lauterbach, bridling, whimpering, gushed boyish gratitude and looked more closely. This was a Potter reborn, not supine and downtrodden as in Batavia but energetic and confident, taking command, a man who still hoped for something from the world. Come to think of it, allowing for the pallid light, he wasn't even pale any more. In fact, he was as brown as a berry.

"Butterflies, old man." His eyes shone with passion. "Don't you know? Really? I should have thought ... This is the best spot in the whole of Java for butterflies. I've been out chasing them for days. There was a report that the Rafflesia had been sighted so naturally I just dropped everything, grabbed my net and ran. Terribly rare. Very exciting. As we speak butterfly buffs from all over Java are converging on this spot. By the end of the week, there won't be a room to be had even for ready money. They'll be pitching tents and Anna will be working her sweet little tush off."

They adjourned to the bar. Potter introduced some skinny fellow lepidopterists who drank till late, recounting former butterflying triumphs and disappointments all over the archipelago, argued on the finer points of butterfly anatomy and grew tearful over sketches of the Rafflesia executed on beermats. Lauterbach pulled Potter aside and shouted confidentially above the barroom roar.

"Listen here, Potter. Can I ask a favour? Please don't tell anyone you saw me here. It's very important."

Potter winked back knowingly, tapped the side of his blob of a nose, squinted still more. "Ah, like that is it? Don't worry old man. I wouldn't dream of it. Married man myself. I shan't say a dicky bird about Anna and all, though I think there's perhaps more to it than that."

"You would do this for me though I am German?"

Potter considered him impassively, whisky clenched in his fist. "You're also a member of my club," he said firmly, like a man adopting the steep and rocky path of a difficult morality. He brightened and hitched up his trousers. "Anyway, if we see the Rafflesia who on earth would remember *you*?"

"Got you!" A heavy hand fell on Lauterbach's shoulder and he jumped like a scalded cat. He turned, heart thumping, and looked into a face with deep blue eyes, cropped blond hair and a skin lined and cracked with laughter lines.

"Engelhardt!"

"Lauter— Oops. Sorry. Mustn't say that word. Good to see you old friend." They both laughed as they hugged. "Come on. Let's get you off this railway station sharpish and under cover. We'll cut through to the harbour and get straight out to the ship.

It was getting dark, the hour where in Europe people would be heading for hearth and home and the world closing down. But in Java that simply meant the night shift was getting into its stride. Barrows were being wheeled into position for the dispensing of chicken and soup and ice chips and crackers and stalls laid out for sarongs and shirts and hats and knickers, along every street in town. People were pumping up hissing lamps and firing charcoal and impaling meat onto skewers. In the teeming throng, no one heeded the two white men threading their way down to the water's edge and the little skiff tied up to the muddy pole of a house. As they climbed aboard Engelhardt looked at his watch.

"Six twenty-eight," He announced, holding up his finger. "Listen." Lauterbach was not sure what he was to listen to – the birds, the waves, the distant sounds of the market or the plaintive call to prayer from a dozen mosques – and then suddenly the background rasping of a million crickets switched into prominence as it was turned off, as though by a single mighty hand. Engelhardt smirked.

"Every evening. Regular as clockwork. Beats me how they do it. You might want to call that the hand of God."

Captain Engelhardt had been in Dutch waters when war was declared and opted for internment in Surabaya rather than fall foul of the British navy lurking offshore. Making the best of a bad job, he had settled in on his ship the *Widukind* and imported his dumpling of a wife to add a pleasing dash of domesticity. Washing and potted plants dotted and shaded the searing foredeck and a strict regime that was wifely rather than nautical kept the old ship spotless amidst the filth and garbage of the reedy backwater to which she had been shifted, linked to the shore by a thin gangplank that was ceremonially lifted at sunset as the German flag was lowered. Since the cabins were too hot for human habitation at this season, Frau Engelhardt had caused a large rectangular tent to sprout on the main deck that caught every waft of breeze and they lived an airy windblown existence behind ghostly sheets of muslin. Meanwhile Engelhardt himself grew orchids, read books, smoked his pipe. He made a small but steady income letting out the cabins to merchants for the secure storage of material too fragile and precious for the normal local godowns.

"When my retirement comes," he quipped, secateurs and watering can in hand, "I shall have to work much harder."

It was the same picture of contentment that had been haunting Lauterbach's thoughts all over Java, the same music played in a dozen different keys, of a simple satiety, the love of a good woman, a life lived fully in the present and secure in its own inherent joy, not one pitching towards some vague and hoped-for future. They sat amidst a mass of hanging, petally flowers whose perfume warred successfully against the outside miasma, drank iced beer, crunched Javanese snacks and reminisced. Lauterbach eased the rest from his limbs by dangling his foot over the rail and staring at the twinkling of the city lights.

"You remember, Lauterbach, that Christmas we got drunk in Hawaii and stole an ornamental turkey from the Iolani royal palace for our dinner?"

"... And it was so tough we had to use a woodsaw to carve it."

"What about the time in Tsingtao, at that party, we convinced a Taiwanese merchant that the Governor would be prepared to swap his wife for a bicycle, so that he wheeled one round to the front door of the Residence the next day and tried to take her away?"

"... And when he complained to us we explained it was because the bicycle was second-hand."

"... And the wife nearly new."

They laughed, clinked glasses, capped one tale with another. Frau Engelhardt sat and smiled and darned ancient socks. She had heard it all before. Let the boys have their fun, their remembrance of what seemed happy only in retrospect. All around them, ships sloshed through the thick, muddy water in darkness. Navigational lights were considered an unnecessary luxury. The gloom hid the tears that had started to Lauterbach's eyes. Nostalgia made him lonely, more proof, as it was, of the inevitable passing of all things. And in the dark a million frogs came out to mock him, shouting "What? What? What?" like red-faced British colonels.

He moved on. He moved east. He was now Lars Renquist, a Swedish traveller, rendered blond in eyebrows, beard and hair by the tender and tittering application of Frau Engelhardt's bleach. The transformation had lent an air of charade to his departure but in his cramped suitcase he now had a compass, a package of papers marked unconvincingly "Secret despatches" in big black letters and a small, sinister revolver given by Engelhardt, a sign, after all, that things were getting serious. The plan was to sail to Manado in North Sulawesi, then try to hop a boat through to Manila where he could disappear beneath the surface of the heavy American traffic to the US, changing identity as circumstances required. His name, his appearance had begun to waver, to become unsure and unfixed in his own mind. When he looked in the mirror he no longer knew unthinkingly what face would be looking back at him, goaty Gilbert, moon-faced Blaamo or scraped Renquist.

The little *Pynacker Hordyke* steamed east in a pall of greasy smoke. The deck-class passengers were fuzzy-haired Ambonese troops bound for New Guinea surrounded by their hushed wives and children together with a mix of Chinese peddlars whose cardboard boxes of merchandise were stacked about them and served as their nightime beds. Cabin-class were British and German with the Dutch and lone Lars Renquist forming an uneasy buffer between them, like mice between two cats.

The food was disgusting, mostly rice and chicken, served day after day in an enduring sameness that robbed meals of their normal shipbound function as markers of time. And at meals the war was an endless source of friction, conversations pitched deliberately loud so that neighbours and enemies should overhear and take offence – rowing by hearsay. It was irresistible.

"Whatever our feelings – as neutrals – about the war," Renquist ventured, " It cannot be denied that some of the men of the *Emden* warrant our respect as sailors." There was a pause.

"Captain von Mueller is a true gentleman of the sea," confirmed the Germans. "He brought great honour to our nation through his daring, intelligence and sense of discipline."

"But wasn't there another officer, a fine figure of a man if my memory serves me well, who distinguished himself for his extreme bravery … ?"

"Ah," said one of the Brits. "You mean von Mueckc of the *Ayesha*? A true seadog in the old British tradition, rallying his men in adversity and bringing them safely to port despite the odds. Mark my words, there must be a drop of English blood in those veins somewhere."

Renquist was nonplussed. "But wasn't there yet another man who went on and did still greater things. Now let me see, what was his name? He escaped from Singapore, crossed Sumatra, brought his men safely to Batavia in defiance of all

217

obstacles."

There was another silence.

"Hang on," said one of the Dutch, stolidly, a pastor. "I know who you mean. I was in Padang when he passed through. It was in all the papers and I actually met the fellow. He was called Diehne. He had the most fantastic tale to tell of having been abandoned by some wretched officer upriver in Sumatra, a man who was running away from prison, I think. Anyway this Diehne was certainly a man of parts. Did you know the British actually put a price on his head? I could see why they wouldn't want a man like that getting back to the front. I say. It seems we all respect these men *as* men. Why don't we drink a toast – all of us regardless of our nation – to their courage?"

There was a grudging, gruffly Adam's appled, murmur of assent. "Hear, hear." "Good show." They scraped back their chairs, rose and chinked glasses solemnly, swallowing each others' pride. Lauterbach drank, smirking fixedly, to von Mueller – which was all right – von Muecke – which was not – and Diehne. That nearly choked him.

The simmering old port of Makassar where naked boys dived in the water to pluck the tourists' small coins from the seabed, on to Manado, home of the industrious Minahasa people, Potter-pale and Chinese-featured. Lauterbach landed in the early morning calm, gripping his small luggage. It was a pretty town sheltered behind a volcanic island, ancient Portuguese ruins swamped in hibiscus and bougainvillea, the port still small and crystal-watered. It smelt of tar, salt and the sea. The Dutch lived in cool, old-fashioned thatch houses shaded by willowy palms and everywhere, soft grass was underfoot. In a hut by the water, they tried to feed him fruit bat but he dined, instead, in a cool breeze on fresh-grilled prawns and nut-flavoured bread leavened with the yeast of coconut water. On all sides plantations flourished, dotted with little churches and schools. The other unmistakable sign of the power of the Christian faith here was the universal presence of chubby dogs.

Disorder and squalour are the measure of a port's importance and by such yardsticks this was a most unimportant port. Still, there was no shortage of loungers and spectators. Lauterbach picked his man and sidled up.

"Mindanao?" he hissed like one offering dirty postcards for sale.

The man laughed, shook his head and repeated the query to those around. They laughed too.

"No Mindanao. All boats here are busy. Anyway, the Dutch do not allow us to go to Mindanao. All traffic has to go to Batavia for control." He spat onto the decking.

"This is not," Lauterbach articulated carefully, "a trading journey. I simply wish to travel there for important family reasons."

"No Mindanao. You ask Master of the Sea, a white man like yourself." He pointed vaguely to the end of the jetty and there, indeed, stood a white man with his back to him and wearing the Mindanao daytime formal dress of cotton pyjamas. Lauterbach picked his way past nets and small canoes and a pile of trussed crabs who glared at him through their eyestalks and, as he neared his goal, the man turned round and was not a European at all but an albino, pink-eyed Malay beneath a broad-brimmed hat and white lashes.

"Mindanao? We are not permitted to sail to Mindanao. You must go back to Batavia and take a ship there. If we go to Mindanao they call us smugglers and confiscate our vessels."

Lauterbach knew that such dogmatic, black and white impossibility could only be the first in a long series of negotiating positions. It was hard to have confidence in someone dressed in the striped outfit of a convict. But he knew the ways of the East and hooked up an overturned bucket with one foot, sat, got out his cigarettes and settled to talk.

He was not Dutch, he stressed. He was Swedish. This was an informal trip, a thing between friends. He merely wished to go across to Mindanao with no merchandise and no great luggage. It was a matter of no great general interest, absolutely of no importance to the Dutch and he had money. The word worked its usual magic. The man seemed to look at him for the first time. There was, it now seemed, one possibility. They could not take him but there was nothing to stop him buying a boat, hiring a crew and doing as he pleased. It just so happened that the Master of the Sea had a friend who …

The boat was about fifteen feet long, old but sound, with classic lines and a single outrigger and a simple sail of some woven plant fibre. The timbers gaped arthritically since the owner had not troubled over much about paint or caulking. It lay on the beach like one of those huge trees washed down from the inner forests, a silver-grey Leviathan, transmuted by the elements into something akin to stone. Lauterbach ran his hand over her bleached and salty flank and thought distractedly of the racehorses he had sent to the bottom in his *Emden* days.

"No problem," assured the Master of the Sea. "The

Batavia. She has been beached for some weeks. Twenty-four hours in the sea and the timber will swell and she will be as good as new. The old lady will become a young girl." He mimed curvaceous breasts on his own board-like chest, threw back his head and laughed. They would find him a crew.

Lauterbach paused. It was one of those moments in a man's life when he is poised on the edge of a cliff and must decide whether to jump or not, knowing he will either fly or plummet to his ruin. The British would by now have boarded and searched the Hong Kong vessel and found no Blaamo. Pale Potter would sooner or later talk, as much from innocence as malice and anyway it was too good a story to keep to himself. It would not take them long to get on his trail and even the Dutch would not want him wandering about where they could not keep an eye on him. Already, they would be checking the sailings from Surabaya and maybe wondering about that very substantial lone Swede, Lars Renquist, who had appeared from thin air. One fear battled with another to create an illusion of courage. He was an experienced sailor and knew the risks of the open sea. But half a dozen islands, dotted in a neat line between Sulawesi and the Philippines would offer some sort of safety net and at this time of the year, the weather should be good. The wind was from the right quarter and the journey would take only a few days. With a bit of luck all would be well. But maybe he had used up all his luck.

As soon as they left the harbour, two large sharks attached themselves to the party and Lauterbach could see at once, from their reaction, that only one of the five crew was a seasoned salt. He pointed at it with his pipe and grinned and giggled as a sailor would. A sign of good fortune, he urged.

"Nasib baik. Nasib baik." Sailors always saw everything as a good omen. They were wrong about that. The two others cowered in the bottom of the boat in terror and cried as much water back in as they bailed out.

The sea rapidly assumed a sullen, leaden aspect and clouds began to boil on the horizon. Soon a furious storm lashed the vessel with buffeting wind and rain and nasty waves that seemed to twist and mangle the creaking boat whose seams still gushed with water. Only with four bailing continuously could they now even keep the vessel afloat. In the flashes of lightning that ripped the black sky, they could see the rubber fins of the cruising sharks, still patrolling around the boat as if impatient for what they knew was already theirs. The wind plucked Lauterbach's hat from his head and whirled it off into the water. One of the sharks thrashed to the surface, grinned and gobbled it down as an appetizer. Slightly shaky, Lauterbach reached for his hip flask of the finest Javanese brandy. There was no need to do this sober. He unscrewed and splashed the raw spirit down his throat. The balers looked up at him appropriately balefully. He stared emptily back, glugged more. This was white man's business. At least the little *Batavia* was flying in the right direction and the seams were tightening. As the wind abated, there came a dreadful calm that left them motionless on a blistering metal sea for one whole day. They sprawled in the wet bottom and groaned and tried to shade their heads and eyes but everywhere was reflected heat and brightness. Sleep was impossible and Lauterbach now regretted the brandy that sucked all moisture from his eyes and mouth. They chewed on cold rice that bound their bowels in a vice-like grip and Lauterbach guarded the water barrel with his revolver, doling out sips with grim egality for them and a slight generosity for himself. He was bigger which gave him both the greater need and the power to enforce it. And that night the storm came on again, dousing them in water, mocking their thirst and heatstroke of the day, till their teeth chattered and their skin cracked open into boils and seeping sores and they clung to any handhold and rode the churning waves miserably. The blow lasted for three more days and when they were so weak and exhausted that they no longer cared to live, an island appeared on the starboard bow and the wind left them, once more, becalmed. Lauterbach cajoled then screamed and threatened so they would take up the paddles but they just stared at him brokenly and hollow-eyed. So he brought out the brandy that was poured out into cupped hands, and cigars that they chewed rather than smoked – and they were revived. At noon they pulled into the port of a small town where a handsome woman of Polynesian appearance and Western self-assurance looked down on them in polite surprise.

"Welcome," she called. "Have you come far? You must be Captain Lauterbach. Do come and meet my husband."

Chapter Eleven

Dear Mr and Mrs McCoy,

I should like to thank you once again for your generous hospitality to a humble stranger in Mindanao. It was so kind of you to offer me the chance to enjoy everything that your lovely house had to offer. I will always remember that wonderful English tea you gave me, with its many delicious and civilised constituents that would have tempted any man's tongue, especially one who had been for so long deprived of the comforts of land. I should particularly like to thank the beautiful Mrs McCoy for serving me with such deep personal attention and showing me the many beauties of the island, especially her lush personal plantation. I still recall with pleasure the fertility of those unploughed soils and the privilege of lying on my back and watching your great, ripe coconuts, bursting with sweetness, swaying above me in the breeze.

Yours sincerely,

Captain Julius Lauterbach

He had perhaps gone a little over the top in his postcard – the *entendres* were not sufficiently *doubles* – but it was at one and the same time a denunciation and an act of shared intimacy for she would have to read it out loud to her husband and could adjust the content as she thought fit. The fact was that McCoy was totally blind and knew only what his wife wished him to know.

Their bungalow was a sort of tropical version of a New England house, lots of white-painted clapboard and a wrought-iron terrace buried under luxuriant creeper built out over the sea. On it sat a very old white man with a long, white beard and matching white cataracts in his eyes, before him a table with a glass of beer and an ashtray. Lauterbach stared at the beer. His tongue crinkled and shrivelled at the sight of it.

"Darling," said the woman touching the man lightly on the shoulder. "We have a guest, Captain Lauterbach. You remember I read to you about him in the paper, the German sailor who escaped from Singapore."

The man smiled and turned sightless eyes on someone slightly to Lauterbach's left. "Sit," he ordered, running his hands through the mass of his white hair, smoothing it down. "Lauterbach is it? America is, as yet, entirely neutral in that little affair of the war so I may extend a hand of judicious welcome." No hand was extended. "We thought you'd be passing through here. It's the only way really from the Netherlands East Indies. Bring the man a beer. He must be parched." The accent was New England too, more of an agreeable twang attached to normal English than something inherently American. Whatever the accent, Lauterbach loved the words. They sat in silence as the woman vanished and swiftly reappeared with a tray. His legs shook as she bore the foaming bottle towards him, condensation trembling on the glass.

"Oohaagh. Oh my God." As he drank, the shaking reached his hands and he thought he might cry. On the boat, at the worst points, he had dreamed of this moment so often that he could scarcely believe it was real and he feared it would disappear in a puff of smoke before he could get it down.

"Thank you. Oh thank you," he gasped. "You must forgive my manners. Yes I am Julius Lauterbach. Whom do I have the honour of addressing? Are you an American colonial official?"

The man looked out over the bay, or at least seemed to and chuckled. "No not an official exactly. My name is McCoy and I have a certain influence in these parts. In fact I own most of these parts. You are exhausted I see. Might I suggest you wash and rest yourself and join us for tea a little later? Tea is the only civilised meal. I imagine tigers eat dinner and breakfast. Only white men take tea." It was said the way requests are made by those used to giving orders. Tea then. Lauterbach would take tea like a white man.

"I first married the sister of Queen Emma of Hawaii," explained McCoy in a droning voice. "A formidable woman in every particular, part white but still very beautiful and in every way a pagan at heart. The Queen devoted herself to good works, schools, hospitals, that sort of thing. Her sister was more interested in making money and we suited each other very well. In those days that was my own principal preoccupation. It was on her death that things became a little crowded in Hawaii what with all the new people coming in and the Americans taking over everything. Many of them were men of very little breeding or talent. People such as myself, the relics of the old order, were supernumary, so I found a new wife and moved out here where the world has been, on the whole, very kind to us."

He fed greedily, great manly bites of unmanly fairy cake, sucking up crumbs from his hand with a whooshing noise. The house was all heavy furniture of uncompromising wood but overlaid with flowery female flummery. Every wall had its samplers and macrame, every table doilies and runners, every chair embroidered antimacassars, a mass of congealed labour and empty time. They were in a cluttered, old-maidish parlour, full of china dogs and gee-gaws arranged on a huge and hideous sideboard, sitting round a table like an altar with a great starched linen tablecloth and a caricature of an English tea set out. Matching teapot and cups with saucers, little sandwiches, small fussy cakes, toasted muffins, a big chocolate confection melting slowly into a mess in the centre. McCoy continued to feed. Lauterbach nibbled. It seemed to him that Mrs McCoy was looking at him more than mere politeness required. He had been too long without relief. He appraised and appreciated the long, shining hair that swung with each movement, the full, curvaceous form, the flawless brown skin. Her teeth were very white against her tongue which, itself, was provokingly pink. She dispensed tea with cafeterial efficiency and flashed a smile at him as she pointed sugar tongs.

"Captain Lauterbach, you look like a man who has two big lumps." She leaned over, dropping them into his cup, showing smooth golden cleavage, "Is there nothing else I can tempt you to? Crumpet?"

He leaned forward in turn. Dare he risk it? He realised that it was not shame that might prevent him but only fear and fear must be faced down though his heart was throbbing and sweating like the boilers on the old *Emden*. He looked across at smiling, sightless McCoy, stared her brazenly in the eye and brushed his hand lightly over her shoulder, pointing at the chocolate cake, so that – if it turned out that way – it could be just an accident. "Might I have a little slice of that? It looks absolutely delicious." His face glowed in shades of sweaty beetroot. His chin, now unused to the military scraping he had subjected it to, was red and inflamed.

"Of course." Said very coolly. She did not withdraw but rubbed herself against the hand, like a cat. It slid down under the stiff bodice. Most Hawaiian ladies wore an unflattering shapeless tube gathered tightly with lace at the neck, a missionary conspiracy against sexual excitement. Mrs McCoy, luckily, opted for lighter American fashions. She arched her neck and groaned as Lauterbach insistently gripped her left nipple between finger and thumb, slowly increasing the pressure. Her black eyes grew wide with arousal.

"Mmm."

"Stop that. I know just what you're up to. Sheer wickedness!" McCoy slapped his fist on the table.

Shocked and shamed, Lauterbach snatched his hand back as if scalded.

McCoy chuckled. "She loves that chocolate cake, Lauterbach, makes straight for it every time. I always have to remind her that tea has a moral dimension. No sticky buns until you've filled up on nourishing bread and butter. You and I will be very lucky to get any. She herself behaves as if she's not had any for months. If I were you I would get solidly stuck in to the good stuff right away before it's too late."

Lauterbach had her top off and was licking the luscious

right breast which she was thrusting brazenly between his teeth.

"Nhhgah! It is true," he panted archly. "That once you have tasted chocolate, vanilla has no flavour."

He gobbled brown flesh, slurped, gobbled again.

"As a man who has travelled much, I wonder if you have noticed the palm trees here, Captain Lauterbach?"

"Gnng. What? Oh … They seem to flourish. Everything here strikes me as remarkably fecund. Many in Manado are afflicted with the blight."

He tongued away gently trying not to leave crumbs around the aureola – which would be as impolite as grease on a cup – and admired, at the same time, his own sensitivity of feeling.

"Your voice sounds a little strange, Captain Lauterbach. Not a chill I hope. Pray take care to cover yourself up well. In this climate foolish exposure can have terrible consequences."

"Excuse me. My manners again, Mr McCoy. Talking with my mouth full. It is so long since I had such a civilising and delicious experience" he stared into her cat's eyes. "In fact I am very warm."

Sweat gushed down his face. He grasped round behind her skirt and wrestled desperately with the complicated eyelets, built for the Braille-educated fingers of a blind man, pulling it down roughly to reveal a nest of jet-black pubic hair and curvaceous golden syrup groin and bent to his task, cushioning her buttocks with his hands as he shoved his face into the coarse underbrush.

"You are very quiet my dear. Might I have a drop more tea?"

She lunged against the table and squealed, grasped the tinkling pot and reached across to slop it roughly into his cup, nearly burning him. "Oops. There, my love. The milk is at your elbow."

McCoy groped and poured, guided by the sound of splashing as a man might pee in the dark. "The point about the palm trees," he continued, placidly stirring, "is that I imported them specially from Hawaii but they seem to have a rude vigour here that they quite lack at home. There is something in the soil that affects them strangely. We get two drops of fruit a year and even the husk is thicker and stronger than the native variety. I have scattered my seed all over the island."

"How fascinating." Lauterbach unbuckled swiftly, spread her from behind and impaled her forcefully on his lap guiding in his rampant penis, feeding it to her slowly and then settling to a slow rhythmic thrust, lifting her whole body at each piston stroke. "Your Hawaiian additions have greatly increased the beauty and desirability of this island." A board beneath them began creaking like a metronome. They fought to control their panting. *Creak*!

"What's that?" McCoy looked quizzically irritated. He laid down his cup and made as if to rise. "What's that noise?" *Creak*!

She thrust down firmly onto him. "The wind blowing that loose guttering. You will remember, my love, that I mentioned it last week but, as usual, no one took any notice. *Creak*! You pay no attention to such things."

"Well it's very annoying. We must get one of the boys onto it. *Creak*! Call Manuel right now and get him to come in and listen."

"Oh darling. He's busy. Anyway, you know tea time is our only chance to get a little peace from the servants." *Creak*! Lauterbach thrust away cheerfully, enjoying the slick friction of membrane on membrane, the slap of sweaty thigh on sweaty thigh. This mixture of exhibitionism and concealment excited him strangely. The Lauterbach torpedo swelled and hardened to a rock as he jiggled and juggled. He was triumphant, all-consuming, pounding like a ship's engine with his mighty shaft.

McCoy chuckled. "May I have my chocolate cake now?"

They sighed and rose, still coupled, a dancing pair in perfect synchrony, shuffled as in a three-legged race round the table and she sliced cake, dumping it roughly on a plate, digging her fingers heedlessly into the icing, and slapping it down. Lauterbach turned her and bent her forward so she could grip the massive sideboard, buried his hand in her long lustrous hair and began pumping towards a climax, giving a slight twist at the end of each stroke that made her shudder as the china dogs tinkled. The muscles of her buttocks were excitingly hard against his groin. In the mirror her face was a savage, snarling mask.

"The one advantage of being blind," McCoy observed smugly, dribbling chocolate happily onto his snowy shirtfront, "is that the other senses become more acute, you actually know more about what is going on around you than the sighted, if you get my thrust. You are probably unaware, for example, of a rhythmic trembling through the floorboards but I can feel it most distinctly. It is the volcano over the other side of the island. Whenever it is set to blow, I am always the very first to know."

Lauterbach felt wave after wave of agonised pleasure tear through his body and gasped aloud, spasmed, gasped, spasmed again. He ground out the afterglow of lust inside her like a cigarette in an ashtray. "Volcano?"

McCoy chuckled. "I hear a tremour in your voice, Captain Lauterbach. You must not be afraid. I am sure you are thinking of those mighty explosions with huge, towering rocks and streams of white hot lava shooting and gushing all over the place that are described in books. But normally, here, it is simply a matter of a few quick spurts of muck, a puff of smoke, perhaps a bit of gas and shaking about and then it's all over and no one the worse for wear. We clear up the mess and carry on as usual. Isn't that so my love?"

Lauterbach lent over the china dogs, chest heaving, taking deep breaths. He was exalted, shriven, but as his manhood collapsed, physical shame crept back in and he turned away coyly to dress. Mrs McCoy returned brazenly to the table, threw back her long hair and dried her face, slick with sweat, on her serviette, towelled off her breasts and wiped between her legs with as little embarrassment as a wrestler.

"Normally, my love." She threw the soiled cloth down on the table with the food and tossed her long black hair out of her eyes. "Normally but not always. You only talk to the men. The women are more affected by these things and some of them speak of experiencing quite considerable eruptions in the past." She rolled her eyes at Lauterbach and mouthed a silent kiss.

McCoy tapped his feet pettishly on the floor, "Shhh!" mimed listening. "There," he smirked triumphantly, in a little high voice "what did I tell you? It's over already. Never much to it."

Lauterbach, reclothed, sank back in his chair sated, now feeling no guilt, no sense of violating his host by giving pleasure to his wife. After all, it was always better to have a happy woman under your roof than a bitter and frustrated one. He had done the man a favour when all was said and done, lubricated the juddering machinery of his household with the sweat of his brow, and he lacked the meanness of spirit that might make him begrudge that another reaped content where he had sown it. Anyway, McCoy was blind and his own attention to the woman was only the due of an otherwise wasted beauty. Blind men? That was what plain women with good conversation had been put into the world for. He deserved a reward. Now how about a piece of that chocolate cake?

Manila stank of woodsmoke and old dishcloths. Lauterbach stalked the Intramuros walled city and rejoiced in the superiority of his own height and girth compared to the local men and the unfeigned beauty of the women. He was billeted on another *Etappe* captain, interned out in the harbour. But the ship was a mess. The young captain had given way to joyless dissipation and spent all day in an alcoholic daze that turned aggressive after dark. Lauterbach could not wait to move on. All around him in the city were the sounds of ordinary life, laughter, babies, soothing him back to normality . Perhaps he would move out, spend some time in a hotel, eat, drink, have a touch of the other.

He settled in a little coffee shop that catered for the foreign trade and leaned back against the ancient, honeyed stone to watch the rich mix of people teeming along the street and let it all wash over him. He blew slow smoke and savoured the neat, light tread of Asia where a walk of provocation was no part of masculinity. Then a tiny urchin came slouching along selling newspapers, leaning back to counterbalance the weight folded over his arm. He appraised Lauterbach dispassionately. He had made an effort to blend in, dressed like a frayed-at-the-cuffs travelling salesman, tried to look ...

"English?"

Lauterbach nodded. His Spanish was that of a sailor, restricted to telling people about their mothers. The boy fished in the pile and drew one out, crisp, neat-edged, today's date, another sign of life and civilisation. Lauterbach paid with a soiled note and received change in coins, plucked from a stack inside the seller's ears as if by magic. He chuckled at this folk version of his own money paunch and then he saw the headline. "*Lusitania* sunk by German submarines. Hundreds lost in cowardly attack on passenger vessel. 123 American civilians, including Mr Alfred Vanderbilt, among those dead. Congress calls for War."

"Shit!" Was there no end to all this? The paper trembled in his hands and he upset his coffee. People at neighbouring tables turned to look at this muttering, dithering madman. Kessel and the Crown Prince had done their work, completely undoing that of the *Emden*. The German navy was evil incarnate. The editorial spoke hotly of nothing but America entering the war within days and opening hostilities against the Hun in Europe. It raged against perfidious Germany, its cowardice, cruelty, the need for swift retribution. And the Philippines were an American colony. And the most unpopular thing to be in town at the moment was a German naval officer who had sunk civilian ships. He was a man running up a blazing staircase with the flames licking ever closer at his heels.

There was no safe way to reach the chaotic neutrality of China. Most of the vessels in the harbour were British and bound for Hong Kong. To go that way was to thrust his head into a noose. Many of the seamen were personal acquaintances from his years on the Asia run and there could be no hope of staying unrecognised for long. The only chance was to take a berth on a Japanese ship where all Westerners looked alike. He ran a finger down the shipping list. The *Otaka Maru*, sailed in two days, via Tsingtao, where he could hop the train straight to Shanghai, simply hoping to remain anonymous for the few hours it would take to get out of the colony. And the only uncompromised travel document he had left was that passport for Pieter Blaamo, purchased from Katsura. It was a sign. He downed the remaining inch of hot coffee – damn and blast- that burned his lips. It was time to move on fast. He shoved out between the tables. Someone had left a custard tart untouched and he crammed it into his mouth as he passed. It was almost an act of compassion. Already the urchin was taking back the newspaper, abandoned on the table, and carefully refolding it for resale.

Back to the ship. The captain could be heard drunkenly mumbling to himself in the saloon, followed by the splintering of a glass, dropped or flung. No need for elaborate leave-taking. Going down to his cabin, he stared at himself one last time in the mirror. Goodbye Lauterbach. He shaved, cropped his hair and became once more a new person. His very features now seemed to swim free of each other and they rearranged themselves into a vacuous moon face. Hallo Pieter Blaamo.

The *Otaka Maru* was not a passenger vessel but a collier,

the sort he had once hunted to near extinction on the *Emden*. That was all to the good. If the captain took him aboard it would be money straight into his own back pocket so he would not want anyone else to hear about it, especially the shipping company. He could be certain of appearing on no passenger list.

Captain Yoshida was a small man, scrupulous within his small corruption, who was only too willing to have a passenger, even giving up his cabin for the journey but was deeply disappointed to find that Pieter Blaamo spoke hardly any English so that conversation was restricted to bows and smiles for Yoshida loved to talk of baseball. But at least Dr Blaamo was no trouble. Most of the time he spent reading in his cabin or watching the British and Japanese navy vessels that teemed like fish in these waters.

Pieter Blaamo, it seemed, was a pipe-smoker and, on the last night at sunset, he was enjoying a pipe on the upper deck, surprised at his own feeling of peace in these hostile waters. Strictly speaking, of course, Tsingtao was not hostile territory but that would count for little if he were recognised. He puffed and daydreamed till his reverie was disturbed by two pigtailed Chinese heads that suddenly popped up from below like prairie dogs. Stokers, he assumed, getting a breath of air. They were silhouetted against the setting sun which made them look even more alike.

"Captain Lauterbach!" He bit down hard on the pipestem, nearly breaking it in two. His armpits gushed sudden fear.

"Who are you?" His whisper was like a scream.

"Gan Poon and Lee Fatt." Of course. They had been on the *Staatssekretaer Kraetke*. Both good men. He had last seen them at the coaling in Pagan. As he had foreseen, the locals were adapting themselves smoothly to the change in administration.

"We see you. We recognise. Everybody seekee Lauterbach. Picture everywhere in Tsingtao."

"Shit!" He was worth £10,000 and they knew it. A rush of blood to the face, trembling. "Who else you tellee?" He hated the tremour in his own voice.

They shook their heads, the way children do when they are lying, swaying their whole bodies from the waist with the movement. "Tellee no one."

"How much you wantee?" A worm seemed to have crawled inside his stomach.

"No wantee dollar. Last time we see you givee watch." They showed their wrists proudly. It was true. In Pagan he had dished out all those useless watches, given by lady passengers, to the crew. "All we askee is paper character so can getee good berth like before."

He was shocked, humbled. He wanted to cry at the simple goodness of poor men. They had the power to betray him for the unimaginable sum of £10,000 and all they wanted was a written reference that cost him nothing. Well he would give them the best references stokers had ever got. He sat and wrote, tears streaming from eyes, described them as angels without wings. They took the papers with solemn grace, folded and stowed them carefully away and waved him farewell, wished him good luck. He swore a silent oath that, when the war was over and he came back to Tsingtao, he would look after them. At that moment, he almost meant it too.

In the early morning, their anchor tumbled into the water of the inner harbour. Pieter Blaamo, face fresh-scraped, already lurked on deck with his luggage. He would have to be alert. Everywhere were people who knew Lauterbach. Gan Poon and Lee Fatt had been set to work on the foredeck and stonily ignored him. ButTsingtao was transformed. He looked around in horror at the devastation wrought by the Allied bombardment. On the waterfront virtually all the solid, stone buildings had been razed and the cobbles torn up in deep shellcraters. Once more, his memories, his youth and much of his optimism had gone with them. The smooth harbour walls were pitted and scored from naval fire and most of the sheds were reduced to wrecks of twisted girders. The sign over the roof garden reading "Dachsaal" had gone and been replaced by a snarl of Japanese characters while the advanced new dry dock had been cut up and shipped off to rapidly-industrialising Japan and now their occupying troops were everywhere, looking every bit as bored and puzzled as the Germans had been before them, only cleaner, and instead of the black-white-and-red of Germany, the Japanese ensign waved arrogantly over the shattered city as if its destruction were a minor irrelevance. Lauterbach felt sad and sick and very old, a well-kicked dog.

In happier days the harbourmaster used to be British, Captain Robertson, a punctilious observer of the old custom of taking a glass with the master of every incoming vessel. It was possible he was still in post and there, suddenly, he was. Lauterbach craned round a corner to see the red boozy face disappear up to the bridge and crept out soft-footed towards the gangway, suitcase under his arm like a tenant doing a moonlight flit.

There, on the mole, in the usual place was a familiar sight, the debauched donkey man, scratching his crotch and waiting, as for many years, for some poor innocent like Pieter Blaamo to blunder into his path. Lauterbach made a great show of hiring two donkeys at absurd prices to transport himself and his luggage to the railway station just as tourists always did. People here were used to comical fat men on tiny donkeys. It was excellent camouflage. Lauterbach would have died first.

Under some odd logic, the Poukow-Nanking line, it seemed, was still operating to a regular schedule and still in German hands. The journey would take three days. But first he made a detour to the harbour postmaster and bought a large envelope. Inside the flap he drew a huge mouth with a finger pressed to it, sealed a soft Chinese banknote inside and wrote "For stokers Gan Poon and Lee Fatt, *Otaka Maru*." They could not read or write but would get his message all right. Arrived at the railway station, he bribed his way aboard, pulled down his hat, *Etappe*-style, and settled down to doze. He was £10,000 pounds, curled up and sleeping like a forgotten deposit account.

Pieter Blaamo perished quite quickly on the Saturday streets of Shanghai. One minute he was walking in spritely fashion down the Bund, convincingly blond, brown eyes hidden behind blue-tinted glasses. The next he was gone, stretched out on the hard paving stones, jauntily hailed to death by an Englishman, walking in the opposite direction.

"Hello Lauterbach. What? You here in Shangers?"

It was Captain Dewar, an old friend from civilian days. Dewar had always been a bit of a dandy, waistcoat with swags of silver chain, boater, spats. He stared at Lauterbach through screwed-in monocle. "There's something odd about you. Those glasses. You look like an elephant in a pink tutu – different."

"Not different enough clearly." There was no point in carrying on this farce any longer. Pieter Blaamo took off the blue lenses and slid them into a pocket. Lauterbach rose again.

Dewar dodged, without thinking, out of the heat into the shade of one of the trees lining the broad avenue and rested his foot easily on a bench. The leaves were beginning to drop and swirled listlessly about them.

"We've been hearing a lot about you. What a lot of trouble you've caused, Juli-bumm. Who would have thought? I'm surprised to see you walking about, bold as brass, like this. Shanghai may be neutral but you know the Brits run the police and the customs. Being massively corrupt is no impediment to patriotism, old man. They've been putting up your picture everywhere and offering a reward. Sooner or later someone's going to have a crack at claiming it. All they have to do is clonk you on the head one dark night and get you to the British consulate-general then whisk you back to Singapore. There are two British destroyers in the harbour that would be happy to do the job." He looked out across the river where sampans swarmed around the big ocean-going vessels heading upriver to Soochow Creek. "Look, there's something else I feel you ought to know. A couple of the chaps whose ships you sent to the bottom are in town and – well – they might bear a grudge too. I'd watch it if I were you. Keep a low profile. God knows, we've got more than enough trouble fighting with the Chinese without letting matters get out of hand between ourselves. We'd better not been seen talking together again for my sake. Sorry but there it is. The German navy's name stinks around here since the sinking of the *Lusitania*. Best of luck to you." He tipped his hat and strolled casually off.

The Bund had changed a lot in the past couple of years and Lauterbach, reborn, sauntered along the busy avenue, a sightseeing boulevardier. All the European nations had their concessions in the city after a century of aggression that seemed to have been guided by a sign he had once seen in a Hamburg crockery shop, "China – If you break it, you own it." The country had, indeed, been smashed and now the business of stripping China of its riches was proceeding at breakneck speed, despite the European war. On the Bund only the pieces of paper to which they were reduced actually moved. and the big European trading houses were still there, hemming in the river, massively pillared and exuding wealthy solidity and were daily being added to. A new heaped-up monstrosity in curlicued Renaissance style called itself the Asiatic Petroleum Building and a couple of doors down was the spanking new Union Assurance of Canton. But the incongruous English Tudor Customs House still stood like a miniature Hampton Court amidst the jostling rickshaws and he paused to set his watch by the clock, known to all as "Big Ching," as he had so often in the past. Then he clapped on speed and headed for the luxurious Palace Hotel for a lunchtime snifter. But here too was change. A sign tacked to the door regretted that there had been a forest fire in the legendary roof garden and the building was closed for repairs. Robbed of his goal, he dawdled outside and suffered momentary panic on discovering that the German Asiatic Bank, where his money was nested, had disappeared but it seemed it had only moved to new and even more prosperous premises a few doors up. He leant against the wall in relief and fanned himself with his hat and then his eyes lighted on number 3, The Shanghai

Club. He was, after all, a member of long standing.

Since he had already been recognised there was no future in hiding any more. His safety would now have to lie in making himself so visible that no one could lay hands on him unobserved. He must be constantly in society. He could head for the Concordia Club at number 22 that catered specifically for Germans but that was too private. He had to make a definitive entrance.

Lauterbach strode confidently up to the marble steps, the uniformed flunky, dressed like an emperor, bowing and flinging wide the door for him, tapped across the patrician tiles, took a deep breath and let his eyes wander the forty-odd feet to the ceiling. It smelled exactly as it always had, of money and power with no hint of the oppression and poverty on which they rested. This was no gentle and companionable club like the sandalwood-scented *Harmonie* in Batavia. This was all about hierarchy and exclusion and rivalry and Lauterbach might not feel exactly at home here – he was doubly excluded by nationality and lack of wealth – but he knew at least that he had a tolerated right of entry as a member of the officer class, the class that ran things without necessarily owning them.

Gilded lifts ran up the hollow centre of the curving staircase lit by the latest American electrical tungstoliers, all brass and razzmatazz. Up there were cardrooms and ballrooms, dining rooms and the rest of it but Lauterbach knew where he must go. He entered the Long Bar, allegedly the longest bar in the world, aware that every one of its 111 feet had cosmological implications, for it was a picture of Shanghai – and thus the world – in miniature. Men ranged themselves from window to door, as in the English church, according to social rank. The big *taipans* – of the Hong Kong and Shanghai Bank and Jardine Matheson – who ran local commerce like warlords, held court arrogantly by the tall windows. The lowest *griffins*, the clerks and scribes in their crumpled suits, stood by the door, constantly pushed back and forth by their betters. The smoke of a thousand cheroots was whirled away by the fans. Women, animals and natives were not admitted under any circumstances. Non-British were barely suffered. Lauterbach headed through the gale of chortle and gossip for the centre where most drinkers congregated, the middle-class demographic paunch of old Shanghai. He stepped up to the bar and ordered a beer, looking up at the great, glowing, stained glass window made of bottles of many colours, lit from behind.

He was served briskly and without comment and at first no one heeded him. Decently dressed, not a local or afflicted with an obviously contagious and loathsome disease, there was no clear reason to deny him the modest place he had chosen. He signed the chit and it was carried off by a boy to be spiked. Then he became aware that the French bar steward was peering anxiously on tiptoe at him over the etched glass partition and talking emphatically to the boy. He disappeared to be replaced by a worried, round-faced man in pin-stripes who looked at him too and blanched. Lauterbach was rather enjoying this. The shit was about to hit the ceiling fans and he for once was throwing it. He lit a cheroot and plumed smoke from all boilers.

Pin-stripes appeared silently at his elbow. "Mister Lauterbach?" he whispered in a voice like a hushed fart.

"*Captain* Julius Lauterbach, actually," he replied loudly. Instantly silence fell around them. Conversation was sucked into the plush carpet. People turned. Those further off noticed the silence and pivoted round to see what was causing it, those yet further off likewise. In seconds a hush had spread over the entire room, except for an aged military man, rendered stone deaf by the guns, who continued to shout into the void a description of a visit to a new low bar in Blood Alley where the cocktail girls specialised in serving drinks by whacking the glass along the polished bar with their bare breasts. The name Lauterbach slithered hissing through the room.

Pin-stripes was sweating profusely and fingering his tight collar. "Might I have a word in private, sir. There is a slight problem with your membership."

"A problem?" Lauterbach sipped beer coolly.

"Owingtoyourlongnon-attendanceattheclub,sir,andnon-payment of dues we have had to reassign membership. You will understand, sir, that there is alway pressure for new members, especially what with the war and so many British gentlemen ..." He stopped, blushed. A sort of collective snarl came from the British *taipans* by the window and a wordless baying that crystallised slowly into a rugger-club cry of "Out! Out! Out!" A nasty predatory expression was stamped on the beef- and beer-fed faces. There could be roughhousing, debagging, maybe something more unpleasant in the way of judicious violence. Lauterbach drained his drink and turned to look at them, trying hard not to make the glass look like a weapon. He put it down and stubbed out his cheroot with slow deliberation.

"Since, it seems, I am no longer a member of this club," he said quietly and with a lazy smile, "I shall leave. But I beg you all to remember that you are permitted to invite me back, at any time, as a guest, and I shall not be too proud to accept."

The baying died slowly as one of the gnarled *taipans* rose silently, and with arthritic difficulty, to his feet. "The *Clan Matheson*," he muttered. "You killed my two beautiful racehorses. I shall never forgive you for that." He was trembling. There were tears in his eyes. "There is no difference in my book between you and those Hunnish swine who sank the *Lusitania* with all those innocent souls on board. You spit on everything, smash everything that's worthwhile. You'll pay for that, Lauterbach. I'll see you pay."

The memory hit Lauterbach like a blow to the solar plexus. "I want you to know," he said quietly and soberly, "that they did not suffer. They were shot before the ship went down."

The old man choked and sobbed. His fellows turned away in embarrassment. Such public displays were unmanly. Lauterbach felt an unfulfillable urge to go across and comfort him but there was no way across that carpet and the tears started to his own eyes. He too had briefly loved those horses as something to be set above the reach of war. He turned and walked with dignity towards the door, the young *griffins* falling back, open-mouthed, to make way for him. He had made his entrance and his point and now everyone knew that Lauterbach was back in town and he stalked through the doors with the steely aplomb of a whaleboned duchess. Over his shoulder, the oblivious military gentleman was still shouting into the silence. "Marvellous stuff. Some of those *songsong* girls, ya know, could shift a pint of Guinness twenty feet with one twitch of the tit and not spill a drop."

Lauterbach swaggered out into the crass sunlight of the street, breathing deeply and caught a tram up Nanking

Road, climbed off three stops later and made for a small, discreet, modern block of flats, standing back from the road. Swallows were building nests in the guttering, flashing off into the sunshine and returning with beakfuls of grass. From a second-floor window a phonograph brayed out a Chinese song sung by the trilling, nasal, female that was the authentic voice of the East. He stopped and listened then laughed as he recognised it as a Mandarin version of "If I knew you were coming I'd have baked a cake." He pulled back the grill on the lift and rode to the fifth floor, looked around the landing carefully before coming out and unlocked a blank door with no number, painted in the shade of red that Chinese Feng Shui declares lucky. There were three small rooms and a balcony, furnished simply and sparely, bought from a speculator friend a few years ago, who had convinced him that this was the future. It had every modern convenience, drains, running water, gas lighting and contained nothing of himself, an empty shell he used as a place to dump his kit and hang his hat when in Shanghai.

The curtains were pulled closed and behind them a fly was buzzing resignedly against the glass. The air was hot and heavy with the stale smell of a place shut up too long. In theory, no one had known he was coming and certainly no cake had been baked. Mrs Chin, the widow on the floor above, had agreed to keep an eye on the place, in return, it was understood, for being allowed to snoop in the closets and read Lauterbach's mail. But now there was no mail and someone else had been here. The drawers on the chipped lacquer commode had been rifled. The bedsheets were tousled as though in some hasty adulterous tryst. The edges of the carpets were flipped back where someone had checked the coins slipped underneath for good luck and marks in the dust showed where ornaments had been recently moved with no time for dust to resettle. Whoever had done it had caused no gratuitous damage but neither had they bothered to conceal their passing.

On a whim, he picked up the telephone and held it to his ear. He had asked for the line to be disconnected, but there came an instant fury of clicks and clatterings down the wire. Lauterbach went directly to the bathroom, climbed up on the seat and fished in the cistern. The water that stuck to his hand was thick and green with slime. Whoever had been here had not had a pee, then, or at least not flushed like a gentleman. He withdrew a key, the key to his safety deposit at the bank, and good householder that he was, clanked the chain to empty the tank and refill it with fresh water. It was time to move his assets west. The dying jangle of the mechanism blended confusingly into a sound from outside where the lift abruptly lurched and rattled back off to the ground floor. Lauterbach pricked his ears and heard it thud to a halt five floors down. He left the flat swiftly, turned the key on the deadlock and hurried down the stairs. On the ground floor below him the grill scraped shut and the lift began to climb back up, groaning and creaking. As he passed through the lobby and hailed a rickshaw, he could have sworn he smelled lavender on the air.

He realised too late that he had been imprudent and that it would cost him his life. The plan had been to stay the night in the Concordia Club dining on fat German sausage. But he had drunk perhaps too much beer, spoken his native tongue too emphatically and inhaled too much German self-confidence in the very cigar smoke. His high-ceilinged room on the first floor lay empty in the early hours of the morning as he had he wandered out from the smoke-filled bar onto the Bund in the moonlight to take the air. A refreshing rain had scrubbed it of its usual acrid tang and lent a delicate sheen to the embankment. The tranquility of the spot, the German cosiness of the surroundings – everything had lulled his senses into woolly content. He had lit a cigarette, as those seeking fresh air often do, and wandered slowly towards the steel ribs of Gardener bridge to stare at the implacable river and the dying lights of the city and suddenly realised that, on the broad, paved avenue, he was very alone.

Wait. No. He was *not* alone. Suddenly there were three men who had been lurking in the black shadows under the trees, coming purposefully towards him in long raincoats, hands in their pockets. He turned. Three more were crossing over behind him. He was cut off. He started to run back towards the Concordia, his unsure feet echoing on the stark cobbles. A late car wobbled over the iron bridge and whined slowly towards them in low gear. He ducked down and used it as a shield between himself and the second group who were dithering across the road. A sudden crack and a bullet starred the side window. The driver accelerated away, his face a white frightened blob under brilliantined hair in the moonlight. In Shanghai you did not get involved in other people's quarrels. Fear trilled through his stomach. In a civilian it would have caused paralysis but now the conditioned reflexes of training cut in. There was only one thing to be done, an ancient naval manoeuvre. Crouching low, Lauterbach ran straight at the closest group and rammed them, barged the larger two to the ground and reeled at a glancing blow from a blackjack or some other kind of cudgel as the third, smaller figure struck out at him and connected on the thigh. The other three were shouting now and closing in fast. His only escape was the river, fast-flowing at the ebb tide. Lauterbach swung himself up onto the stone parapet under a hissing gas lamp like many a festive drunk before him but his leg lay dead from the blow, and he hesitated, looking down sweatily into the turbid water wondering whether to jump. The little figure made the decision for him, leaping up to grab at his good leg, unbalancing him so that they both tumbled forward. He just had time to recognise Katsura's terrified face and then the filthy Huangpoh boiled over his eyes and ears and the next he knew he was gasping and striking out for the far shore, fighting the panic of the cold water and the bullets that were fired off randomly into obscurity. Getting a grip on himself, he began to tread water and breathe deeply and floated gently downstream in darkness until he accosted an astonished sampan.

"Taxi!" he called in his most patrician tones. "You takee German ship, chop-chop." He clambered aboard and gushed filthy water on all sides. The boatman stared, open-mouthed. "Chop-chop," snapped Lauterbach sitting down primly by the stern as if this were a totally regular means of hiring a taxi.

The French concession in Shanghai was one of the more relaxed. It financed itself largely through the pleasures of the flesh and many of the girls who worked in the Lane of Lingering Happiness housed in the cheap tenements around the Avenue Joffre. The German concession lay just north of it around Kraetkestrasse, a place of offices and counting-houses, and the familiarity of the name, the same as his old ship, leapt at Lauterbach as he swung down from the tram and picked his way carefully over the rails. His thigh still ached.

The German consul, Herr Wolf, was a fussy little man after whom no ships or roads were likely ever to be named and he operated from a darkly panelled office that concentrated down the sticky Shanghai heat and made it totally intolerable. Thick carpet kept noise and humidity in. The only dry thing was the rasping tick of a heavy wallclock in a marble case. the shape of the Brandenburg gate. Lauterbach appraised it charitably. A clock in an office always added a touch of class. They sat across a desk with great bow legs like his grandmother's sideboard.

Herr Wolf had a cold. "Lauterbach?" he sniffed. There was a shaving rash under his left ear. "Don't know you do I? You must make an appointment, I'm afraid. I have an urgent meeting across town." He snorted tiredly into a handkerchief and looked at the clock as if expecting it to confirm his story but the golf bag leaning against his chair spoke louder.

Lauterbach sighed, unintimidated by this sheep in wolf's clothing. "Herr Wolf. I have with me certain secret documents from our Batavia legation that I have carried at great personal risk and I am eager to disembarrass myself of them before they fall into the wrong hands." He pulled the packet from his side-pocket and pushed it over the desk so that it came to rest on the blotter where Herr Wolf sat and looked at it appalled, careful not to touch. To touch would be to assume responsibility.

"This is really most irregular." He reached for the phone, thought better of it, sneezed, and put his hands in his lap. Then he reached for a pencil and poked at the despatches as at an unclean thing. "They are not, I note, actually addressed to me. How am I to know they were intended for myself and not another?"

Lauterbach shrugged and stared at the Emperor's portrait nailed to the wall. There was something odd about it. "No doubt the first letter contains information about myself and the content of the other letters, if you care to look at it."

"What? Have you read these papers?" Wolf was becoming as angry as his rash and he scratched at it in rage. "That too is most improper and an offence under German law." He sulked and breathed heavily through his mouth. Lauterbach realised what it was with the portrait. A house lizard had got behind it and was rocking up and down so that the imperial moustache twitched as though in patrician distaste. Lauterbach had confidently expected a warm and enthusiastic welcome, *Etappe* housing, a fake passport or two, more money. This would not do at all. Wolf sniffed back snot.

"You will have to come back tomorrow. I cannot possibly deal with such an extraordinary matter now." He pushed the letters back with his hankie and made the face of a man straining against constipation.

"And what if the British shoot me dead in the interim?" Lauterbach shoved them back yet again, stuck out his jaw. "They have already made one attempt on my life."

"In that case do not come back. Atchoo!" Witty. Very. The man was a fool and this was a waste of time. No matter. Lauterbach knew his way around this town and had more than one string to his bow. There was a squeal of tyres and a furious honking outside. That would be another of the strings. Without another word, he stood up and walked out, leaving Wolf looking down stupidly at the letters.

Rosa was Eurasian and of good Shanghai patrician family which is to say that her father was an English trader while her mother had formerly worked in the entertainment business but was now redeemed as a devotee of bridge and lawn tennis. Rosa had clearly got her legs from her mother. Lauterbach looked at her fondly as she sat smoking in her little yellow convertible outside the German consulate. A knot of tangled emotions stirred in him. Was this love? The word was difficult. It was at least affectionate lust that stirred in his breast and elsewhere. He walked over and knocked on the window.

"Darling!" Her whole face lit up. She leaned across, wound down the window and kissed him briskly on the lips. He opened the door and slid in beside her. She was about thirty-five, dark, with big, brown, almond eyes and those tiny even little teeth only Asians can have. She exuded warm feral odours. The Lauterbach torpedo armed itself as he slid a hand over her shoulders. He should have brought the traditional flowers – what Schwabe termed "a bundle of plant sex organs." Women liked that sort of thing.

"Thank you for coming."

She laughed. "So formal darling. Would you like to have it off?" Shock showed on his face. She laughed again. "The *roof*, you idiot. Shall we have the roof off?"

"Better not." He settled back into his seat. "As I explained on the phone, I need to hide out for a few days. I wondered about that big old house of yours in the country? Do you still have it by any chance?"

She started the engine and shifted into gear, the slit in her skirt showing a haunch of appetising pale thigh. "No problem. These days you can't give away an old pile like that. Anyway," she laughed and looked at him fondly, "I'd do anything for an old shipmate."

They had met on the old *Staatsekretaer* a few years back and one thing had led to ... a repetition of that one thing throughout the journey to their great mutual pleasure. He had written to her from the camp in Singapore and she had sent a reply of such anatomical intimacy that the shocked censor had let all future letters through unopened. Rosa was an independent woman who ran her own club, The Wild West, in the lively Foochow district. Having noted the relatively high pay of American doughboys, she had set up a cosy bar to cater specifically for them, American drinks and music, a decor involving table lamps in the form of the Statue of Liberty and girls who might or might not be nice but were always clean and had no holes in their underwear.

They bowled along beside the Huangpo river, heading out for the expansive countryside otherwise known as China. Lauterbach kept an eye out for anyone who might be following them but once they were outside the foreign concessions, vehicles were few and they were virtually alone on the dry dirt road. After a while the lanes lost their obsession with straight lines and settled to a meandering pattern between parched fields, as though their course had been fixed by a man chasing a pig. Ten miles further on, they took a right turn and drove slowly down a rutted track to a big placid house, transplanted from the Surrey hills and hidden in pine trees. Ancient gardeners bowed deferentially as they crunched past. They seemed older than the trees.

"It looks just the same."

"Of course, darling. We sometimes use it for weekend

parties, politicians and such but it's the quiet season." She squeezed his hand. "Just us."

The next two days passed in a golden haze of the senses. They ate, drank, made love and then, one night, he said.very deliberately, "I want you to do something for me."

Rosa burst into tears. "Sorry," she sobbed. "I've been waiting for you to say that. I know this can't last, that we have to have our fun while we can and not take things too seriously. We both knew that from the start and I'm not complaining." He said nothing, just hugged her in the dark till his arms ached and she fell fitfully asleep. She was a grand girl and of his 'ladyfriends' she was closest to being a proper *friend*. But his mind tossed and turned in the night. He quarried her sleeping silence for proofs of his own failings. What was it he really wanted? Freedom or security or simply that constant alternation that is the sailor's life? Sailing the seas thinking of home or sitting at home missing the sea? Caring for someone made you strong but it also made you weak since terrible things could happen to them. Caring about anything was dangerous. He had intended to ask her to sell the flat for him but now he could not. He would have to leave it as an unredeemed pledge that he would be back after the war. No, wait. The property market was at its peak. He would quietly ask someone else to sell it and then, if he returned, go back into the market at a lower price. Surely, there was no harm in that? Rosa would never know. He sighed. He wanted to be happy but feared that God had simply made him sad. With the clarity of vision that comes in the dark, he realised that his lovelife was organised on the same model as his looting forrays on the *Emden* – a dispassionate inventory, followed by a ruthless ransacking that met his immediate needs, followed by moving on. He lay awake brooding muzzily until the early morning grey crept through the frilly curtains. Just as he fell asleep, Rosa awoke and drove back in the first light to the city, leaving him alone. He awoke sad and with a terrible taste in his mouth. Perhaps it was the taste of melty love but more likely just a tongue parched from too much snoring.

Two days later she was there again, smiling, makeup bright and cheerful, dressed in a fresh new two-piece, the car full of parcels.

"Here you are darling. Everything you wanted." They went giggling up to the bedroom where Lauterbach excitedly tried on his brand new uniform of a sailmaker's mate, first class, in the US navy. A few weeks before, to crown an evening of hard socialising, petty officer William Johnson had engaged in mild fisticuffs at The Wild West and so lost his wallet, passport and other documents as well as two teeth. The papers had been adjusted to fit Lauterbach. Last, she gave him an envelope containing a ticket aboard the *SS Mongolia*, an American-registered Pacific mailboat, sailing for San Francisco via Nagasaki and Yokohama. The froth of US war fever had now subsided as swiftly as it had boiled up and there was no longer an immediate risk of a declaration of hostilities and the sailing was in two days' time. Rosa did not cry again and wore a constant bright smile that was more frightening to Lauterbach than tears. And that night she broke a long-standing house rule and made love to a man who wore the uniform of the US navy.

CHAPTER TWELVE

Dear Detective Namura,

Many thanks for the guided tour of Yokohama. Without your help I should never have gained access to the many interesting experiences vouchsafed by that fair city whose hidden side you know so well. I assume you have still not fulfilled your dreams by arresting that desperado from the Emden *whose capture was such a focus of your concerns when we were together. Look at my signature and hang on to a single thought – that you briefly held ten thousand pounds in your hands but let it slip through your fingers. Think what you might have done with that money! Thank you for the Hawaiian shirt. I have had it made into a dress for my mother and the rest of the material makes an excellent bedspread.*

Yours sincerely,

Captain Julius Lauterbach

Lauterbach made his entry aboard the *Mongolia* in style. Rosa had borrowed the steam launch of a fabulously wealthy Chinese *taipan* and decked it out with three large versions of the Stars and Stripes and a small brass band. The British officials, scanning the faces and documents of the many furtive passengers aboard the normal tender, were dazzled by the boat's sheer chrome and mahogany razzmatazz. A cast of Rosa's friends had been recruited to wave tearful farewells. Lauterbach stood tall in his new uniform. Looser and less tapered of cut and of thicker material than his German outfits, he had the feel of a man sleepwalking in pyjamas. Another friend, an employee of the *American News of Shanghai*, had slipped a short notice into the paper to the effect that Julius Lauterbach had been "reliably reported by wireless telegraphy" as taken into custody aboard the *SS Mounteagle* off British Columbia. It was speculated that he would be returned to Singapore for trial. Lauterbach read it with pleasure. He was getting used to reading his own obituary and it had become a sort of proof he was still alive and kicking.

He went below to his cabin but the presence of his travelling companion, a devout and fussy clergyman who took an impertinent interest in the state of his soul, irritated him and anyway he did not want too much time to sit and think about Rosa, so he was driven back on deck. There is a tireless fascination in sea departures and his practised eye was soothed by the regular flow of goods and supplies, the hundred little preparations for sailing that are the mark of professional seamanship. But all at once the good order was disturbed by a sudden flurry of activity near the gangplank as a team of British customs officials with clipboards came on deck and started checking identities. That he did not like that at all. Shanghai was normally so relaxed that even passports were not strictly required. He turned on his heel and wandered away, keeping just ahead of them, towards the middle deck. Ducking down a corridor he came to the barber's shop, empty of course at this stage of the voyage, and pushed through the swing doors, swathed himself in a large towel, chose a chair with its back to the door and draped his American officer's jacket ostentatiously over it, then hastily soaped his face from neck to eyebrows and worked it up to a thick lather. He settled back cosily in the chair like a waiting customer and lit a carefree cigar. The customs men appeared in the door, saw the uniform and foaming Lauterbach raising his hand, in the mirror, in friendly – Hi folks – greeting. They smiled, saluted and withdrew. Twenty minutes later, amidst honking and the ringing up of commands, the *Mongolia* finally weighed anchor and set sail.

The ship soon settled to a regular routine with Philippino stewards ranging the corridors with their tinkling gongs to entice passengers to eat. There were other US military travellers, a loud and opinionated general and entourage, a dour admiral, a couple of rangy, hard-drinking colonels always the last to desert the bar at night. Lauterbach decided they were best avoided as too many akward questions could arise that might not be covered by a simple claim of good German-Milwaukee ancestry. There were ladies enough to be beguiled by a well-cut uniform but he was still sated and doggedly depressed from Rosa and so the Lauterbach torpedo slumbered sullenly in its cradle. He drove people away with deliberately plebeian habits, smoking a foul-smelling pipe, digging with his fingers in his nose and examining the product against the light and spitting about the deck, lavishly and with bad aim.

There was no lack of Japanese, either, pattering about the ship and initially he found himself keeping a wary eye open for Katsura. Time could be spent agreeably enough playing cards with some commercial gentlemen or reading in the library and he took pains to be the first to the dining room, ordering the simplest dish and dashing away wiping his mouth before most had even finished dressing. An aged English lady, dry as a tortoise, challenged him to a daily game of scrabble after lunch, drubbed him regularly but accepted all his wilder spelling mistakes as correct American orthography. It became just another regular feature of his pensioner's schedule.

Three days' sailing brought them to Nagasaki. The usual medical officer came aboard by launch to enquire into the risk of infectious disease on the vessel. Lauterbach, posted on deck, noted carefully the standard yellow flag, flying from the back of the launch. He knew from experience that Japanese doctors took themselves seriously at such formalities, sometimes insisting on examining tongues as well as passports. But this doctor did not come unaccompanied, indeed a whole troop of uniformed officials followed on his heels and, worse yet, all passengers were summoned to appear in the smoking saloon with their travel documents. Fear gripped his bowels. Escape was impossible, since they were anchored well out in the roadstead and there was no hope of slipping over the side and swimming for it. Moreover, this was the most well-disciplined harbour in the East and no small boats approached the big liners as in other ports, so he would have to take his chances with the rest. The little revolver weighed heavy in his jacket pocket. They would not, he resolved, take him without a fight.

The saloon was a big, frowsy room, smelling, appropriately enough, of cigars and a lot of the ladies were doing a business of sniffing and clamping little white hankies disgustedly to their faces. The Japanese officials were seated stiffly at a card table with manifests and such like before them. Lauterbach settled to wait as far from them as possible, eyes and ears alert. A little man with thick glasses and bandy legs, clearly the senior officer, stood up with the authority of his shiny boots. "Is there an American officer here called Johnson?" Blood thundered in his ears. They knew! Someone must have seen him in Shanghai and sent word via the undersea cable. He looked round again for Katsura, somehow convinced he must be behind this.

"Mr Johnson please. Is there a Mr Johnson?" Lauterbach sat firm on his fat sofa at the far end of the room and stared into space. They would have to ask him to his face. He would pretend to be deaf. He would clutch at his heart and faint. Another Japanese took up the cry.

"Please pay attention, ladies and gentlemen. We are looking only for Mr Johnson. No one can leave the ship until he reports to us."

The old scrabble lady was looking at him significantly with her watery eyes, hand half-raised like the class sneak, as if to denounce him with a seven-letter word. Would she really remember his name? He realised suddenly in despair that it was all pointless. He was only putting off the evil moment by a few more minutes. Best get this over with and hang on to a little dignity. No wait. Sod dignity. Every minute was precious. He turned to see one of the boozy colonels stepping up, with care, to the table, cigarette in hand, dark glasses over his eyes.

"Johnson?" he asked with deep south, mint julip courtesy and breathed smoke. "I guess you gentlemen mean me – sorry I'm late – we had quite a session at the bar last night – but it's not Mr It's Colonel Johnson."

Lauterbach went weak at the knees, collapsed heavily, whimpered thanks to the deity. Two Johnsons! There were two Johnsons on board. Thank God he had chosen such a common name.

A smirk like a disfigurement spread across the face of the senior officer. "Oh *Colonel* Johnson," he snickered and bowed, grinning round at the others. "Please forgive me, *Colonel*." He reached up and whipped the dark glasses off the astonished American's face, then snapped out an order and his henchmen circled round behind and gripped the colonel by each arm. "We are not deceived Mr – Colonel – *Captain* Lauterbach. You will please accompany us to headquarters where we shall look into your story. Do not worry. We shall arrange to disembark your luggage since you will not be on board when the ship sails," They swaggered off, frogmarching him away protesting, raging, crying out for the help of the divinity and the US consul. Lauterbach rose shakily. It seemed too dangerous to stay on the ship and risky to try to get off. And then he saw the American admiral, blah-blahing and dawdling with a group of obsequious staff officers towards the gangplank. As they passed down each snapped off a salute at the Japanese officer on duty. Swiftly, he attached himself to the rear of the line and did the same, striding onto the bouncing tender as if he belonged. For the moment, he was free.

The day in Nagasaki was very long and he was painfully visible. Here, there was no possibility of merging into the landscape as in the Indies. He hid all day in a dark bar, drinking gassy beer, fearful of a tap on the shoulder. If he missed the boat, they would pick him up in a matter of hours. At dusk, he reboarded the ship on payment of another sharp salute and went back down to the cabin. For the moment, they had been thrown off his trail but, when they had established the authenticity of Colonel Johnson, would they think to look for a second Johnson aboard?

His cabin door, as he approached it, was open and a bar of light fell out into the corridor. Inside was a man with his back to him, bending over his open suitcase. Katsura? He was a small man but Lauterbach felt in his pocket all the same, where the revolver gave a warm glow of reassurance. He pushed the door wide and stepped in, closed it again behind him in case there was noise to be kept in.

The man looked up and grinned without shame. He was Japanese all right but not Katsura, young and cheesily handsome with slicked down hair. He reached into an inside pocket and drew out a badge. "Hi! Namura, detective." He slid the badge back in the pocket and returned to rummaging in the suitcase. He would find nothing in there.

"If you told me what you were looking for I might be able to help you."

"Just looking. Just a poor working stiff doing my job, Joe."

"My name's not Joe. It's William." Hang on better not talk about names.

"I thought maybe I'd find me one of them German officers." He held up Lauterbach's Chinese silk underwear quizzically. Japanese, Lauterbach recalled, wore a sort of primitive cotton loin cloth under their trousers, a *fundoshi*. "Weird. You know Joe I love my job. The things you learn about folks" he straightened and stared Lauterbach in the eye. "You know there's a price on the head of those Germans, the ones on the run from Singapore?"

"Well I'm only an American officer. You wouldn't get much for me. You speak very good English by the way, detective Namura."

Namura blushed with pleasure. "Oh, I guess I read a lot. Then I learned plenty over the years doing the Hawaii run. Met lots of great guys and ..." he winked hideously, "Dames."

"I bet."

"You'd be surprised how many white dames want to try a bite of real fresh-rolled sushi as a change from the old meat and potatoes."

"I'm sure."

Namura straightened up and squared his shoulders, threw out his pigeon chest. Instead of bowing, man of the world, he extended a tiny hand, seized Lauterbach's paw, squeezed pathetically hard.

"I expect you're wondering about my shirt?" Lauterbach looked. It was a curious garment, several sizes too large and cut of the loud and distasteful sort of cloth used for cheap ladies' kimonos. Namura held back the wings of his jacket to allow greater admiration. Frail Japanese boats crashed through huge, white-crested waves over his shoulders and chest. "Great huh? From Hawaii. My uncle's got a business there making these for the plantation guys. They just eat 'em up. One day I'll move over there and go in with him and get rich. One day even old guys like you will be wearing these. Great talking to you, Joe. Say, you know Japan?" He reached for the doorknob.

Lauterbach shrugged. "No. Alas I was only in Shanghai for a short time and had no chance to visit Japan."

Namura grinned and straight-armed him to the shoulder.

"Tell you what. When we get to Yokohama, I'll look you up, show you the sights. Got to go. See you round."

Lauterbach ran a rapid inventory of his belongings. Nothing was missing but then everything of importance was in his cummerbund pocket. Did Namura suspect something? Was it possible he was as simple as he pretended? By the time they got to Yokohama, he would surely have forgotten all about Lauterbach.

He kept a low profile. This was the most dangerous and restless part of the journey as the ship steamed peacefully in the pale sunshine of Japanese waters. What had happened to the other Johnson? Even Namura had mysteriously disappeared.

At Yokohama, he resurfaced in a police boat, surrounded by eager young men in smart blue uniforms, waving up to Lauterbach. "Hey Joe. Come on we're all waiting for you. Yokohama's waiting for us like I promised." They all grinned with naughty excitement, just like the *Emden* boys had whenever they had been heading for shore leave. There was no way out. Lauterbach shrugged. Where, after all, could he be safer than hidden amongst a bunch of roistering baby policemen? Anyway, he needed a little harmless relaxation after the tension of the ship. Then he raised his eyes and saw a familiar complex of black steel girders at the far end of the harbour that looked very much like the floating dry dock the Japanese had stolen and towed away from blasted and looted Tsingtao. It provoked an impertinent pang of conscience and duty trying to transform the happy policemen into what von Muecke would call "the evil enemies of his nation". Well, he wasn't having it. He suffocated the thought at once, put a smile on his face and tripped gaily down to the launch. They hauled him laughing aboard like a sack of coal.

Namura was a stern guide. Yokohama was the most progressive city in Japan and Lauterbach was called upon to admire the modernity of every brick building, tramline and dock installation that were a Western commonplace but a Japanese novelty. He led them all to Moto Mati to see this latest wonder, a department store, where money whooshed in cannisters on wires over the customers' heads. Lauterbach nodded dutiful astonishment like a bumpkin. But Yokohama was also the home of the Chinese traders of Japan and Lauterbach looked on their pigtails and stiff tunics with something akin to homesickness. Chinese ways too were all the rage though despised as un-Japanese. They slurped hot noodles at a Chinese stall, giggled over woodprints of drunken sailors in a Chinese shop, drank plum brandy that tasted like rancid seawater in a Chinese toddy house and all the time they sneered and giggled loudly at the Chinese.

"How you like, Japan, Joe?" asked Namura, ordering more food for his gobbling, nodding chicks.

"Marvellous," grinned Lauterbach with total sincerity, feeling himself back in old Tsingtao. There had been so much intermarriage, so much taking of Japanese ways by Chinese and vice versa that it was sometimes hard to tell them apart here. It was odd the way that people who hated each other, Chinese and Japanese, British and German, were always indistinguishable to outsiders.

Then Namura marched them off to the Sankeien Park to stare at gloomy pools and tortured firs and bought cheap souvenirs that he heaped on Lauterbach as they drank beer in a tea house. They drank a great deal of beer. As they left, all the police cubs gathered round a tree at the entrance and gave vent to a hot and happy discussion. Threading his way, swaying, to the front, Lauterbach saw that the talk was a all about a police poster. "Twenty-five thousand yen reward," said Namura headshaking. It was a picture of himself, fortunately a very bad, fuzzy picture from the Singapore internment, a pudgy and fair Lauterbach, beard and moustache spreadeagled misleadingly over his face like a birthmark and eyes squinting into the sun. "If only we could catch this guy," Namura sighed. "That guy they hauled off the boat today don't look like the right gee to me but all red-faced southern barbarians look the same to us. See, he even looks like you."

Lauterbach by now had enough drink in him to sup with the devil. "I will keep my eyes open," he promised. "My trained vision can spot the difference between Westerners in a way yours cannot. If I see him Namura-san, I will tell you at once and we will split the money."

Tears sprang to Namura's eyes. They had been drinking steadily all day and, as night fell, alcohol was fermenting into maudlin sentimentality. He looked at Lauterbach with fuddled love.

"Miyozaki," he croaked with finality, raising a finger. The word was like a magic spell. Silence fell over the policemen. The group huddled together and the word was hissed back and forth with electrical excitement.

Rickshaws were called up. Shoulders strained and feet padded to whir them out of town on a long straight road that led through a sort of dank swamp till, in the distance, an ornate gateway reared up. A temple? No. As they wheeled to a halt, painted girls looked out of upstairs windows and tittered. It was the pleasure district. Lauterbach dispensed generous gratuities to the rickshaws to cries of polite Japanese protest from the policemen. He was their guest. He must not spend his money. The manager, a fat man who had seen too much of the world, looked out without relish. Policemen did not pay for the pleasures that they took yet, in an age where licence required its own police permits, they must not be crossed.

Namura guided them confidently inside, slipping off shoes, bowing, grinning, leading Lauterbach by the hand to a tall room with tatami mats and low furniture. After some whispering with the manager, three ladies with musical instruments shuffled in on their knees and set up a discordant plonking and wailing that Lauterbach recognised as the universal sound of high culture. On the whole, the West had escaped fairly lightly with Wagner. Pots were brought and set in charcoal burners sunk into the tables with heaped up vegetables, meat and pickles on platters and Namura rolled up his sleeves and began to seethe and cook with his own hands while hot and cold sake alternated round the guests. As soon as Lauterbach touched his glass it was refilled with bowing ceremony.

"So Joe, where you from in the States?"

"Milwaukee." Lauterbach told travellers' tales of this place that he had never visited. He spoke of the farm where he had grown up. Its chief problem was that the grass grew so tall and lush that the cattle were constantly getting lost and they finally had to build a tall tower to spot them at milking time.

There were toasts . "To America." "To Japan." "To the Allied Victory." Ah, no. There Lauterbach invoked, twinkling, the obligatory neutrality of a member of the US armed forces. Then they pushed back the table and Namura began the singing with a spirited rendition of what he believed to be the American national anthem, Yankee Doodle Dandy. Lauterbach responded in a fine bass voice, "Zu Lauterbach ... Oops ... Oh where oh where has my little dog gone. Oh where oh where can he be? With his ears cut short and his tail cut long ..." It was, translated at length by Namura to his chicks, a sad song about a man who had lost a dog that he, personally, had mutilated in a dozen different ways before it escaped. Long Oooh's of comprehension. Then a man with a droopy moustache sang a strident song about the beauties of Kyoto and another sang happily that there was no music as sweet as the sound of a panting woman. A panting woman? Oooh. All eyes turned on Lauterbach. Which, Namura asked smirking, was the most beautiful of the three discordant ladies. Lauterbach looked them over in his state of high inebriation. It was clear to him that they were very much the rough end of the geisha market. The thick, clownish makeup, the shape-hiding clothes did nothing to arouse the torpedo. Still politeness demanded a more gracious response.

"That one," he pointed. "The one who looks like a whitewashed horse."

They drank more, went back to the plum brandy that tasted of sea-water. He became aware of a furious whispering, a surreptitious passing of money – no one passes money as dicreetly as a policeman – and suddenly he was being led, lurching to a side chamber where there was a mattress spread on the floor and pushed into darkness. No not darkness, there was a vague muted glow. The horse woman was in there. This must be her stall and Lauterbach was sprawled on the bed with her pulling his clothes off and giggling. He was intrigued by the overwhelming smell of hot sugar and scorched paper that she somehow exuded. He did not resist. Why should he? She lit a thick joss stick and waved the new sickly perfume over him like the whore of Rome. He knew how this worked. It was part of the international lore of sailors. He, or rather they, had paid for the time that it took for one joss stick to burn down. If she took against him, she would blow softly on the stick as they made love to make it burn faster. To a stupid client it was the sound of a panting woman. She laid him bare and stared down at the Lauterbach torpedo – that immediately rose to the challenge, armed and cocked itself – and gasped. Then, she grinned at him and lifted up the joss stick, stuck out her tongue and gammed at the shaft, soaking it with strings of gross saliva. Now it would smoulder wetly for hours. She grinned horribly with incense-stained teeth, whinnied faintly in Japanese, cooed damply like a dove and came for him on her knees like a dog for a bone.

He arrived back at the boat with Namura, just an hour before she was due to sail, and once more his cheap souvenirs were pressed upon him. Both he and Namura were totally wrecked in body and soul, debauched, physically ill and hardly aware who or where they were – all in all a most satisfactory shore leave. On the way back, he had identified as "clearly German" two French sailors almost as extravagantly drunk as they were and the baby policemen had hauled them away with whoops of triumph to police headquarters.

On the dock, Namura gave him a final present of a gruesome Hawaiian shirt. It was cut large even for a man of Lauterbach's proportions and featured multiple images of Mount Fuji. Both the volcano and the sky were the same shade of blue so that the mountain only appeared through the outline of white snow on its peak and sides. When he wore it, Fujis would swarm all over his body like a plague of boils. He thought it was the most beautiful thing he had ever seen and burst into tears.

"Here you go, Joe." Namura hugged comfort and, snufflingly, handed over brothel joss-sticks. "Any time you want to remember the beauty of Jap dames, just light one of these. I'll come see you one day in Milwaukee. Say what's your full name?"

"Ah ... Just ask for Joe and look for the tower. Everybody knows me as Joe. I'll send you a postcard. That's a promise."

Colonel Johnson had been returned to the ship sporting a black eye and a tale of indignity and abuse that shocked the American passengers into tut-tutting outrage. He had been harangued, punched, threatened with bamboo sticks and fed nothing but sticky rice. The Japanese police had sent him back huffily with scarcely a word of apology as if he had let them down by being the wrong Johnson. His dark glasses, moreover, had disappeared and been lost for ever. Another tragedy of the war. He brought with him two hundred delicate Japanese ladies, brides for the gaudy-shirted workers on the Hawaiian plantations, each chosen from her photograph. Perhaps it would work out but Japanese did not seem to Lauterbach very good at recognising people from their photographs.

Lauterbach was in a slightly difficult position. The next stop was Hawaii and if he entered American territory with a false identity, or bearing arms, or in a fake US uniform he might be interned. He waited till they were beyond territorial waters, dropped the revolver over the side, put on Namura's

Mount Fuji shirt as his only civlian clothes and went to have a word with the captain in the strictest confidence. Within an hour he was the talk of the ship. The long, slow days of scrabble were over. Now he waddled the decks displaying himself, twirling his growing moustache, dispensing grinning gallantries to all and sundry. Much of the afternoons was spent in the swimming pool with single ladies, amongst whom he was greatly in demand, and evenings in drinking and carousing in the bar with the men. As he returned to his cabin at three in the morning a door opened and a large blonde in a small nightdress looked coyly at him round the edge and twirled a lock of her hair.

"Captain Lauterbach," she cooed. "I couldn't sleep and was just thinking about what you said earlier, in the pool, about torpedoes."

He clicked his heels and bowed with tired gallantry. "Madam, with regret, the torpedoes of His Majesty's Imperial Navy are faster, bigger and pack a greater punch than any others in the world. But like all torpedoes, they can be fired only once. I wish you good night."

CHAPTER THIRTEEN

The picture of Colonel Johnson looked somewhat surprised on the front page of *The San Francisco Chronicle*, as he shielded his weak eyes from the reporters' flashbulbs. Well he might. The headline read "Captain Lauterbach arrives in San Francisco." It was followed by an account of a completely imaginary and sensational interview, invented presumably by the reporter rather than poor Colonel Johnson. Lauterbach smiled fatly and folded up the paper. Such confusions were the best sort, like weeds, endlessly replicating themselves and the more people tried to root them out, the tougher they became. At this moment, British agents would be carefully cutting out the picture all over the States, as his own, and thus repeating the mistake of the Japanese.

Lauterbach plunged beneath the surface of Chinatown, whence, a few days later, Dr Larsen, a large and amiable Dane, set off untroubled across the continent by the Pan Pacific Railroad. With him he took a large quantity of Lauterbach fanmail, offers of accommodation, employment and marriage, delivered to the German consulate by avid newspaper readers. He looked at his reflection in the window. Would they be disappointed or pleased that this, Lauterbach's face, the face that had sunk a dozen ships, was not also the face of Colonel Johnson? The journey took six days during which Lauterbach revived slowly, idling in the club car, looking out on this vast, milk-fed continent while coloured boys, all teeth and shoeshine, waited on him hand and foot. He ate lobster and strawberries and washed them down with the curiously insipid American wines. The food was stolid and unimaginative, the way he liked it, not like on French trains where he had once been served a horror of raw meat and egg that he remembered ever after as "steak catarrh." He watched his fellow passengers and liked these big-boned, beef-bulked people with their slow assurance and lack of fear.

Sometimes complete strangers tipped their hats to him in the restaurant car and offered a card. Alarm bells shrilled in Lauterbach's Old World head but they were always inoffensive travelling salemen, assuming a fellowship of the road.

"Good day, sir. Milton P. Goosewang, at your service, travelling in leather goods. And yourself?"

"I am a crocodile trainer by profession."

"That so, sir? Well that's mahty fahn, mahty fahn."

At night the train often glided just a few feet from the windows of remote towns and he could peer in and catch glimpses of these little domestic heavens and hells, hermetically sealed like fortune cookies. Sometimes they rattled through empty forest or across vast, cultivated pariries or crept through big cities. The smeared smokestacks of Chicago greatly impressed him, an inelegant city dedicated to the mass evisceration of cattle and swine. But before all these Lauterbach did not pause, wafted past, a rolling stone, perpetually unmossed and wondered whether he was blessed or cursed. Arrived in New York, the new Grand Central Station was a Beaux-Arts thing of wonder with vaulted ceilings

NIGEL BARLEY

and classical gods in stone though gobbed-out chewing gum already marred the marble floors. He stepped outside to marvel at the soaring skyscrapers, amongst the Babel accents of the city, with their magic names of Woolworth and Singer and his heart soared. From a slick hotel on Lexington Avenue, with rubber flooring and glass ceilings, he sought out the German consul.

Herr Flick was all smiles in an office with views over the New York skyline. "Glad to meet you captain. I must say you don't look a bit like your picture in the paper. Have you heard the good news?" He arranged the blotter on his desk, aligned a pencil with the grain of the wood. He was a very fussy man in a nice dove-grey suit.

"What news?" Lauterbach was installed in a leather armchair, his overcoat retained despite the unseasonable autumn heat.

"Your superior, von Muecke," Flick smirked, "What a man! He's fought his way across Arabia and turned up, out of the blue, in Constantinople." He frowned. "Of course, he shouldn't really have had to *fight* his way since the Turks are our allies and that's their patch but still ... At least Germany has a real hero at last. They've been in rather short supply of late. They're shipping him back double quick and organising a big bash in Berlin, bands, march-past, the works. The Kaiser himself will make a speech."

"I see." Lauterbach wondered sourly how many of the men had died along the way, sacrificed to von Muecke's aggressive heroism.

"You don't look too happy about it. Oh, I see. Yes of course, it must be a bitter blow that you can't be there to witness his moment of glory. Well that's war." He swigged excellent coffee, puffed on a fine cigar to show he knew what the sufferings of war were all about. "So what about you?"

"The first thing," Lauterbach interposed swiftly, "is some cash. I've been living on my wits for months now." It wasn't quite true but anxiety gnawed at his stomach despite the cash paunch. He needed urgently to feel he had some more dollars coming in and that he was not simply wasting away.

"Not my area. I'll give you a note for the cashier. She may be able to find a mark or two but you'll have to come out of the naval allocation and that's a bit tight till the end of the financial year. As long as you move on ..." He seized the pencil, made a note, stared at the point as if annoyed. It was no longer perfect. He took out a sharpener, twirled the pencil a couple of times and blew away the dust, then sat looking at it on the carpet.

"No hurry is there? I thought, maybe a bit of propaganda work over here. I could travel around, talk about the *Emden* and my own poor adventures? Some clubs, a few universities, ladies' groups, you know the sort of thing." He saw absolutely no reason to rush back to the austerities of wartorn Europe. Life was evidently very comfortable here in America. He sipped his own excellent coffee, sniffed Flick's cigar that perfumed the air. The British, surely, would dare to make no move against him on American soil. At night, he had begun to dream happily of milk-fed Milwaukee. He actually missed those cows of his imagination, mooing plaintively, lost in the lush grass, tended by apple-cheeked girls in more of those lacy frocks the Chinese wenches had once worn in old Tsingtao.

Flick sucked air over his teeth and shook his head. He took out his handkerchief and began to rub fingerprints off the pencil-sharpener. "The moment for all that has passed,

I'm afraid. The idea at this point is for the navy to keep a very low profile over here, what with the unrestricted submarine campaign and all that. It looks like the policy on that's going to have to be reversed – which will cause another fearful stink. I'm afraid Lauterbach you're going to have to be hushed up. Your only use to us is if you get back to the fatherland. Then you'd come in really handy at home as a stick to beat British stupidity and arrogance. Over here, ideally, we prefer our naval heroes to be dead – less bother all round. Since bolstering the wobbly neutrality of America is our principal concern at the moment, I couldn't risk getting involved in your travel plans myself, of course, but I'm sure you're a resourceful fellow. And no rush. We could give you a few weeks to get back across the water. I don't imagine you'd want to take more than that. You're not formally on leave you see and the navy gets horribly awkward about pay and availability for active service and all that rigmarole and you have been wandering about for some time now on a sort of holiday. We really don't want our people hanging around in New York without any means of support and doing nothing. It gets us all a bad name."

It was true. In the bourgeois enclave of Harlem Park, where the Germans strolled on Sundays, he had encountered the military band of Tsingtao, gold braid dimmed by wear and tear and all marooned high and dry. Since they had only worked as stretcher-bearers by day, the Japanese had decently released them as non-combattants. The British, on the other hand, insisted on treating stretcher-bearers as ordinary soldiers, so they dare not continue their journey home. If the British got them on the Atlantic they would stick them in a prison camp and throw away the key. So there it was. They sat in an arid New York park with their hats on the ground and oompahed glumly for their supper while Flick washed his hands of them. He should have known. He was not to be celebrated as a hero after all but to be cruelly abandoned here, thousands of miles from home, ignored with no more than a twitch of the nostril like a fart in a public place. Their ingratitude, lack of vision, administrative sloth – anxiety gripped him as usual in the belly. "I'm going to need quite a bit of money to get back," he said defiantly, grasping his paunch again.

When he left the building, it was immediately obvious that he was being followed. Was it the British, the Americans or even the Germans? He could not be sure. Sometimes it seemed there were two separate groups on his heels. Sometimes they seemed to give up on him and just follow each other. He saw a lot of them over the next few days. He liked to visit Grand Central, lead them through the crowds, duck down the tunnels and up the stairs. He went to art galleries in one door and out the other. In restaurants, he often left through the kitchens, impervious to the staff's shouts and curses. When all else failed he would slip into a skyscraper and ride to the fifteenth floor, cross the landing and ride straight down again on the other side. Sometimes hc just turned on his heels while walking and came straight back at them, enjoying the horrified looks on their faces as they darted across the road or cowered in doorways. He made their life hell.

Then one day, he went back to the hotel and there was a familiar figure sitting in the lobby, staring into space and fanning himself with his hat. With his other hand, he tumbled a bullet relentlessly base over tip. Lauterbach was suddenly very tired of all this. He went and sat next to him. They stayed there for a minute or two in silence, both unwilling to transform their austere and wordless relationship and engage in what might be a difficult, even unpleasant, negotiation.

"Who are you?" Lauterbach asked finally. The smell of lavender was very strong, made worse by the fanning business.

The man sighed. "My name doesn't really matter. It changes as often as your own, Captain Lauterbach." He was very lean and wiry, something of the sportsman about him, and still sporting a tropical tan. "We won't let you get back to Europe you know. There's too much at stake. It would be much better all round if you just elected to stay here. We could all live with that. I could even give you my word that when America comes in on our side, as it surely will, we would make no move to extradite you. Absolutely. Arsehole-hooter-minty as our Italian friends say."

"'When' not 'if' and who is 'we'?" There was an accent there. "Are you Australian?"

The man sucked in his cheeks. "'We' is the British. The Allies more generally, if you prefer. No I am not really from Australia. I have a poetic soul and what poetry can there be in a country whose name rhymes only with 'failure' and 'genitalia'? If you stay here, we can call that a kind of victory and I'll leave you alone. But try to get back to Germany and I'll do for you. We'd have no choice really after what your blokes just did, putting that captain of a ferry boat before a firing squad for trying to run down one of your subs off Antwerp. Public opinion, I'm afraid, would insist upon our stringing you up. It's me or you old chum. You must remember that it's different here. This isn't Asia. The Atlantic's our home territory and we keep it locked up tight as a drum. You've made me look very foolish one way and another, spat in my soup and made me drink it. Good luck to you. But you see, now my expenses need to be justified or they'll send me to some bloody hellhole in Africa. No shortage of those in the Empire. I need you Lauterbach."

At least somebody did. But expenses? Was this some great truth? Was the whole war nothing to do with national pride and the realities of politics and personal honour? Was it for everyone ultimately about nothing but trying to look good to the boss and justifying one's expenses? Herr Flick had said much the same thing, so had Kessel in Batavia and as for himself, expenses had been a fundamental article of faith. But he had always regarded himself as a lone visionary and, of course, it wasn't that simple. There were plenty of people like von Mueller and von Muecke, the true believers. But then maybe they were the true source of all the trouble in the world.

"I'm tired," said Lauterbach. It was true. "I cannot hide the fact that I have been thinking about settling down here."

"Best thing," said the lavender man, coolly. "You have a good think. You Germans are patient chaps, something to do with the language I expect, all that waiting for the transitive verb. I'm sure you'll agree it's best all round. You settle down, get yourself nice and snug – *gemuetlich*, as you say. You may not be seeing me again but I'll certainly be seeing you." He rose, plumped his hat on his head and strolled elegantly away without looking back. Two old friends. A very civilised chat. Lauterbach was a little surprised that neither had offered the other any money, though which way the cash would have passed was unclear. Could he be trusted? Of course not. This was the man who had tried to have him shot down like a dog in Shanghai. As soon as America came into the war he'd sell him out in the interests of his expenses and, anyway, Lauterbach couldn't let him get away with a smooth exit like that.

"My regards to Katsura-san," he called.

Lavender man paused and looked genuinely puzzled. "Mr Katsura is dead," he said slowly turning. "It seems he had an accident one night and fell in the river in Shanghai. He could not swim. I thought you knew." He seemed suddenly angry. "Remember what I said Lauterbach. I'll lay you a thousand dollars, here and now, you don't make it back to Germany."

Lauterbach stared him in the eye. "Done." It was now a bet and he was immediately astonished that something so stupid should lift his spirits as he felt it did. The world and his movements in it had a clear, direct purpose again. It was all just a bet. This must be what it felt like all the time to be von Muecke.

That afternoon, a reinvigorated Lauterbach walked swiftly through the Broadway entrance of Macy's Department store, rode the lift to the Men's Outerwear department and shrugged on a mackintosh before crossing over to the neighbouring building and diving down the stairs to exit at the rear. Then, he made his way cautiously to his favourite place, a smoky bar called *The Stockfish*, down by the Battery, haunted by Baltic sailors in ancient, lumpy pullovers that smelled of sweat and fish. There were already the first leaves blowing in the streets and the first icy note sang in the wind. He talked Swedish, gave himself out as an old salt looking for a berth home, bought some disgruntled seaman's papers cheap and kept his ears open. A Danish boat, the *Frederick VII* seemed the best bet, bound for Copenhagen. The captain was a regular at *The Stockfish*, a seasoned tippler of aquavit. Over a drink, Lauterbach broached the subject of a job. The captain looked at him evenly enough but his hands trembled on the glass. "I am looking for a stoker. I think you are not a stoker. You are Swedish but I think maybe not too Swedish. You look like a man of experience but then experience is just a kind name we give to all our mistakes. Times are hard. I tell you what I do. I take you aboard but you get no pay. Instead you give me two hundred dollars and I ask no questions and tell no lies. Is good?"

They shook hands on it. Was good.

The *Frederick VII* was not a graceful ship. She was an old rustbucket weighed down by a cargo of tinned goods, bacon and fresh fruit and gobbled twice the coal a more modern ship would have. After six hours' stoking in heat and dust, Lauterbach felt he had worked himself sufficiently into the role and went to the captain. A little more money changed hands and the rest of the journey consisted of light duties, polishing brass, oiling valves, painting hatch-covers. Lauterbach had always disliked the Atlantic, a nasty cold sea that amplified the greyness of life. It was vicious and hostile and featureless. Glumness was somehow also the natural idiom of the vessel and its crew and, as the journey wore on, he felt himself becoming nordically depressed. They were tossed back and forth by storms for weeks till the smell of decaying fruit began to invade the galley and chase out that of fish while the captain drank himself from black moods into blacker ones and sobbed alone in the wheelhouse at night. Once, after midnight, he had barged into Lauterbach's cabin, wild-eyed and distraught. "People are pears not apples," he had raved a propos of nothing. "They rot from the inside out, not from the outside in!" and plunged back into the storm, tearing his hair.

The crew sulked and groaned in Swedish and Norwegian and other Nordic tongues that had no name whenever the slightest effort was asked of them. No one shaved. Few washed. Evenings were spent playing patience alone. Everything was just too much trouble and life was a burden to be borne. They even lacked the energy to fight with each other. Then the British came.

They came unobserved because no one could be bothered to keep a proper watch and nearly opened fire when their orders to stop went unheeded. Finally the crew were roused by a shot across the bows. It was a big, armed auxiliary and they sent over a boarding party. The petty officer in charge was a fussy man and became obsessed with the amount of bacon they carried. Why so much bacon? And to a country that produced its own bacon in abundance. Was this bacon not intended to bring comfort to the German army? Was it not a fact that Germans lived almost exclusively on bacon? He felt sure it was. They were ordered into Kirkwall in the Orkneys. The crew groaned and the captain sobbed but, in the icy wind, Lauterbach saw a familiar face at the rail and felt a knife twist in his stomach. It was lavender man, waiting to come across.

The boarding was sloppily done, not as Lauterbach would have handled it. There had been no checking of lists against names and engine-room crew had been allowed to stay at their posts. He had planned for this. Above the scalding boilers he had constructed a nest shielded by metal plates from below, so that it looked like a mere continuation of the boiler itself.

It was as hot as Hades but bearable for short periods and he shoehorned himself in, gulped water from a store laid to hand, slapped a soaked towel over his head and settled to sweat it out. Half an hour limped by. Then his foe appeared below, looking suspiciously in all directions, opened doors, checked lockers and moved with painful slowness down the aisle between the throbbing machines. He stared the crew boldly in the face, stopping them at their work and turning their heads with his hands as if they were pots he was thinking of buying. None of them – Lauterbach was sure – would give him away by a word or an upward glance. They were too depressed to look anywhere but at their feet. Lavender man came to rest right beneath the roaring boiler and glanced up at it as if he could see Lauterbach up there, smoking like a kipper, and fanned himself aggravatingly with his hat while Lauterbach stiffened and felt the sweat gush down his chest to drip sizzling on the hot metal. His guts gurgled like the boiler pipes around him and he strangled a fart behind his sphincter and thought he could almost smell the lavender but such a thing was – surely – impossible over the reeking smoke and oil. Gazing down, he felt rage and hatred and then a sudden stab of pity, like his dyspepsia, at the incipient soft baldness of the man's crown, normally concealed by the hat and now revealed in all its babylike vulnerability. Then the man reached into his pocket and pulled out the bullet that he began working through his fingers like an infant sucking on a joyless dummy. Suddenly, Lauterbach was assailed by dizziness. He blinked, shook his head and swam in fumes and fear and, finally, when it seemed he would topple at his foe's feet, the man passed on. Lauterbach stayed a few more minutes and emerged light with terror and dehydration. The

British vessel returned to station, leaving only a skeleton crew in occupation. His enemy was gone.

They spent five bleak days in Kirkwall. Lauterbach looked out at the grey joyless town built of cold granite and felt even more depressed. To be hanged in this place would be terrible indeed. They were questioned every day by a thin-faced British officer in a duffle-coat as gales howled around the ship. If they were kept much longer, there was real danger that the auxiliary, complete with lavender man, would return to this, its home port, for resupply and then Lauterbach would swing at the yardarm. He had to dig deep into his childhood memories of Sweden to give a plausible account of himself and his family and it ended up sounding like another version of imagined Milwaukee. Fortunately the interpreter was incompetent and his own halting command of the language passed muster. The nastiest British trick was swooping down on them in the early morning and shouting them awake in German to test their response. On Lauterbach this was wasted. He responded to no human language at that hour. Then they started on about the bacon again. Lauterbach snarled back. What in God's name did he know of bacon? He was a stoker. One, he realised suddenly, with awkward, lilly-white hands so he put them behind his back but again the British did not notice. After five days they were given leave to go and take their bacon with them. That night, they were hauled over by a German submarine that raked them with its searchlights and questioned them through a loud-hailer. Satisfied of their neutrality it vanished back into the depths. Finally, they arrived in toytown Copenhagen that crackled with a layer of silver ice and the whole crew sobbed with sated homesickness. And just as suddenly, in the chill air,

Lauterbach froze solid.

He had been driven round the world and, in an instant, could move no more, like a donkey that will suddenly endure any amount of beating and just digs in its heels, lays back its ears and refuses to budge. Unafraid of the cudgel, it will die first. He checked into the best hotel in town and went to bed, summoning occasional meals to his room. The thick curtains were pulled over views of the frozen harbour and untrammelled heat puffed and hissed into the room through clanking radiators. Lauterbach lay under the flounced eiderdown and stared at the intricate moulded ceiling for hours, days. Or he would break out in a cold sweat like a corpse on a marble slab and lie naked, listening to the boiling and rumbling of his guts as they merged with the sounds of the heating. The fragile gangplank that connected him to the rest of the world had collapsed and sunk. He was all at sea and the ice was forminh again over his head. In the carpeted room was not Asian time, or American time but Lauterbach time, dictated by the rhythms and needs of his own body. It was the time of the sickness experience, when the whole world shrinks down to your own flesh and each breath requires a conscious act of volition and each minute is felt in every quivering nerve, not assumed and lived *through*. To forget to breathe is to die. He moved between bath and bed and no further. Sometimes he cried but did not know why and when he gazed in the mirror he saw a succession of tear-stained strangers staring back with eyes devoid of self-knowledge. Was he an apple or a pear? He did not know. His identity was a pen that he had left on a table, a dropped cufflink, a sock abandoned under a bed or perhaps by a stream and he had simply lost himself and did not know where to look.

He could not remember what name he had signed in the register downstairs for the months of imposture had brought no flash of self-knowledge about the core of his being, as it often does. On the fifth day, he reached into his cummerbund pocket and counted his money, again. There were the familiar Chinese bedsheets, the crisp dollars, the arrogant pounds, the clenched and curlicued Reichshmarks spread out on the bed. He smoothed them and smelled them as they soothed him with their innocence and he fell asleep with his nose buried in their slim solidity and woke to find them soaked in his drool and his mouth dry from snoring. That afternoon he washed, shaved and went to the German consulate. He had rebirthed himself but had been born an orphan.

"Officially, you don't exist," they told him. "You have no passport, no right to be here. Our records mention no Lauterbach. Nothing from New York. Go away or we will have you arrested."

He walked through the limpid sunlight, as light as a ghost, the air sucked out of him, leaving no shadow. On the street was a woman handing out biblical tracts to all and sundry. He passed her three times and she offered him nothing. He was invisible. He headed for the offices of the Hamburg America Line, his old employer.

"Of course we know you," they said, gathering round, smiling, handshaking, offering a glass, pouring substance and sensation back into him. "Shanghai, Hong Kong, Tsingtao. Good old Lauterbach." The clerks were called in, the manager came down from his high office. His boots refilled with comforting solidity, his swimming senses returned. There followed aquavit, beer, more aquavit, a pickled salmon meal in the steam of potatoes in a restaurant down by the port.

"Here's a note to the Naval Attache. He'll sort you out."

He had danced and boasted and proposed toasts and awoken dry-mouthed beside a mousy-haired, dog-faced woman whom he did not remember and who spoke no language known to Man but demanded fish for breakfast entirely in gesture. He was alive.

On Sunday morning he took the little pot-bellied ferry to Warnemuende and, as the boat puttered towards land, he was surprised to see people on the beach. It was not the holiday season and the sea, for locals, was exclusively a place of work. But nobody worked on a Sunday. Here there was no gangplank and he took off his shoes and socks and clambered down onto the honest wet sand, enjoying the worms of sludge sliding up between his toes, a childhood memory. Germany. He had never been very good with the pomposity of abstractions. He was rooted again, earthed. A loud cheer rang out and he looked up to see a little brass band fighting down the beach and striking up a ragged rhythm.

"In Lauterbach I lost my sock / I won't be going back there. / But if I went to Lauterbach, / I'd once more have a pair there."

"Three cheers," they shouted. "Three cheers for Lauterbach, the hero."

They rushed up, good-natured, pig-faced people with fair hair and heaved him, grinning and grunting, onto their strong, fat, pink, shoulders and ran him around the beach. At least this time, they weren't making him wear a turban and someone, somewhere, finally owed him a thousand dollars.

It was a bitter November day in Bremen and a stiff wind

whipped around the empty flats of the shipyard before rushing out over the sea to smack the waves into life. Even though it was a festive occasion, there was a chill, funereal feel in the air, for it was a season for past memories not future hopes.

All the worthies from the city of Emden were there in the stands, clothed in deepest black, astrakhan-collared and well upholstered, fortified by hip flasks and heavy breakfasts as at a graveside. Their women were with them with dead foxes wrapped round their necks and hands thrust into fur gloves. Below, stood the workers in their rough serge and best caps, grimly determined to make the most of a rare day off work. The launch of a ship was always losing a daughter more than gaining a son, though the order book was full enough at present to make up the heavy loss of shipping in the endless war. She was a light cruiser whose principal distinguishing feature was a great, clumsy Iron Cross welded to either side of the bow and her name was picked out in white against the dark grey – *Emden II*. There was a long, bombastic speech with enough hot air to fill a Zeppelin. At the back stood two naval officers, one pared and thin, the other bulky, a comic pairing from the motion pictures.

"So Lauterbach. You have had a good war" stated von Muecke, eyes facing ahead, not without an edge of bitterness. "Out of all of us you seem to have come off best. So you are now a great hero? Who would have thought it?"

"Well, that is what the Kaiser says, so I suppose it must be so. It came out of the blue. They wrote about me in the newspapers and the Kaiser reads the newspapers. You might say I am a hero by imperial decree." Lauterbach twitched his sleeve with its extra bands of gold. He was not just a hero now but also a Lieutenant-Commander of the Reserve. Von

Muecke had stuck at Commander. The difference in rank should be noticed. They eyed each other's rows of medals and ribbons cautiously, like boys appraising each other's conker collection. Lauterbach had more crosses than a Catholic altar.

"You have lost weight," observed von Muecke. "You have been on recent active service?" The slimmer waist was from the absence of the cummerbund, replaced by a more conventional nest-egg in non-inflationary gold, stowed under the floorboards at home.

"I have just got back from the Baltic with my First Commercial Protection Half-Flotilla," declared Lauterbach. "When I was in Hamburg, I asked to be posted back East so, out of spite or miscomprehension, they sent me to the Baltic – east after a fashion." Not the east of Rosa. A pang passed through his stomach. God this Western world was grey. But Rosa would never do here, a Eurasian wife, a 'Chink', to be sneered at as inferior by tight-mouthed locals. He sighed. The loss of the East was not, for him, merely a matter of imperial pride. He felt it in his flesh. Yet, he had compromised and already put down a deposit on a serviceable Hamburg fiancee. He even had a marmalade cat.

"What is that, 'Commercial Protection'? Is it anything to do with the Seagoing Circus?" Von Muecke seemed to sneer but then whenever he smiled, he sneered. It was not his fault. His face was just made that way. Ask a shark to smile. But he looked older; more lined and the skin had an odd, variegated look, more like an old crocodile. Perhaps that was from the terrible sunburn they had all suffered. In fact, now he thought of it, von Muecke resembled one of those Iron Men, wooden carvings of warriors set up all over Germany, so that the patriotic could pay good money to knock nails into them and raise cash for the war by this odd fetishism. He also gave off a smell of stale laundry but then so did many people nowadays. Lauterbach sniffed unwillingly. He fished out a cheroot and lit it. In its turn, it tasted of old tea-leaves and floor-sweepings.

"What they call the Seagoing Circus is von Rosenberg's operation, an amateur thing of mine-laying and -clearing. We're different, the mystery ships. You know? You don't know? The mystery ships are chamaeleons. We pretend to be merchant vessels to lure in enemy submarines but actually we are heavily armed and as they close in to attack on the surface, we sink them. We got three in the past year alone."

"It does not sound entirely honourable."

Lauterbach bristled. "Honourable or not, it's bloody dangerous. My ship just got blown to bits by British destroyers and I sustained wounds that were accounted honourable enough by the Kaiser." He shifted stiffly. His leg was playing up. He had broken it falling down the stairs to get to the boats but a wound was a wound as surely as one Reichsmark was worth another. "And you?"

"There was a lot of trouble over my report concerning the *Ayesha*. It was all politics. I am a naval officer in the service of his country and politics are not my concern. I would not lie. But they did not like the fact that I mentioned the treacherous collusion of our Turkish allies in the attacks on my men in the desert. You may have noticed my books?" He looked at Lauterbach with a small hope.

Indeed he had. Two best-sellers, all about von Muecke, snapped up by blind patriots and star-struck little boys. The vanity of authors. He was now a famous writer about the war and prouder of what he had written than what he had actually done. His life had become an object for him to possess. Lauterbach saw in a flash that he, himself, had never really cared about *things*. True, he liked money but that was for its sheer ethereal beauty, that it could magically transform into anything. When he was last in Berlin, von Muecke had been giving rousing, ticket-only, lectures on the *Emden* and *Ayesha* to packed houses and talked of conferring immortality on the dead heroes by his own deathless prose, proof enough that it was his own eternity he was concerned with. Lauterbach eyed his thick, non-regulation overcoat. He, too, had made a pretty penny, one way or another, out of the war and should not complain.

"No. I didn't know you had written books."

"Well I have. Some few people have heard of me." Now he was piqued. "You know, Lauterbach. You should write your own life story. I am sure it would be not without a certain rude interest. Writing is an excellent discipline. I could put you in touch with a publisher, if you like."

Lauterbach shivered. And clapped his gloves together. "Not my sort of thing at all, Number One. I've never been a man of words." He put a manly gleam in his eye and thrust out the jaw like the prow of a battleship. "Deeds perhaps – words, no. Anyway, what can there be left to tell? You must have said it all."

There was a crack, a smashing of glass and a cheer, drowned in a swelling rumble of iron on iron. The ship was sliding down the slipway, the chains and the great hydraulic pistons groaning and screaming. It was a foul noise, drowning out the band with its "Deutschland, Deutschland ueber alles" and the cheering mob. Cold sweat dewed Lauterbach's brow and he staggered back against the rear of the grandstand in sudden vertigo. The birth of a ship was the same sound as that of one dying, tearing itself apart, summoning up the ghostly legions who had perished on the first *Emden*. Ashes to ashes, rust to rust. He wiped his gloved hand over his face and looked at the glistening black leather as if he had never seen a hand before.

"And von Mueller? What of him. The last I heard, he had been transferred to England."

"I had not heard that. I thought he was still in some prison in Malta."

"At least we are free, Lauterbach."

They looked at each other again. They would never be friends – there could be no melty love – but they were forever shackled together by too much shared history, like family, not to feel something. Indeed, there was a proposal before the Kaiser that all crew members of the *Emden* and their loved ones should be allowed to hyphenate the word '-Emden' to their surnames and so become truly family. That ship would follow him around all his life, forming him, dominating him. Soon he would be Julius Lauterbach-Emden, hyphenated genteelly enough, but von Muecke would be hyphenated *and* still hang on to his aristocratic 'von' so that the distance between them would be maintained. Free was it? No. He would never be free.

"We should send von Mueller a postcard," suggested von Muecke. "A card in prison to cheer him up."

Lauterbach paused. "No. I don't think one of my postcards would be quite the thing. But let's go somewhere and have a drink to him," he offered grudgingly. It occurred to him how few real friends he had and how often he ducked behind a shared drink like a barricade.

Von Muecke nodded. "Yes. A good idea. And it will permit me to raise another matter of the greatest national importance that I want to discuss with you in strict confidence." They picked their way carefully down from the grandstand, decorations tinkling like two Christmas trees in the wind, von Muecke swollen by the importance of his undisclosed mission.

"You were always a man of great resourcefulness, Lauterbach. I concede it. It was something I always admired in you and a quality of great service to the Reich, in its way. You are now in a position to perform another great deed for your country. With the British blockade, there are strategic shortages everywhere, things that simply cannot be had on the regular market and with your irregular contacts you may be able to lay hands on them when the rest of us cannot."

What was this? Soap! Soap had completely disappeared from the shops six months ago. Everyone stank. Was it possible he was after Elysium-brand toilet soap?

Von Muecke was embarrassed, looking down like a blushing schoolboy at his iron crosses. "You are even close to the Emperor. You could speak to him on this matter. Personally." There was reluctant awe in his voice and rage at the injustice of the fact. "At this stage of the war a pen may be as lethal as a ten-inch gun."

Lauterbach paused and stared into the impossibly vivid blue eyes that still glowed with undiminished zeal. He felt suddenly immensely tired. "What exactly is it you want of me, Number One?"

Von Muecke, seized him passionately by the arm. "For a patriotic writer, such as myself, at this time of the year, one thing is quite indispensable. Gas mantles, Lauterbach. For God's sake, for Germany's sake, find me some gas mantles."

Lauterbach opened his mouth to speak but was cut off by a tweaking at his coat. He thought of scuttling shipbound rats and shuddered but, looking down, saw the grubby hand of a child tugging at his fine worsted. It belonged to a waif, blue with cold, with symmetrical snot trails as if two snails lived up its nostrils.

"Mister," it sniffed, holding out an envelope, already creased and seamed with grime. "A gent arsed me to give this to ya."

"Gent? What gent?" Lauterbach took it cautiously from the chapped and slightly sticky fingers. Was this some trap? He looked around. Everyone was watching the ship. No one heeded their odd little group. The child scanned the crowd and shrugged. "Dunno. E's gorn. Said you'd give me summink."

Lauterbach dispensed small change and the delighted child scuttled away. He tore the flap open with clumsy, gloved fingers, aware of von Muecke's curious gaze. Inside was a smooth, beige sheet of paper with writing in a scrawled, ugly hand. He held it away, at arm's length to focus and peered down his nose. Age was catching up with him. Perhaps, as he grew old, he would become metaphorically as well as literally farsighted. It was an IOU, signed "John Smith", made out for one thousand American dollars. The notepaper bore the address of a London gentlemen's club, not – he thought – one of the best but the sort frequented by ambitious tradesmen who, like himself, were not *quite* gentlemen. Without thinking, he put it to his nose and laughed as he smelled fresh lavender and laughed again to see von Muecke's shocked face at his receiving a perfumed *billet doux*, in public, from what must be a female admirer. Wait, there was something else in there. He tipped the envelope and something rolled into his palm, a little jewel, shiny and patinated from much handling – a bullet.

The thing had been nicely done, with a judicious ambiguity. To von Mueller, who saw war as a sort of gentlemanly sport, it would be the punctilious payment of a patrician wager but implied a certain mercenary quality in the receiver who exchanged honour for cash. And Lauterbach could not actually attach the money since it lay in an enemy country and under a false name. Moreover, the mere fact of the IOU's smooth delivery carried a smug message of superiority. It was effectively worthless and downright condescending. And the bullet said "Bang! Bang! You're dead," claiming a kill its owner had not quite been able to make. The challenge rankled at the back of his throat like the aftertaste of a good pickle. Never mind. He pocketed it up smiling. The smile would be observed somewhere in the crowd. He had an address. Now that *was* a project worth one of his postcards. Smirking, he began composing it in his head.